BLOOD & MAGICK

THE WITCH'S MONSTERS BOOK 4

Blood and Magick
The Witch's Monsters, Book Four
Copyright © 2022 by Sarah Piper
SarahPiperBooks.com

Published by Two Gnomes Media

Cover design by Luminescence Covers

v5

E-book ISBN: 978-1-948455-60-2
Paperback ISBN: 978-1-948455-39-8
Audiobook ISBN: 978-1-948455-67-1

BOOK SERIES BY SARAH PIPER

GET CONNECTED!

I love connecting with readers! There are a few different ways you can keep in touch:

Email: sarah@sarahpiperbooks.com

TikTok: @sarahpiperbooks

Facebook group: Sarah Piper's Sassy Witches

Twitter: @sarahpiperbooks

Newsletter: Never miss a new release or a sale! Sign up for the VIP Readers Club: sarahpiperbooks.com/readers-club

1

JAX

I was an immortal fucking demon. I'd lost my humanity centuries ago.

But I wasn't so old I didn't remember what pain felt like. Human pain—the crushing immensity of it. The helplessness. The way it could steal the breath from your lungs and make you feel as if you'd never be able to breathe again.

I'd been human when my kid sister died in my arms. When my original family sold me to hell. When the cruelest, most vicious monsters in the pit tortured me until everything mortal about me had finally fled, leaving only a broken, brutal demon behind.

And as that demon, I'd endured brutalities that made hell look like Disney World, especially here. Even when we'd escaped to New Orleans, I couldn't shake free of Midnight's nightmares. Of that feeling of loss and emptiness more vast than the Boiling Glass Sands, so dark and bleak I was certain one night it would swallow me whole, spit me out right back into the bowels of hell.

But tonight, when that stupid, infernal, *reckless* fae fuck shoved me out of the way and I watched from the ground, powerless to do anything but gape as the fog just... just fucking *pureed* him...

I'd sworn my insides disintegrated right along with his.

Saint—my enemy, my bane, my brother and best fucking friend, was dead.

And I finally understood—as the wet, wine-dark spray of him slid down my face—that I'd never really known pain at all. For all that I'd suffered, I'd never even come close.

I was still blinking the blood from my eye when Hudson came into view, his face a mask of death. He knew at once what'd happened—witnessed the whole thing from above and just couldn't fucking get to us in time.

I saw the rage come over him then, his eyes smoldering with it, his muscles spring loaded as he leaped back into the air and went after the closest raven gryphon. They attacked him ferociously, but in the end, the gargoyle proved victorious. He took down two of those fucking hellspawn beasts—a shower of blood and bone and black feathers—before the witches called off their storm and retreated.

Hudson and I scoured that mountainside for hours,

desperate for any sign that Saint had escaped—that somehow, the scheming bastard had found a way to pull off the ultimate trick. To beat death. To come back to us, but... nothing but blood and mist and memory.

It wasn't a fucking trick. Saint had sacrificed his life for me. For all of us. Even after all the horrible things I'd said and done. The cruelty of it all, and he was just...

Gone.

Fucking *gone*.

The storm had long since passed, no sign that the witches planned to return with reinforcements, but Hudson refused to fly. We trudged up the path in silence. Shock. I kept telling myself it was the cold, even though the snows had eased. I kept telling myself it was the cold because the alternative—that grief had rendered him flightless—was too much to bear when my own heart was already shattered.

With every step, the silence of Midnight grew more deafening. My chest tighter. Breathing more impossible because my lungs just couldn't fucking expand under the weight of the ugly truth filling up my heart.

Yet still, my mind refused to budge.

Saint would be waiting for us with Evander and Haley, it kept insisting. We'd get to the cave, and he'd stand up from behind the fire, a bowl of stew in hand, that cocky, crooked smirk shining out across the dim. *Took you long enough, brothers,* he'd say. And sure, maybe he'd be high again, maybe—ever the schemer—he'd be laughing his stoned ass off that Hudson and I had so thoroughly fallen for his ruse. I'd beat the shit out of him, but I wouldn't be mad. Wouldn't judge or condemn him for his antics or his little black pills. No fucking way. Never again would I so much as glower at him in distaste, if only... if *only* he'd just fucking *be* there.

But now, as we finally neared the cave at the top of the rise, the entrance glowing with firelight from inside, the soft and all-too-intimate sounds of Haley and Evander drifting out on the chilled breeze, that stupid hope inside me guttered out.

She was in there with our warlord. Our captor. Saint's brother.

She was... for now... happy.

And I was about to fucking destroy it.

No, not out of a jealous rage.

But because someone she loved had died for me, and I couldn't bring him back.

I turned to look at Hudson. He held my gaze a long moment, defeat casting his eyes in shadow. His wings had been torn in the fight. His spirit broken.

I nodded once. I would do this alone. I would fucking do this, because Saint died for me. For my pathetic life, and I owed him this much. I owed *her* this much.

Giving Hudson a moment of privacy, I stepped inside.

Saw the whole scene spread out before me, just as I'd feared.

Haley and Evander, naked before the fire. Embracing. Laughing.

I didn't know what was worse—the fact that he'd made her laugh, or the fact that it might be the very last time I ever heard it.

"*Haley*," I said, my voice hoarse. Broken. I dropped two packs on the ground—mine and Saint's.

She gasped and jumped to her feet, grabbing a shirt to cover up.

His shirt.

Evander rose behind her. Nude. Erect. Proud and smug, glaring at us as if we'd better have a good reason for the interruption.

"Jax!" she cried out, her smile breaking my heart a little more. "You made it!"

I tried to memorize it. That smile. The light in her eyes, no matter who'd put it there. The warmth. Tried to hold on to it, knowing I was about to blow it all away.

I drew in a shuddering breath, trying to find the words. But before I did, she saw it in my face. My eye, that fathomless window to the dark soul inside.

"I... what's wrong?" she whispered. "What happened?"

I glanced at Evander. Still nude. Still smug. His shoulders tightened under my gaze, though. And there, behind all that self-righteousness, I sensed it.

His fear.

Sharp and acute.

Hudson finally entered the cave, silently looming behind me. Blood dripped from his hands—his blood. The raven gryphon's. Saint's. The blood snow that'd finally vanished from the skies but still stained his skin.

Haley's eyes widened as she took in the sight of his torn wings.

Her fear spiked, the scent of it mingling with Evander's.

"Hudson?" Haley gasped. "What... what happened? Where's Elian?"

Evander's fear morphed into pure terror. He met my gaze again, his face etched in shock, the first glimpse of real pain flickering beneath.

My legs could no longer hold me up.

I dropped to my knees. Stared down at my useless, blood-stained hands. Tears blurred my vision.

Blood dripped onto the floor behind me—the last of the snow melting from clothes and shoes and packs. The fire crackled and hissed, and I finally lifted my head to look into Haley's eyes.

"I'm so sorry, angel," I said, every word scraping my throat raw. "Saint... Elian... he died."

And as I watched the look—*that* fucking look—bleed into the eyes of the woman I loved... the woman who loved Saint more than all the stars in the Midnight sky... I was reminded all over again just how little I'd known about true pain.

Endless. That look in her eyes was endless.

Haley fell to her knees before me. And Keradoc— Evander—whoever the fuck he was now finally had the decency to put on some pants.

"What happened?" He crossed the chamber, knelt down beside Haley. He wrapped a hand around the back of her neck, steadying her. "Where the fuck is my brother?"

"The—the witches," I stammered. Helpless. Dying inside. "They conjured the fog and he just... He saved my life. I didn't even see it coming, but he... One second he was across from me on the mountainside. He dropped his pack, the two of us bracing for incoming witches. And then... A flash in his eyes. A blur, and he just..."

The images rushed through my mind. Torture. Fucking *torture* as I'd watched my brother turn into red mist. A body made of muscle and bone, blood and hair. Silver eyes and a rare but wicked laugh. Memories and mistakes and loss and loyalty... An entire fucking immortal existence... All of it rendered utterly insubstantial by the fog. The cold, cruel breath of the realm blew across the mountain pass, and Elian was gone.

The Saint of the Hollow, the Saint of New Orleans. Just... gone.

The cave walls wavered, and Haley touched my face,

her own pinched. Tears glazed her eyes, but they didn't fall.

"It's fine," she whispered. "*He's* fine."

"No," was all I could manage.

She glanced up at Hudson. Frantically shook her head. When she spoke again, her voice had risen in volume and pitch, echoing throughout the cave. "You guys are being ridiculous. We just need to... We need to go out there and find him, is all."

"Angel," I breathed, reaching for her, but she was already getting to her feet, flitting away like water, like smoke, and I stayed on my knees and kept right on reaching for her as if I could grab her and hold on long enough to make this okay. To fix it.

To bring him back.

My fingers clutched at nothing but the chilly air, and I watched with my heart stuck in my throat as she quickly dressed and then knelt before Saint's pack, her hands trembling.

"He needs... something," she murmured, yanking open the ties. "Warm clothes. Maybe different boots... Is it still snowing? He'll definitely need good boots if it's still snowing. These mountain paths are no joke."

Evander got to his feet. Offered a hand to help me up, and I took it, both of us exchanging a pained glance as Haley carried on, babbling as if Saint had merely lost the trail. As if he actually needed boots. As if he still had feet to carry him back home.

Releasing Evander's grip, I forced myself to go to her. I had to make her understand. To accept this, no matter how devastating.

Hudson still hadn't moved. Hadn't made a sound but for that blood still drip-drip-dripping from his body.

I slid my hands over Haley's shoulders, my touch unbearably gentle when all I wanted to do was crush her against my chest and never let her go. Never let her take a step outside of this cave, because inside it maybe there was a chance... A chance I could keep her safe. Keep all the cold, brutal things from ever laying a hand on her. Keep her whole and warm and fucking *alive*.

Hear that laugh again, even if it was Evander who brought it out.

"Haley, listen to me," I said, struggling to keep my voice from breaking. My fucking heart. "I know this is hard, but you need to hear this. Saint is gone. He's dead, Haley. He's not lost. He died. We have to—"

"*Find him!*" she shouted, rocketing to her feet and whirling to face me. Her green eyes flashed—not with grief, but frustration. Fury. "We have to find him, Jax!"

I wrapped my arms around her. Held her tight, even as she beat her fists against my chest. Even as her whole body shook. Even as she just kept saying it, over and over.

Find him. Find him. Find him...

The agony in her voice ripped me to shreds all over

again, and I knew—I fucking *knew*—it didn't matter if I chained her up in this cave for the rest of her life.

This pain, right here, was worse than any brutal thing that existed outside these walls.

And I—an immortal fear demon forged in the bowels of hell—didn't have the strength to protect her from either.

2

HALEY

For the first time in my life, I had absolutely *zero* tears for Elian. Seriously—not a single drop—not even when the hopelessness in Jax's voice threatened to break me. Not even when the dark clouds in Hudson's eyes were so all-encompassing, I worried they might swallow us all.

Nope. Not going there.

Because if I let even one stupid tear fall, it would mean I actually had something to cry about. And I didn't. All I had was something to be *annoyed* about—that Elian had gotten himself hurt and separated from the others, and now everyone was staring at me like I'd lost my damned mind just because I wanted to go back out there and get him.

Well, they'd obviously been through hell fighting off those weather witches. Hudson was in rough shape. Jax

II

was completely out of sorts. Both of them were bloody and filthy. They could stay here by the fire—clean up and recuperate, if that's what they needed—no judgments.

But me? I needed to get back out there and find my man.

"Gloves," I said firmly, freeing myself from Jax's crushing embrace and returning to Elian's pack. "*That's* what he needs. Maybe some hiking socks, too. You have to protect the extremities in cold weather, right?" I fished a pair of soft leather gloves from the pack, and something else fell out with them, hitting the cave floor with a quiet tick.

A piece of paper folded into a square the size of a cracker.

I picked it up, gently unfolding it. Smoothing out the creases.

Even as my hands trembled, blurring the image before me, I knew at once what it was.

Holy shit, he must've been carrying it with him all this time...

I felt Jax hovering behind me, his breath catching.

"There was a street fair in Blackmoon Bay," I said softly. "This guy was doing caricatures and portraits—I dragged Elian over to him. Elian laughed and rolled his eyes the entire time, but he indulged me." I traced my fingertips along the lines—me, sitting in Elian's lap, my smile wide. Elian whispering in my ear, a glint of mischief in his eyes.

I still remembered what he'd said that night. That moment.

When we get home, you're going to pose for me, naked and blindfolded. And I'm going to lick every part of you until you're singing all my favorite songs...

The lines of my face were smudged and faded, as if he'd unfolded this paper and ran his fingers across it ten thousand times.

How many nights had he spent looking at us? Touching my face the way I now touched his? Remembering me, missing me, when all along I'd thought he'd forgotten?

Grief wrapped my heart in a vise, but I refused to let it break me.

I folded up the paper and tucked it back into the pack, resuming my hunt for warm socks.

"Snacks," I said. "He might need snacks. Is there any cheese left?"

The light flickered as someone moved closer, footsteps like whispers in the darkness. I hoped it wasn't Evander. I couldn't look at him now. Couldn't risk seeing even a *glimmer* of his twin's face...

But it was Hudson who came to stand behind me now. I felt his love for me through the bond, sweet and all-encompassing. His sadness, too, as heavy and immovable as the mountains themselves. All of it slipped beneath my ribs, and the defenses I'd built up around my heart began to crumble. A crack. A fissure.

I sucked in a sharp breath and closed my eyes, willing away those fucking tears that stung the backs of my eyes...

No. Do not *cry. Do* not *fucking cry for him...*

The air shifted, and my gargoyle knelt behind me. He was in his human form now, the blood vanishing along with his wings. He rested one strong hand on my shoulder. Warm. Solid. Reassuring.

His breath stirred my hair, and then his voice was in my ear, the soft rumble making me shiver. "Babygirl, I can't pretend to know how you're feeling, but—"

"*Worried*, Hudson. That's how I'm feeling. I'm worried about Elian because he's out there somewhere, alone, scared, injured... and we need to find him. We just need to *find* him, okay?" I nodded as if to affirm it for myself, cementing all those words in my mind. What choice did I have? I certainly wasn't going to sit around wringing my hands over it. Searching for him was a thing I could actually *do*. My one fucking piece of lasagna, which was about all I could manage in that moment.

Hudson squeezed my shoulder, but didn't say anything else. Didn't even move.

"You're injured," I finally managed.

"I'll heal."

"But... there was so much blood. I saw it."

"Gargoyles have a lot of extra blood vessels. It's what helps us shift so quickly. But I'm okay, babygirl. I promise."

I turned to meet his eyes, and he watched me for a long beat, his face tight with the effort of holding back his pain. No, not the pain of his torn wings, his surface wounds. But something I refused to truly see. Refused to acknowledge, because for him to be in pain like that could only mean...

Nope. Not possible.

So I turned away from him and dug around for the damn socks and told myself, again and again and again, that he and Jax were being overdramatic. That they'd misinterpreted what they'd seen out there. That the stress of fighting off the weather witches and the raven gryphons, of making their way up the mountain through the blood snow, of finding their way back to me had simply confused them.

I took another deep breath. Focused on the scents of the cave—the wood smoke. The stew Evander had made for me, remnants congealing in the pot. The lingering warmth of our desire, the bedrolls not yet cool.

A spark of magick skittered down my spine, settling low in my stomach. Across the chamber, someone else inhaled sharply.

I knew without looking up it was him. My warlord. My dark lover. He'd sensed that spark—felt it—because the magick of Midnight belonged to him as well. It bound us to each other. To this land and all its beautiful darkness.

The thought should've brought me comfort, but it only cracked another chunk off that wall around my heart. The edges of it flickered with pain. Raw. Exposed.

"Haley," Evander whispered, but I still couldn't bring myself to look at him. To acknowledge the loss looming over us like a dark, inescapable cloud.

The magick inside me finally fizzled, and a tremor rumbled up through my legs. For the briefest instant I worried the ghouls of Beggar's Moat had come for me, tracked me through the mountains to finally claim what I'd denied them the night the guards left me for dead. I stared at the ground between my knees, waiting for the crack in the earth. Waiting for the bones to rise. To drag me to the deep places of a world without light. Without hope.

But it wasn't the ground that shook, I realized. It was me. A great wave rippled up from my feet, through my legs, into my chest and arms. My teeth chattered, every cell in my body vibrating with the effort of keeping my heart from exploding.

"Hey," Hudson murmured into my hair. He gripped my elbows, his massive hands warm and steadying as he gently urged me to my feet. "Mind if we step out and get some air? Something I need to tell you."

Still shaking, I nodded, grateful when he scooped me into his arms and tucked me in close, relieving me of the burden of having to walk even a single step.

I think we both knew that if I so much as tried, I would've collapsed.

I had just enough strength to reach up and touch his face, and when he met my eyes, I said the only word I could manage just then.

"Fly."

3

EVANDER

I watched, stunned into silent paralysis, as the gargoyle carried Haley out of the cave.

How was it possible that only minutes had passed? Minutes since I'd held her in my arms? Since I'd kissed her breathless and she'd filled up the emptiness of this dark cave—of my heart—with her terrible singing?

Since her men had returned without their third—without my brother?

I blinked slowly, as if my mind simply couldn't keep up with the turn of events.

Across the dim space, Haley finally spared me a glance, her dark head lifting over the gargoyle's shoulder to meet my gaze. I don't know what she saw in my eyes, but her own suddenly filled with a terror so plain, so sharp, it tore through me as readily as a blade.

With that single look, I understood why the demon had fallen to his knees.

The helplessness I felt in that moment threatened to rise up and sweep me clear off the mountain.

The magick that had bound me to her faded, and it was only the demon's hand firm against my chest that made me realize I'd moved at all. That I'd reached for her as she vanished into the starry dark void beyond the cave entrance.

I blinked away the haze and looked at him, that blue eye glaring at me, glassy and raw, mirroring Haley's pain.

"She needs time," he said.

"We don't have the luxury of—"

"*Evander*," he snapped, and I finally relented, backing off.

"And you?" I asked, if for no other reason than to provoke him into conversation—*any* conversation. Anything other than the deafening silence of the dead. "What does her demon need?"

He groaned and scrubbed a hand over his face, massaging the skin above his ruined eye. Phantom pain, perhaps.

I suppressed a shudder.

"I don't know what the fuck I need," he said. "But even if I did, I sure as hell wouldn't be getting it from you."

I let it go without a response, and he turned his back and stalked toward the entrance. He didn't leave, though.

Just leaned against the stone, arms crossed over his chest, eye undoubtedly roving along whichever route Haley and her gargoyle had taken.

Never before had I felt so torn between opposing worlds—opposing lives—as I felt in that moment, standing immobile between the darkness beyond the cave and the fire burning within it. My brother—their friend and ally—was dead. That alone should have given us some common ground, yet I was no closer to the demon than I'd been the night I'd put him on his knees in the throne room and watched as my guards riddled him with bolts.

I searched my heart for an ache, but found none. Only a deep, endless longing for the woman who no longer needed me—if she'd ever needed me at all. And why would she? Haley had her gargoyle and her demon now. Men who loved her. Men who loved my brother, when all I could feel was... empty.

And I'd meant what I'd told her earlier—time was not on our side. Regardless of the ill fortune that had befallen Elian of Autumnshire, I still needed to reach the fae who dwelled beneath this mountain range. Still needed to convince them to fight by our side, even if I had to do it alone.

I finished dressing in silence, then checked my pack, picking up where I'd left off just before she'd told me the story of my scars and the silver wolf who'd given them to me. Before she'd wrapped her arms around me and upended my entire world.

"Going somewhere?" the demon finally asked. He didn't turn from his watch beyond the cave, but still, I felt his gaze on me. His judgment.

"Melantha's army continues its advance through the desert. I don't believe she's manifested yet, but her presence grows stronger—I can feel it in the magick. It's... changing." As if it were listening in, the magick rippled through the surrounding stones. Barely perceptible, but there. Making itself known. Present.

I wondered if Haley could feel it now, too. If this magick would always tether us. Change us.

"I need to move forward with my plan," I continued, closing up the pack. I kept it light—either I'd find the fae and convince them to aid me, or I wouldn't be making a return trip. "We need allies, and—"

"Your brother is dead, Evander."

"So you've said."

"Your brother is *dead*," he repeated. "Your brother."

Again, I mined the depths of my heart, searching for something beyond that yawning dark emptiness.

But there was only the dim echo of memories I could no longer reach. Memories that belonged to another man in another time in another realm, as lost to me now as the brother I would never know.

4

HUDSON

*P*lease tell me you've got the words to make this better, Hudson. *Please...*" Haley's voice broke, and whatever was left of my heart fucking cracked in half.

The one time I needed words more than anything, I couldn't find them—not even for her. Because the words to explain this fucked-up mess didn't even exist.

Ignoring the pain in my tattered wings, I'd shifted back into warrior form and flown us out about a mile down from the cave, desperate to escape the crushing sadness inside those suffocating stone walls. Now, Haley and I sat side by side on a nameless rocky ledge, legs dangling out over nothing but black air, the sprawl of Midnight's darkness stretching on for an eternity below.

All I could think about was the fall.

Would death claim us as swiftly as it'd taken Saint? A

blink, a breath, and then... nothing? Would we find peace? Had *he* found peace?

Fucking Saint. All those pills. His pain. Was it possible he'd finally escaped it?

I tried to hold on to that thought. To the blind hope that no matter how badly the rest of us fucking hurt to lose him, maybe Saint was... maybe he was finally okay.

But I couldn't know that for sure, and hope and pretty wishes would never be enough to calm the storm raging inside me. To dry the tears from Haley's eyes and bring that smile back to her face.

Saint. Elian. Our brother. Our family. He was... gone.

"Tell me this isn't happening," she whispered, and I shuddered, desperate to keep the full extent of my pain inside. In that moment, it felt so fucking sharp I was pretty damn sure it would slice her up if she got too close to it.

I closed my eyes and squeezed her hand tight. Blew out a long, broken breath. Didn't matter how many times I'd witnessed death up close and personal, how many fucking times I'd seen the most violent, gruesome shit imaginable. It *never* got any easier, and it never made any sense. How could someone be standing there one second, and then—in a single heartbeat, in a *literal* blur—just stop fucking existing?

Still wordless, still spinning, I pulled her onto my lap and held her against my chest, tucking my torn wings around her as if that alone could keep her safe.

"He's not dead," she whispered, her whole body trembling in my hold, voice softer than the breeze. "Elian... what we had... what we *have*... If he were truly gone, I would know it. Deep in my heart, I would know it."

I stroked her hair, wishing like hell I could just leap off this fucking mountain and fly her somewhere else—to some other realm where the light still shone, where darkness and pain could never touch her again.

"Do you know what I told him?" she asked. "One night when we were still back at the apartment in Amaranth City? I told him that after he left me—after I was sure he was never coming back—I would fantasize that he'd died. He stood right in front of me, and I looked him in the eyes and told him I wished he *had* died, because it would've been easier than watching him disappear a little piece at a time... God. How could I say something like that, Hudson? How could I be so cruel?"

Tears blurred my vision, the breeze cold on my warrior skin. I could feel her pain through the bond. Her desperate ache. The dim flicker of hope that somehow this had all been a mistake.

"I just got him back," she said. "I spent five years hating him. Five years wasted to anger and bitterness, and all along, he was here. He was here with his brothers, fighting for you all, fighting for what he thought was right, and I finally... I finally *understand* him, Hudson. I understand why he made the choices he made. Turns out all those things I cursed him for are all the things I most admire about him, and if he's gone—truly gone—then I'll never get to..."

She sucked in a sharp, shuddering breath and pressed both hands to her chest, as if she could keep her heart from leaping right out and splattering on the rocks. When she opened her mouth again, no more words came out. Only gasps. Sobs.

Agony.

"Breathe, Haley. Please, babygirl. Just breathe." I could no longer keep the pain from my voice, from spilling right out of me like blood from a wound. I felt it wrap around us both, heavy and endless, as dark as the Midnight sky. I ran a trembling hand down her back. "I need you to breathe for me, because if you don't, I can't... I can't get through this without you..."

"I'm falling apart, Hudson. I'm falling apart and you have to tell me it's okay. Tell me this is just a nightmare. One of Elian's schemes. A trick of the realm. *Something*..."

Fuck, I wished I could lie to her, just this once. She wanted it so badly. Needed it—all that sugar coating.

But that's not how it worked with us. Never would be.

I slid my hand around the back of her head and held her against my chest, my tears soaking into her hair as hers spilled all over my skin, and I whispered the only words I could find.

"I got you, babygirl. I fuckin' got you."

She went boneless in my arms, and a howl so vast, so desperate, so full of anguish exploded out of her, the sound of it carving me out inside, my wings trembling as she clung to me and sobbed, and in that brutal moment, it was only my love for her—my fated promise to take care of her—that kept me from shifting into my human form, closing my eyes, and jumping right over that black fucking edge.

The cold wind scraped across my skin, and in the light of the triple moons, there we sat, the warrior and his witch, his mate, both of us succumbing to that gaping, gnawing hurt.

And then, finally... breathing. Just fucking breathing.

I didn't know how much time passed before the trembling stopped—hers, mine. The mountain itself. But eventually she pulled back to gaze up at me, and through them tear-soaked lashes, the change came over her swiftly.

Grief faded from her eyes, and in a blink, that fierce, steely, Haley Barnes determination lit a new fire behind them. A bright fucking blaze in the darkness.

"I know Death," she said. Then, in a whisper that sent a chill slithering down my spine, "I can bring him back."

My arms tightened around her instinctively, as if she

might bolt right out of my hold and throw herself off the mountain just to find her way back to him.

"Haley..." It was a warning as much as a plea. "*No. Necromancy is...* No. Saint doesn't even have a—" I clamped my mouth shut over the word. *Body*. He'd been liquified by the fog. *Liquified*. All that remained of my brother had soaked into the Midnight soil. Into my skin. Jax's.

I could still taste his blood in my mouth. Smell it. Feel it.

But Haley was already shaking her head and wriggling out of my embrace, this new mission giving her strength. Purpose. "You don't understand, Hudson. I know Death. Literally. From everything in Blackmoon Bay... Death is one of my sister's mates, only he became mortal and the death mantel passed on to..." She swallowed hard, then said, "Reva. She was one of our witches. A kid—teenager. She helped save us from Darkwinter but she... she didn't survive the final battle. Not as a mortal girl, anyway. But Liam—Death—he found a way to... I'm not sure exactly how it all happened, but I know her, Hudson. So if I can find a way to get to her before Elian's soul crosses into the Shadowlands, maybe she can send him back to us."

The Shadowlands. The place where the dead found their eternal rest.

Assuming they made it that far. Assuming they weren't bound for hell.

But Saint... no. He wasn't going to hell. Not after all he'd sacrificed for us. If that's how the universe worked, then Death and everyone else involved could go fuck themselves, far as I was concerned.

"The Shadowlands weren't meant for the living, Haley," I said, as gently as I could. "You're talking about risking the loss of your own soul and facing down Death— that's assuming you can find her. Friend or not—*teenager* or not—it won't be an easy battle."

"If that's what it takes to save him? If there's a *chance*?" She wiped away the last of her tears, the color returning to her cheeks. "I don't care how hard it is. I'm doing it. And I'd do it for you and Jax, too. For... for anyone I care about."

"Evander." The name was out before I could stop myself. Stop the flames of jealousy that had flickered to life the moment we'd returned to that cave and still hadn't yet dimmed, despite the weight of everything else.

"Evander," she said firmly. It wasn't a question, but I could tell from the look in her eyes she wanted my thoughts on the matter.

I took her hands in mine. Pressed a kiss to every one of her knuckles, then released her hands so I could cup her face. "Evander... Saint's brother..." I shook my head, still not quite believing how much had happened in the last couple nights. "If you're telling me you care for him, and you're telling me he's worthy of it... Then hell. Doesn't matter what I think of him. You know I support you, Haley. Always."

A nod. A faint, relieved smile. "But it *does* matter, Hudson. It matters to me. For better or worse, there's something that connects him to me beyond the fact that he's Elian's brother. And that means he's connected to you and Jax as well. To all of us. I don't know how it happened, or why, or what it all means... And maybe I could make sense of it if I had more time. If we weren't facing this war and Melantha and everything with..." She sighed again, her lashes lowering. "With Elian. But that only makes me realize how important all of you are to me. Logical or not, we were meant to find each other. All of us. Which is exactly why I need to bring Elian back. To bring our family back."

Fresh tears slipped down her cheeks, wet and warm on my hands, but they weren't tears of grief. They were the tears of a fighter preparing for battle. Tears of a warrior who was ready to face down death for the man she loved.

I stared at her, awed and humbled. Still so fucking gobsmacked that the fates had seen fit to bring her to me. To make her mine. Ours.

I thought I'd understood loyalty. Bonds. Saint and Jax and me—we were brothers. Even without the blood oath and the tattoos, we were fuckin' *brothers*. But Haley? Her loyalty was unparalleled. She was talking about fighting

Death. Literal death just for a slim chance to bring him back to us.

Now, looking into her infinite eyes under the triple moons of Midnight, I smiled. "I said it before and I'll say it again. If anyone can save him, babygirl, it's you."

"But you... you don't think it's possible." Her shoulders slumped.

"I don't think it's *likely*," I answered honestly. "But... That ain't a reason not to try."

She nodded and let loose a heavy sigh. "So you didn't bring me out here to convince me to just... accept that he's gone? To let him go, once and for all?"

Another shudder rippled through her body, and I drew her close and pressed a long kiss between her brows, wishing I could make sense of the feeling burning in my heart. Wishing I could turn it all into words so she would know—truly—what I felt.

My whole life in this body, in this universe... a thousand fucking years... and I could count on *one* hand the people who'd fight for me like that. Saint. Jax. And now...

"Haley, I'd no more try to talk you out of fighting for the man you love than I'd try to talk you out of casting spells or growing them gorgeous black roses. It's all part of who you are, part of the woman I fucking love more than all the stars in the sky, in this realm or any other, and I don't want to change that about you. Never. *Never.*"

She climbed into my lap again and I ran my hand

down her back and buried my face in her hair. *Mine.* My fierce little monster girl, my mate.

"I brought you out here," I whispered, "because I need you to know you're not the only one who loves him." I closed my eyes as my throat tightened around the words. "I need you to know how much Saint means to *me.*"

5

HUDSON

"You never asked me about the not-talking thing," I said softly. "Why it took me so long to open up to you, even though we clearly had a connection from the start. Why I still find it hard to talk to everyone else."

"I figured you'd share if and when you were ready. And if you didn't, well..." Haley's breath misted against my chest, her fingers tracing idle patterns along my forearm as I held her tight. "It's the same thing you said about me, Gargs. It's all part of who you are. Part of the man I love. Words or no words—that doesn't change how I feel about you. Doesn't change our bond."

"No, but knowing this... It might help you understand things better. Me. Saint. Why he... why he sacrificed so much to get us out of Midnight."

She stiffened, the weight of my old ghosts pressing in close. I knew she could sense it through the bond—my shame. My private darkness. The rage that would continue to simmer inside me until Mad Marco and the last of his traitorous fucking crew were dust in the wind.

But I had to tell her this story. Had to get it all out, once and for all, because I needed her to know it. To know all those things that'd made me the man she loved.

And to know how much Saint truly fucking meant to me, just like I'd said. Not just because I wanted her to know, but because I wanted him to know, too. And I never got the chance to tell him.

A fresh bolt of pain shot right through me, but I welcomed it. Pain like that... it meant I'd lost something fucking important. The fact that I'd even had it at all was a blessing.

Keeping my wings tucked close around us, I shifted partially back into my human form and turned my right arm so she could see the tattoo—a field of wildflowers hacked by a bloody scythe, bright blooms scattered along the ground.

"I call it the reaping," I whispered, the word sending a cold shiver down the back of my neck. "Not a day goes by I don't look at this tattoo and remember it. Feel it."

She traced the outline of the scythe with her fingertips, down the handle and across the blade. When she spoke again, her voice was reverent. Awed. "What does it mean?"

"It means I'll spend the rest of my immortal life atoning for something I can't change." I turned to lay my cheek on the top of her head and breathed in the scent of her. Sweet. Home. I'd meant what I told her before the weather witches attacked—she *did* make me strong. Brave. And I needed every ounce of that courage to get this story out.

"Like all of Midnight's gargoyles," I continued, "I was born in captivity, bred at the behest of the dark fae nobles who saw us as little more than cattle. Most of us were used for grunt work—transporting goods, fighting on the front lines of their bullshit territorial skirmishes. Others, they..." I swallowed the knot in my throat. "...experimented on."

Haley gasped. "Do they still do stuff like that?"

"Experiments? Yeah, I'm sure they do. I mean, all this was even before Keradoc's time—the *real* Keradoc—but one look around will tell you... Ain't much changed. Same shit, new warlord, you know? Anyway, they had me working in the Stone City mines at first, digging up gems or metals or whatever the hell else they thought they could turn into currency. I was good—strong, fast. Did the job of guys twice my size in half the time. Eventually, the owner of one of the mines—an original Midnight royal, this guy —he took notice. Saw what I could do and decided he wanted me in his elite guard. Given the alternatives, it was a fucking honor to be selected for work like that, so off I went."

"But you had to leave Stone City?"

"Had to leave everyone and everything I'd ever known, yeah. But still—it was a better shot than what most of us ever got. So I said my goodbyes and went willingly. Did the job with pride. Wasn't a bad gig, honestly. For the most part, he and his family treated me fairly."

"For the most part?"

A hollow laugh rang out, the old resentments twisting through my gut. "A slave is still a slave, Haley. Not like they set a place for me at the dinner table, or even called me by my name, for that matter. I was just 'gargoyle' to them. Sometimes 'guard,' but never more than that. The kids, though? They were the good ones. Still young enough that the whole fucked-up system hadn't yet crushed their spirits." I laughed, remembering how they used to climb all over me whenever I walked into the room. Beg me to take them out flying, even though their parents had strictly forbidden it.

I told Haley a bit about my life at the royal estate in northern Amaranth City, not far from the sea. How I'd spent my nights guarding the noble lord and his family, telling the kids stories about life in the mines. Occasionally accompanying the lord on so-called diplomatic missions to territories beyond the wall, where I'd slaughter his enemies and let him bask in the glory, claiming another plot of Midnight wasteland just because he could.

"The royals never visited their claimed territories," I said. "Only time they ever left the safety of the wall was to wipe out some faction or another—expand their pointless empires. Whole thing was fucked. Always has been, always will be." I closed my eyes and shook my head, those old resentments turning into a quiet rage that rippled through my muscles.

Haley tucked in closer, her touch once again easing the ache inside me.

"One night," I said, "the lord of the manor decided to head out beyond the wall with some of the other high fae fucks on a hunting expedition. Looking for dragon's eggs, supposedly—way too precious a treasure to risk bringing a lowly gargoyle on the trip. I was left behind to look after his wife and their four children. The lady had heard whispers of a growing threat against the royals—the usual unrest. She'd begged him to cancel his trip, but he chalked off her concern to hysteria and left me to deal with her.

"She'd just put the kids to bed when we both heard it —a commotion on the roof. We grabbed the kids from their rooms, and I secured them with their mom in the master suite, then headed up to check it out." I sucked in a shuddering breath, no longer able to keep the quake from my limbs, the frantic pounding from the warrior heart that'd never forgotten its most brutal betrayal. "They were waiting for me up there, babygirl. Fuckin' ambush."

"Gargoyles?" she whispered.

"A half dozen of 'em, yeah. Three I'd never seen before. Three I'd once considered friends." I opened my eyes. Met her green gaze in the moonlight. "Garrison, Draven, and Mad Marco."

6

"I am... saddened by the news of Elian's passing," I finally managed, the lie leaving a bitter taste on my lips. "But I didn't know him as you did. I didn't know him as my brother."

"Because you threw away the chance. Even after learning who he was. Even after he fought by your side against your own guards in the Sanctuary. Even after he agreed to accompany you on this... this doomed mission."

"He was your friend," I said evenly. "That I *do* know, and for what it's worth, I'm sorry for your loss. But—"

"But you're leaving us, anyway. Leaving *her* when she needs all the support we can offer."

Something about the "we" in his statement sent an unfamiliar warmth unfurling in my chest, making me itch.

"War rarely gives us the luxury of doing what's right. Only of doing what must be done."

"Spoken like a true warlord." A dark laugh slithered across the chamber. "Tell yourself whatever you need to, Evander. Whatever gets you through the night, right?"

"And what would you have me do, demon?" I stood and crossed the dim space, joining him at the entrance. Outside, the darkness of Midnight shone like a black jewel, haunting and fathomless. "Shall I fall to pieces and weep for a brother I likely mourned centuries ago? Ask the kind, compassionate soldiers of Darkwinter for some bereavement time for a man who, until last night, was nothing but a fugitive of my realm? Perhaps I can inform Melantha and her Army of the Dead that we'll need to reschedule their sacking of the kingdom on account of the death of a vampire-fae who sacrificed his life for *you*." I fisted his shirt, hauled him close. So close I could see every scar and divot in his ruined face, harsh and cruel in the firelight. "Do *not* presume to understand my feelings on this or any other matter, *demon*."

A deadly smile slid across his mouth, and his eye blazed bright. Brighter still, until it was nearly glowing. A chill crept into my skull, scraping across my mind like a bitter wind.

I didn't resist the invasion of his power. His manipulations. I merely returned that smile—the grin of a corpse who didn't have the good sense to know he was already dead. In a dark whisper, I said, "If you honestly believe you can conjure a fear more terrifying than the nightmares haunting my head, be my guest."

Behind us, a log shifted on the fire, the flames hissing and popping, shattering the tense moment.

His smile faltered. The gleam in his eye finally dimmed.

That cold, invasive power retreated at once, leaving only shame in its wake.

"I'm... sorry," he said, and when he finally lowered that unnervingly intense blue eye, I knew he'd meant it.

I just didn't know what he was sorry for, exactly. That he'd invaded my mind? That I'd lost a brother I didn't even know? That Haley was in pain? That we'd nearly drawn daggers over all of it?

He let out a dark sigh and said softly, "I should've... I should've been able to protect him. He was my brother and friend, and I was supposed to have his back."

And there was my answer, right along with the common ground I so desperately sought.

No, it wasn't loss and grief that bound us now.

It was guilt.

All the anger inside me crumbled into dust, unleashing the dam on my own dark confessions. The first bite of pain lanced my heart, and I whispered, "I... I let him stay and fight while I retreated to the safety of this cave."

"You were merely protecting Haley."

"Still, I… I sent my brother to his death believing I wanted nothing from him but his unwavering allegiance. Nothing but what he could offer me as a soldier and spy. And now I'll never…" My voice splintered, and I closed my mouth, admonishing myself. It was more than I'd meant to say, more than I'd meant to reveal to the demon I'd treated as poorly as I'd treated my twin. My blood. My worst enemies.

"It was Elian's choice to join this mission," he said, plainly and without judgment. "All of us made the choice to back you, Evander. Same as Haley. And we'd do it again in a heartbeat, even knowing the risks."

"For her."

"For her," he confirmed, leaving no doubts about the limits of their loyalties.

And how could I blame them? Until last night when I'd finally revealed my true identity, I'd been their captor. The cruel warlord who'd threatened them, forced them to do his bidding, put their lives at risk again and again, all in service to this war.

My war.

And tonight, they'd walked into this cave carrying the weight of Elian's death—their brother's death—only to discover I'd bedded the woman they all loved. The woman he'd loved, too.

A surge of guilt burned away the last icy vestiges of his powers lingering in my mind.

Hastily, I stepped into my boots and grabbed my cloak.

Shouldering my pack, I said, "Keep her here. Keep her safe."

"What about you?"

"Watch for me by the second moonrise tomorrow. If I haven't returned, I want the three of you to gather what supplies you can and retreat to—"

"*Retreat*?" The hissing voice that broke across the night was not the demon's, but something unfamiliar, terrifying in its utter lack of warmth. Of humanity. "Such is the way of cowards and thieves."

The demon and I reached for our daggers and turned toward the cave entrance just as the pale faces came into view. On silent footsteps, they marched inside uninvited— a dozen feral fae soldiers, skin and hair as colorless as the first moon, all of them armed with swords carved of bone and obsidian. Three ancient dark fae witches accompanied them, magick curling from their very skin like glittering smoke.

Just beyond the cave, the shadows of two raven gryphons darkened the path.

Before I could even speak, a dark spell wrapped an invisible fist around my throat, squeezing. Crushing. The demon choked and gasped beside me.

"So tell us, *warlord*. Which one are you?" The general stepped forward and narrowed his ancient gaze, his black eyes like twin pieces of coal sinking into that eery, milk-white face as his witches surrounded us, the ancient magick crackling as it feasted upon the very breath in our lungs. "A coward or a thief?"

7

HUDSON

It was the fight of my life, Haley," I said. "For *hours* the six of 'em taunted me. Tag-teamed me like a rat in a maze, no escape. I left more blood on that rooftop than I've spilled in the nine-hundred-some years since, but no matter how hard I fought, there was never a chance for victory."

"*Assholes*," she seethed. "You were outnumbered six to one. By your own fucking kind."

"Wasn't just the numbers. Whole thing was rigged from the start. The fight was just a way for Marco to... I don't know. Feel like a man, I guess. Toy with me before the real attack came down."

"*Real* attack?"

"He and his boys had gotten tight with some dark witches. They were packing a sunlight spell that could immobilize any gargoyle on contact."

"Like the bullets from the night of the feast?" she asked.

I nodded. "Same shit, only this one was like a goddamn nuke compared to those bullets. One minute I'm on the ground bleeding, trying to think through some kind of plan. Then there's a flash and a fire across my skin like nothing I've ever felt. Next thing I know, I'm stone."

I shuddered again, the rest of the gruesome story boiling up like hot poison from the darkest, most ancient parts of me.

"I could see, hear, and feel everything around me," I said. "And they knew it, too—that's exactly how they planned it. I was trapped, Haley. Trapped and paralyzed as they broke through the wards in the house, dragged the woman and her servants and children out onto the grounds and... and did the most unspeakable... The way they... they violated them, and I just..."

My words tangled into knots and fell away on the Midnight breeze, tears leaking from my eyes. My girl didn't say anything, though. Just wrapped her arms around me and held me tight, giving me the space to catch my breath. Letting me find my way through the darkness, back to the tangle of my words. Back to her.

Long moments passed before I could speak again, and when I did, my throat ached with the effort. But I couldn't stop now. I had to get it out. All of it.

"I found out later that Marco... His family had paid off

the nobles to get him out of the mines, but they'd chosen me as their guardian instead, keeping the money and denying they'd ever had any dealings with Marco's family. So Marco took it upon himself to exact his revenge—on me and the family both. In the end, he and his boys slaughtered everyone who lived on the estate. The lord and lady's siblings, random cousins. All the staff. Hell, even the mares weren't spared the wrath of the Stone City gargoyles. And the whole time—the whole fucking time they tortured those people, spilled all that blood—there wasn't a damn thing I could do but scream inside my prison of stone. Scream and fucking *scream* until it felt like my throat was shredded, but no one heard a sound.

"When they were sure all the fae and their servants were dead, they dropped me in the middle of all that carnage, still in my stone form. They painted me with the blood of the dead and left the bodies strewn around me like it was all some kind of... ritualistic sacrifice. I... I ain't never seen anything like it. Not before, not since. And I pray I never have to. Not with kids. Not like that."

Haley was crying now, too, the two of us clinging to each other in the darkness as the gruesome memories scored my heart all over again.

"When the spell wore off and I could finally move again, I was... I was beside myself, Haley. A total fucking wreck." I ran my thumb along the tattoo. "I kept thinking about wildflowers cut down by a blade—that's what I saw when I looked at those poor fucking kids. And all I wanted to do was find a way to put them back together again. But there was so much blood and... and it was too fucking late. They were just... gone. Exhausted, wasted, I fell to my knees and wept, but when I tried to scream again, no sound came out. So I stopped. Stopped screaming. Stopped fucking talking altogether. Words wouldn't bring them back, so what the fuck was the point?"

She laced her fingers through mine and squeezed.

"When the lord returned from his hunt the next night and saw what'd happened," I said, "I still couldn't speak. Couldn't bring myself to give voice to what I'd witnessed. He knew I wasn't the murderer—knew I loved his fucking kids like they were my own. But it didn't even matter, because my true crime was much worse than the murders. I was a gargoyle—*their* gargoyle. Slave or not, I was still honor- and duty-bound to protect that family at all costs, even if it meant sacrificing my own life. And in that single, most important mission, I'd failed.

"I remained in my human form, naked and vulnerable before him. I knelt. Bowed my head, hands clasped behind my back. I wanted him to execute me. Waited and wished for the bite of his sword. It was his right—I was their guardian, and I'd failed them. Completely and utterly failed them. But of course, an outright execution would've been too kind a punishment."

I rubbed the back of my neck, the dull ache where I

sometimes still felt the blade that had never come. Still felt like I deserved it.

"He cast me out beyond the wall," I went on, "forbidding me from having any contact with other gargoyles. I wasn't allowed to return to Stone City. Wasn't allowed to meet my... my mate." I blew out a heavy sigh. "Yeah. Nine hundred years ago, I had a mate—only other time in my life. She was another gargoyle—one I didn't know. Felt the first tug of our bond just a couple months after the slaughter, knew it was my fated duty to protect her as well. But I couldn't—couldn't risk even acknowledging that pull. If I disobeyed the lord's command and returned to Stone City, I knew he'd find my mate and slaughter her as readily as Marco had slaughtered his family. The irony of it, though... Fuck *me*, Haley. She died anyway. A few years later, Marco took her out. I don't know how he found out she was my charge, but he did."

Another audible gasp. Haley tensed in my arms, but I pushed on. Hell, I'd kept the story locked up inside me for so long, I never thought I'd ever give it room to breathe again. Now that I had, I couldn't stop. Not until I got back to the fucking start of all this.

To Saint.

"Cutting a gargoyle off from his wards, from his pack... it does something to us," I said. "Not just emotionally, but physically as well. We *need* to protect. We're driven by that need, fed by it. Out beyond the wall, no charges to mind, no friends... I was dying, babygirl. Night by night, breath by breath, I was literally fuckin' dying."

At this, she cupped my face and looked up into my eyes, her gaze turning fierce as she caught my tears with her thumbs. "But you *survived*, Hudson. You were a gargoyle on your own, and somehow, you made it through."

"But that's the thing, Haley. I wasn't on my own. I felt something out there. Some kind of... spark." I lowered my mouth to hers, stealing the ghost of a kiss—the barest brush across her sweet lips. Then, in a voice as soft as the breeze, "I think it was you, babygirl. The promise of you. It'd be several hundred years before you were even born, but fate already knew you'd be mine. Not just a mate to protect, but a woman I might actually fall in love with. A woman who might fall right back. And even the idea of it... of you... It just... just gave me that little nudge. A reminder that life was worth fighting for, even if it would take me centuries to realize why."

She smiled and pressed a hand to my chest. To my heart. I covered her hand with mine and held her there, once again borrowing her warmth. Her courage.

"I decided to trust that little spark," I said. "Somehow, I made my way back to the wall. Snuck inside with a trading caravan. Changed my identity, started picking up odd jobs —mercenary work, private security detail for some of the most unsavory motherfuckers you can imagine."

"Unsavory..." Haley narrowed her eyes, the tiniest smile turning up the corners of her lips. "Let me guess. That's how you met Elian and Jax?"

"Hundreds of years and thousands of unsavory assholes later, yeah. That's *exactly* how I met them. Keradoc—the real one—was Midnight's ruler by then, making life hell for everyone—more hell than usual. The boys needed my help keeping their asses safe during their various... business dealings."

"Smuggling drugs, weapons, and secrets," she clarified. "Jax told me about it the first time I saw the corpsevine fields."

"Hey. Ain't none of us ever pretended to be the good guys." I sighed. "Despite all Midnight's bullshit, though, I was content. For the first time since I'd left Stone City to serve the nobles, I had a family to protect again. A purpose. Fucking *brothers* I could take care of, who took care of me just by being there. Letting me in. I wasn't naive enough to think it'd last forever—that's the first lesson you learn growing up in a place like Midnight. Don't get too fucking comfortable, right? But I *did* get comfortable. So much so that I almost forgot about my old ghosts. Forgot that they never really die, even if they lay low for a time."

She reached for my forearm again, fingers gliding across the wildflowers, making me shiver. "What happened?"

"One night, I was coming out of the tavern after a few drinks, and there he was."

She knew at once who I meant. Could probably hear my damn blood singing the fucker's name.

"Mad Marco," she whispered, and I felt the answering fury rise inside me all over again.

"He attacked me again, but this time, he was alone. Without his boys or his precious dark fae witches backing him, I beat his ass in a heartbeat. Would've killed him too, right there in the streets of the Hollow for all to see. But he reached out to Draven through their gargoyle bond, and the fucker showed up and saved him. They could've double-teamed me, but they didn't—just took off. I knew right then I was in deep shit—no way would they leave a loose end like me hanging around. Sure enough, the fuckers reported me to Keradoc as a fugitive. Said they had irrefutable evidence that I'd slaughtered the fae nobles all those centuries ago—an unsolved crime so heinous, it'd sent the noble lord and the remaining members of their bloodline fleeing to the mountains, never to be heard from again."

"Hudson... wait. The mountains? The... oh my *god*." She shot to her feet, the last pieces clicking into place. "The fae nobles... You're talking about the feral fae. The ones Keradoc wants us to meet."

8

HUDSON

aley's face paled as I confirmed her suspicions about the fae.

"Those children are still... they kept them," she said. "Not alive, but..."

"Yeah. I know." Sickness roiled inside me, and I reached for her hands and tugged her back down into my lap again, needing to touch her, the softness and warmth of her skin the only thing keeping me from absolutely losing my shit at the thought of facing those fae again. I had no idea whether the noble lord himself was still alive, but it didn't matter. His bloodline lived on—all those who hadn't dwelled at the estate, anyway. And those poor fucking kids, kept in some kind of twisted magickal stasis, never allowed to find peace...

That alone was enough to make me rage.

"I... I didn't know," she said softly, tucking herself

53

inside my hold once more. "When Evander told me about them, he mentioned the attack in passing. I didn't know you were involved."

"Pretty sure he didn't know it either. It was before Evander's time as Keradoc, and I've never spoken of this to anyone. Not even the boys know the whole story."

"You shouldn't be here. You shouldn't have to face them. To live through that again."

"There's a whole lot of shit none of us *should* have to face, but we do it, Haley. We fucking do it for the ones we love. So yeah, I absolutely *should* be here, because here is where *you* are, and if you think for a second there's anywhere else I'm gonna be, you need your head examined, woman." I ruffled her hair and leaned in close, stealing another kiss before she could say anything else on the matter.

When I finally drew back, she said, "How did you find out Marco reported you?"

"Keradoc gave his lieutenant general the order to hunt me down."

"Wait..." Her brow furrowed. "Oona?"

I nodded. "Saint never really trusted her, but apparently the two of them had worked out some kinda truce for Jax's sake. Soon as she got the order, she told Saint about it. Said she didn't want to do it—had no reason to hunt me, to deliver me to the dungeons for an eternity of torture. But hers wasn't the only crew out looking for me. It was a death sentence either way—I could either let Oona turn me over to Keradoc, or bide my time until Marco and his fucking lackeys found me again. And that was fine—I was ready for death. Thousand years was a good run, I figured, especially for a gargoyle of Midnight. But—"

"But Elian wouldn't let you die," she whispered, barely holding back a shudder as the reality slammed into us both. The reminder of why we were out here having this conversation.

My chest tightened, images of Saint getting swallowed up by that fog slicing through my mind once more.

"Saint gave me the lowdown from Oona," I said. "Told me not to worry—he was already working on a plan to get us the fuck out of there for good—all three of us. I didn't want him and Jax risking their asses for the likes of me, but Saint... You know how stubborn that bastard is. He dug his heels in. Refused to leave this place unless all three of us walked out together—those were his terms."

I shook my head, a sad laugh escaping as I remembered the look in the sonofabitch's eyes that night. The warning he gave me. *You bail on us now, brother, you're condemning us to this nightmare world for an eternity. So unless you want me to beat your ass until you're talking again, you're walking through that portal with us.*

"I didn't understand the hows and the whys at that moment, but I wasn't about to hold them back—not when he was flat out refusing to leave without me. I only knew that it would cost us—that we'd have to keep the business running in New Orleans, that Gem and everyone else would get a cut of the profits in exchange for keeping our escape secret. But there was dark magick involved, too."

"Fucking Melantha," Haley gritted out. The very mention of her name seemed to shift something around us, turning the air foul. Far in the distance, a strange indigo light flickered along the horizon.

The Dark Goddess and her army were getting closer. Stronger.

"For me, leaving my homeland *was* the price," I said. "Midnight was my last connection to my people, to the gargoyle I'd been for damn near a thousand years. The goddess knew I'd never really fit in down in New Orleans, even as I kept watch over Jax and Saint. And a place like that—all the sunshine? I spent more time as a statue in Saint's garden than I did anywhere else. Felt like my damn wings had been clipped, but still. Small price to pay to avoid the dungeons, and to keep Saint and Jax safe, too.

"The three of us never talked about what she demanded from us that night. No reason to—we got out, started over in New Orleans, and that was that. I always assumed that's why Jax had lost his eye—figured it had something to do with his powers. But with Saint, I had no idea. Until now." I slid my hand into her hair and fisted it tight, tipping her head back until she met my gaze. "It was you. You were the price Saint paid to get me out of Midnight."

It wasn't a question, and she didn't respond with anything more than a dark sigh.

"That's why he doesn't touch you," I said. "Even though you're both still so in love with each other, even a blind man could see it. You and me? We got a mate bond, Haley. But you've got a bond with them as well. Different, but just as real. Just as true. And when I see you and Saint... Fuck. Every time one of you walks into the room, the other one lights up like a damn star shower. Didn't make any sense to me—how even after you told us you wanted us all to be together, he still sat on the sidelines, watching us like it was tearing him apart inside not to touch you."

"He told me Melantha cursed us," she whispered darkly. "That if we ever touched intimately again, if he ever tells me how he truly feels... I mean, how he *felt*..." She trailed off into a silent sob.

Fuck. I hated everything about this.

"It destroyed him, babygirl," I said. "He never said it out loud, but that man was haunted. Utterly haunted. And I get it now. Holding you in my arms, breathing you in, falling in love with you... I finally fucking get it. What it cost him. What it did to him to lose you." My voice broke, every word a struggle to get out, but I had to. I fucking *had* to make this vow—to her, to Saint, to myself. "God *damn*, For *me*. He did that for me. And I swear to you, Haley, here and now, by all the stars and moons in the sky, I will spend the rest of my immortal life trying to be worthy of it."

Another sob rattled through her body, but she didn't flee. Didn't rage. Didn't tell me I could never possibly earn that sacrifice. She merely wrapped her arms around my neck, brought her soft lips to my ear, and whispered, "You already are."

Her words, the warmth of her breath, the promise in her touch... I closed my eyes and fell into her, wrapping my wings around us again and just holding her. Protecting her. Loving her in the only way I knew how.

With every fucking thing I had left.

"Thank you for telling me," she whispered, settling back into my lap.

"I never wanted to," I admitted. "Never wanted you to know about all the terrible things that stole my words all them years ago. That brought me to Amaranth City. To Saint and Jax. How we all got out of Midnight. But tonight... Fuck, Haley. You need to know you're not alone in this. You need to know how important he was to me. To Jax."

"Not *was*, Hudson. *Is*. How important he is." She closed her eyes and pressed her lips together, and I knew my woman well enough now to understand she was gearing up for something, that smoldering fire inside her sparking to life once more. And sure enough, when she opened her eyes and met my gaze again, I saw it. That familiar blaze.

That determination, undimmed by even *this* tragic fucking nightmare. "Elian is *ours*, Hudson, and it's on us to help him. You said you felt the spark of me all those centuries ago—the promise of your future mate? Well, I feel a promise like that with Elian, too. A promise that he's still out there—in some form. That he hasn't crossed into the Shadowlands yet. I know it sounds crazy—I'm sitting here listening to myself and I'm like, girl, you're out of your damn *mind*. But you know what? Nothing in Midnight is as it should be. Nothing—not even death. So I'm not leaving Elian behind just because *this* realm says he's dead. I can still feel him, Hudson." She pressed a hand to her heart, her voice trembling with conviction. With love. "I can *feel* him."

"*Haley*." I fisted her hair with both hands. Touched my forehead to hers and breathed her in deep. "I'd *never* leave him behind—you have my fucking word on that, and you know better than anyone I don't give out them words lightly. So if you're telling me there's a chance... even one fucking *sliver* of a chance that he's still out there some-where... that we can bring him back before he crosses over... I don't give a fuck how crazy it sounds, babygirl. Say the word, and I got your back on this. Hundred percent."

Her face lit up like the brightest star in the sky. "You mean it?"

"You know I damn well do, babygirl."

"Will you take me to him, then?" She wiped away the

last of her tears, brow furrowed with renewed intensity as her mind undoubtedly cobbled together a plan. "To where the fog came down and he... If there's anything left of his physical form there, maybe I can sense him. It's the best chance I've got at doing a spell and making the connection."

I'd watched the Fog chew Saint up and spit him right out again, and I knew—without a doubt—there was nothing left of him there but blood and memory.

But Haley was right. Nothing in Midnight was ever as it should've been. It was a place where all things were possible—the most terrible as well as the most miraculous.

So yeah, maybe it was fucking crazy. Stupid, even. But maybe—with a little faith and one fierce, beautiful, badass blood witch—we really *could* find a way.

With a grin that mirrored hers—a grin that matched the hope rising inside me for the first time since we'd set foot on these treacherous mountain paths—I stood up, shifted fully into my warrior form, and tucked her in tight, ready for the jump.

"Oh, one more thing," she said, and I braced myself for whatever law she was about to lay down next.

"Out with it, babygirl."

"If I *ever* see that fucking dickless gargoyle stain again, I *will* kill him. With a dagger, with magick, with my bare hands if I have to. Marco is a *dead* man if it's the last thing I ever do in this fucking realm. You have my word on that."

A low chuckle rumbled through my chest. "I ever tell you how sexy you are when you threaten my enemies?"

"If you think I'm sexy when I threaten them," she said with an adorable shrug, "wait until you see what happens when I mutilate them."

"Looking forward to it, my spooky little monster girl." I kissed her temple, then said, "Now, let's go get our boy before he fucks himself off to the Shadowlands for good."

HALEY

The blood snow had mostly melted, leaving a swamp of dark red mud along the path. Aside from a few sharp stones, there was very little to differentiate one wet patch of earth from another, but Hudson was absolutely sure about the location.

I felt it, too. The void left behind by a life unfairly taken. The absence of something that should've been there. That should've fucking *lived*.

I hadn't wanted to believe it before. Not when Jax had told us the story in the cave. Not when Hudson held me as I cried. Not even now.

But standing here, the chill creeping into my limbs, the smell of recently spilled blood a rich tang on the air, I could no longer deny it.

Elian was well and truly... dead.

The heaviness of it pressed on my heart anew, merging

with everything Hudson had just shared about his past. About Marco and the fae nobles.

The dead children.

The sheer immensity of all that darkness and despair threatened to overwhelm me. My vision blurred, my heartbeat kicking into overdrive, my breath coming in short, staccato bursts...

No. If Hudson could survive that brutal massacre and everything that'd come after, I could certainly survive the telling of his story. And if Elian could survive death, then...

Then I would do whatever it took to bring him back.

"Okay, babygirl?" Hudson's voice rumbled against my neck, warm and comforting. And one touch, one gentle stroke of my gargoyle's hand over my head, and everything inside me settled. I felt his love for me through the bond. His belief in me—belief that I could actually do this.

"Okay," I said, sure of it now. I *was* okay. I *had* to be.

Then, steeling my spine, I sucked in a breath and knelt down in the mud.

Hudson moved around me like a silent sentry, keeping watch along the paths and in the skies in case the Darkwinter witches and their raven gryphons decided to return and finish the job.

I closed my eyes. Pressed my palms against the dirt.

Magick tingled at once across my skin, and the chilly breeze shifted, carrying his scent right to me—bergamot and rain.

"Elian," I whispered. "I... I need you." They were the first words that came to mind—the absolute truth—so I spoke them into the night, fingers sinking deeper into the muck. Into the Midnight earth soaked with his blood.

"I need you," I whispered again. "I *need* you."

Warmth filled my chest, and in my mind I saw the glint of his silver eyes, felt the touch of his silver-white braids falling on my cheeks as he lowered his mouth to mine and...

I gasped as the memory took root and bloomed. Our first night together, warming up in bed after I'd pushed him into the bay and then jumped in after him.

Our first kiss. Our first... everything.

Now, kneeling in the cold mud, I felt the gentle pressure of his lips on mine, tasted the sweetness of that long-ago kiss. Felt the hot slide of his fingers between my thighs, the scrape of teeth as he closed his mouth over my nipple and sucked.

The memory speared my heart and split me in two, every part of me throbbing with pain. Images continued to unfurl in my mind, each one revealing some deeply remembered facet—the sound of his roguish laugh, the way his cocky grin pulled up higher on the left side than the right. The warmth of his breath as he dragged his mouth across my skin, kissing me from one hip bone to the other. The firm press of a hand splayed across my stomach, holding me in place as he teased and taunted. The mischievous light in his eyes when he caught me touching myself in the shower, fantasizing about him. Singing after that sweet release.

The swirl of butterflies inside me the first time he brought his hot mouth to my ear and whispered, *Sing for me, little sparrow...* The nickname that would always remain. The name that'd made me his.

Every last one of those memories collided and shrunk into a single pinpoint of light, a bright spark I wanted to claim and swallow and keep inside me forever. In my mind, I tried to reach for it, but the moment my fingers brushed that tiny spark, it exploded, unleashing a hundred more. A thousand. A million.

My body trembled with the force of it, the force of *him*, the force of the love I'd never been able to bury—not even when I thought he'd turned his back on me. Not even when I thought he'd forgotten it.

Now, it thrummed inside me like a second heartbeat, and I knew he could no more forget than I could. Knew that not even death was powerful enough to smother this flame.

The dark, ancient magick of Midnight snaked up through my arms and into my chest, twining with my own and coiling around my heart, and I bent all my energy, my will toward finding Elian. Toward reaching out across the realms, across the void and shining a light so bright it would illuminate the way back to—

"Haley!" Hudson snapped. "We got company. Move!"

I barely had time to shake myself out of the near-trance before the gargoyle grabbed me, hauled me to my feet, and shoved me against the rocks, his body and wings instantly turning to stone around me. Protecting me, as only he could.

"Shit," I hissed. I'd gotten only the barest glimpse of the approaching figures before he'd encased me in his stone shield. I had no idea who or what was gathering behind him.

Darkwinter? The gargoyle traitors I'd vowed to eviscerate?

Through the gap between the bottom of his stone wings and the ground, I watched dark shadows ripple across the earth.

I pressed a hand to his stone chest, trying to get a read on the situation through our bond. I sensed his fear for me. His fierce protective instinct.

"Assume your human form, guardian," came the command, no more than a whisper on the wind, the scrape of metal against raw bone. I couldn't even tell whether it'd been spoken aloud or was just some spell rasping through my mind, but the order sent a chill down my spine.

"Release the woman and change form," the whispers continued. "Or you both die."

Not gargoyles. Fae.

I sensed the intrusive touch of their magick like an

echo in the wake of their threat—a tingling on the back of my neck and a slight pressure around my chest, like zipping up a dress that didn't quite fit.

It didn't feel like Darkwinter magick. None that I'd come across, anyway. But they were definitely dark fae. As in... not friends.

My blood turned to ice as the realization dawned.

These were the fae Evander sought. The whole reason for our journey.

No one else lived in these caves. And any Midnight foes who would've risked their lives to follow us up this forsaken mountain would've killed us already.

The shadows shifted on the ground. They were closing ranks around us.

"We don't have a choice," I whispered, my hand still on Hudson's stone chest. "We can either fight them or try to talk our way out. But right now, you have to do as they say."

I felt his frustration, his fear for my life. The fact that he'd trapped me here rather than flying us out told me just how quickly—and silently—the fae had come upon us. By the time he'd noticed them, it was too late to do anything but put up the shields and hope for the best.

"Please, Hudson," I said. "We both know there's no other way out of this. You can't shield me here forever."

A flicker of agony through the bond. An apology. Shame, like a dark serpent slithering through his heart.

I didn't have time to tell him it wasn't his fault before

he transformed, the stone protector turning into the man I loved, his chocolate-brown gaze catching mine for the briefest instant.

I smiled, if only to let him know I was okay. To give him some shred of hope to cling to.

Slowly, he turned to face our foes, keeping me tucked behind him. The well-defined lines of his massive, fully inked body glimmered in the moonlight, raw power locked away in every muscle. Even as a man, he was damned formidable.

"You are trespassing on sacred lands." Another hiss, another chill slithering down my spine. I peeked around Hudson's arm and spied the speaker—a tall, reed-thin fae male with hair the color of old parchment and skin so bloodless it was nearly translucent. He leaned on a gnarled wooden staff that looked even older than he did, but I wasn't foolish enough to think it was just a walking stick.

With his bulging muscles and imposing stature, Hudson may have looked every bit the deadly warrior he was. But this fae was just as treacherous. I saw it in his eyes—that gleam of violence. The hunger for it.

It reminded me of another kind of hunger. One that twisted up my insides.

Elian got that same look in his eyes whenever he'd gone too long without the Black.

"State your business," the old fae demanded. His voice had progressed from the raspy hiss to a watery calm, and he leaned on that staff like a frail creature, as if the night breeze might blow him clear off the mountainside.

A ruse. One that ignited a fierce rage inside me.

I stepped out from behind Hudson's shadow and opened my mouth to suggest the *perfect* orifice into which he could firmly shove that staff, but before I could get a word out, Hudson grabbed my hand. Squeezed. And did something that nearly stopped my heart.

Spoke to a stranger.

"We've come on behalf of Keradoc of Midnight," he said firmly, no hint of fear or uncertainty in his tone.

The hunger in the fae's eyes burned bright. "What does the warlord of the realm seek from the fae who dwell here?"

"An alliance."

A cruel grin split the old one's face, revealing a row of small gray teeth filed into razor-sharp points. Too many teeth, I realized. Far more than any fae I'd ever seen.

Darkness claimed us before I could even finish counting them.

10

ELIAN

I need you...

The river churned and roiled, pushing me toward some unknown end as the current sucked and clawed at my limbs. Every surge of icy, dark water felt like another fist. Grabbing and pulling. Tearing. Dragging me under and drowning out the sounds of her voice.

I need you...

A voice I knew, but couldn't... *Fuck.* I just couldn't place it.

My thoughts scattered as the water yanked me in deeper, submerging me in its endless depths. Thick and red like wine. Like blood.

No... Not *like* blood. It *was* fucking blood—blood full of Devil's Dream. And I was drowning in it.

I kicked hard, bursting through the surface and

sucking in air. Tainted blood ran into my eyes, into my mouth, the sickly sweet taste of the Black making me equally hungry and repulsed.

Fangs burst through my gums, everything in me burning with desperate need, but some deep, ancient part of me knew not to drink the blood. Knew if I swallowed even one drop, it wouldn't just trigger a relapse.

It would end me.

Swimming hard against the current, I glanced around as best I could, frantically trying to get a sense for where the fuck I was. What'd happened. Why I was so alone.

Didn't I have... friends? A family? Love?

An ache blossomed in my chest, crushing my lungs. Somewhere in the dark recesses of memory, that voice echoed... *I need you...* But the harder I concentrated, the quicker it faded away. When I looked around again, there was only the red river and a barren wasteland that stretched on for an eternity in every direction, the earth so black I couldn't tell where the horizon rose and the night sky began. Overhead, not a single star fractured the endless dark. But there, high above...

A quick flash of a white wing. Then another.

A glowing white raven gliding on the current. Following the pull of the river. Following me.

I fought to keep my head above the surface, my eyes fixed on the raven as the dark river carried me down, down, down, straight into the heart of the dead lands until it finally spit me up onto some rocky, unfamiliar shore.

Coughing up the strange blood, I dragged myself onto dry land, jagged rocks slicing through my palms. Behind me, the river vanished, but I could still taste it. Blood and Devil's Dream coated my mouth, ran down my chin. Slicked my skin, shining like black rubies under the moonless sky.

It was only my vampire sight that allowed me to see any shapes and colors at all.

In this wasted place, there was no light. Only death.

Spitting out a mouthful of blood, I rose, took a deep, trembling breath, and glanced up into the night sky. The raven circled, riding the currents lower and lower, its massive wingspan cutting through the inky darkness.

I stared at her for so long, the world began to spin beneath my feet. The tremble in my lungs spread to my arms. My legs. But at least I was on solid ground again.

For all the good it did me.

Every step was agony.

Blood continued to fill my mouth. To squelch up from the cold black mud between the rocks. My feet were bare, and for some inexplicable reason I was dressed in white robes as thin as sheets, every inch of fabric stained red. Clinging to my skin. Dripping.

So much fucking blood...

My fangs throbbed. Nausea twisted my stomach into

knots, and an old companion flickered to life on my shoulder.

The devil I'd never quite left behind.

Swallow it, asshole, he whispered into my ear as my mouth continued to fill with that tainted blood. *Just fucking swallow it. Give the Devil one more dance. Let him take away your pain...*

I closed my eyes. Tried to sort through the feelings flooding my heart as swiftly as the blood filled my mouth.

Temptation. Shame. Hunger. Resignation.

I sank to my knees on the razor-sharp rocks. More blood spilled from fresh wounds. My muscles quaked. Heart pounded. Fucking *burned* for it, the promise of sweet fucking oblivion already humming through my veins...

That's it, the devil whispered. *Taste it. Just one taste. Remember how good we made you feel...*

I opened my mouth. Let the Dream-soaked blood spill out, but it just kept coming, filling me. More. So much more. Tears slid down my cheeks, tremors wracking my body, every part of me pushing me closer to that edge. The final one. All I had to do was close my mouth and swallow. Let it wash away the last of my sins on a wave of fantasy.

Let it wash away the last of my very existence.

A crack split my head in two, the pain like lightning. Like fire. My veins felt as if they were boiling inside me, then drying up. Blowing away.

I need you...

My heartbeat began to slow from a thunder to a trot. A throb.

I need you...

And fuck, how I wanted to give in.

I need you...

No more than a faint pulse now, the heart that'd once beat so wildly.

Elian, I need you...

Elian... the name as familiar as the voice. Lingering just at the edges of memory. If I could just... just fucking *remember* it. Just reach it, somehow...

"Elian," it came again—closer this time. Louder. The musical echo of a thousand voices, ancient and all-knowing. Not locked in a memory, but here. Now.

My name. I was Elian. Elian of... of Autumnshire.

And then...

The faintest breeze rippled across my face.

"I can end this for you," the voice promised. "Truly end it. Your struggle. Your pain. You've only to take my hand."

I spit out another mouthful of blood. Opened my eyes. And watched as the white raven landed on the earth before me, transforming into a figure enshrouded in a hooded cloak as colorless as her feathers, her pale hand outstretched in offering.

In her other hand, she held a scythe almost twice as tall as she was.

Her face was hidden in shadow, but I knew at once who she was.

"Death," I whispered. The word sent a bolt of ice to my gut, but I clung to it anyway. "Death," I said again, grateful for the shape of it in my mouth, for something other than the blood, which had finally stopped flowing.

The fog cleared from my mind, the pain in my head receding. I rose to my feet, standing once more on limbs that didn't tremble. The blood vanished from my wrappings, leaving them as bright as the moon.

No, not moon, but *moons*, I remembered suddenly. There were three of them. But... where?

Something shook loose inside me, and the memories rushed back, almost too fast to process.

I clutched my forehead, trying to slow the images. The feelings.

Midnight. Blood Before Roses—my brothers. Keradoc. Evander, my twin. Melantha and the Army of the Dead and Darkwinter and—

"Haley," I said out loud. Gasped as a new pain gripped my heart. "Sparrow..."

Loss. Regret. Longing. Love.

I need you, Elian...

"There was a fight on the mountain," I said. "Weather witches. Hudson tried to... But then Jax, and the Fog, and... oh, fuck." When I lowered the hand from my head and tried to search the face of Death, I found nothing but those shadows. "I'm dead. I died on the mountain. The Fog took me."

At this, she finally inclined her head, still not revealing herself.

"But I... no. Not possible. I'm immortal! I..." I paced the black earth before her, trying to sort through it all. How much time had passed? How long was I stuck in that river?

Was I in hell? Some kind of purgatory?

"Not purgatory," Death said, though I wasn't sure if it was because I'd spoken the thoughts out loud or she'd simply plucked them from my mind. "You're in the border-lands between realms. Take my hand, and together we'll cross into the Shadowlands where you shall find your eternal rest. Or..."

"Or *what*?"

She sighed and finally lowered her outstretched hand, and behind me, the blood river appeared once more. Wilder this time. Darker. Carving through the black earth like a wound.

In that same spectral voice, she said, "Or you return to the river."

"Return to *that*?" I asked as I watched the rapids whip the blood river into a frothy, red-black soup. Shadows moved beneath the surface now—some unnamed beasts ready to devour.

The old devil laughed in my ear once more. *Should've taken my offer, asshole...*

"What happens then?" I asked.

"Then," Death said, her otherworldly voice turning dark, "you will struggle mightily, but you will ultimately succumb, only to be delivered straight to hell. And there, your eternal hosts will make your worst nightmares feel like the *best* of friends."

11

EVANDER

Fire flickered behind my eyelids, the scent of wood smoke and magick slowly drawing me back to consciousness.

Blinking away the haze, I waited for the blurred shapes around me to solidify.

A cave. They'd brought us to another cave. Moonlight filtered in through the cracks and crevices, and judging from the position of the shadows cast upon the rock walls, we weren't too far from where they'd found us.

I wasn't sure how much time had passed, though. How long we'd been under their dark enchantments.

The demon and I were chained to the wall by our ankles and wrists, shackled by iron and magick both. The metal bit into my skin, burning my flesh and draining my powers. Beside me, the demon groaned, fresh blood spilling from the side of his mouth. Iron couldn't hurt him, but magick... I had no idea what kind of spells they'd hit us with.

But for now, we were alive. Awake.

The fire burned before us, illuminating a large chamber bustling with activity. At least two dozen fae and several dark witches moved about, some carrying food and jugs of water, others consulting the general who'd taken us. Three fae males were busy carving symbols around the cave's wide entrance and down along the front wall—a fae language I didn't recognize from any of the hundreds I'd come across in Keradoc's library.

I wondered if they were wards. Or perhaps some sort of reckoning. Despite the current frenzy of activity, it didn't feel like the cave was any sort of residence or permanent gathering place.

I glanced over at the demon, wincing as the iron cut deeper into my wrists. "Are you hurt?"

"Nothing I can't handle," he said. "You?"

"The iron is... most unpleasant."

The demon turned his head and spit out a mouthful of blood. "Fucking fae pricks."

"On that, we can agree. Unfortunately, we still need to convince them to—"

"You were not given permission to speak, warlord." From the opposite side of the chamber, the general reprimanded me, his tone ice cold as it cut through the din. Two other advisors had gathered with him around a stone altar, and they stopped whatever they were doing to turn and glare at us. I could just make out the feathered hide of some poor, small creature bound to the altar with ropes, its blood long since drained.

I wondered if that's how they kept control over the much larger raven gryphons. Some dark sacrificial magick.

It certainly didn't bode well for us.

"Still want to make friends?" the demon whispered, his eye fixed on that dead, bloodless thing.

"Can you access your abilities?" I asked, lips barely moving as the fae general stalked toward us.

"No. Whatever their spells, I'm effectively neutered. I can't get a read on any of these assholes."

So manipulating their fears was out. I tested the iron again, wrists straining against the binds. My skin blistered at the effort.

No chance of breaking free by force, either.

"Making friends it is," I grumbled.

As the general reached us, I forced a note of politeness into my voice and asked him, "Do you speak for the fae who dwell beneath this mountain?"

The question earned me a snarl and a backhand across the mouth. Before I even tasted the first trickle of blood, something flashed outside the cave entrance, and the murmuring around us fell silent.

More magick. I could taste it on my lips, in my lungs. The sharp, telltale bite of it.

I watched as several new fae stepped into the cave, dragging two more prisoners in behind them.

Haley and the gargoyle.

"Fuck," the demon hissed.

I yanked hard on my chains. For the effort, I was rewarded with a wave of nausea that made the room spin before my eyes. A gift from the iron that had no intentions of letting me go unscathed.

Haley and her mate were unchained and appeared unharmed, but a dark haze clouded their eyes, their movements sluggish. Their captors led them to the fire and ordered them to kneel.

Neither obeyed. Neither seemed to even understand the command.

"Kneel!" he bellowed again, kicking the gargoyle's legs out from under him.

At that, both of them dropped to the ground, palms splayed out on the rock to break their fall. Two heads dipped low, hair sweeping the ground, eyes downcast.

Defeated.

A new fire blazed inside me, burning away the lingering nausea.

"What do you *want*?" I demanded, no longer attempting politeness. "You've captured four innocents without cause, and you have the nerve to call *me* a coward? State your demands or release us."

Next to me, the demon whispered, "Apparently you

missed the class on how to win friends and influence people."

A grin of ice and shadow slid across the fae general's mouth, his pale skin gleaming. "Those who trespass on our front door are hardly innocents. You of all fae should know that, warlord. Or is that wall around your city merely a decoration?"

"What do you want?" I asked again.

"As *you* are the ones seeking *us*, I'd hoped you might answer that question for me." He snapped his fingers, and in response, the shadows along the cave walls shifted, peeling away like phantoms, materializing before our eyes.

Three fae witches as pale as the others, but glowing with an ethereal light. Not the clear white light of the stars, but the deep violet light of Midnight herself. Its truest, most ancient magick.

Original magick.

It washed through the cave, through me, so raw and powerful it brought tears to my eyes. My own magick tingled with awareness, seeking the connection to its dark counterpart. Finding it.

The iron chains melted away, freeing me. Freeing the demon.

The general gasped, and in that instant, I felt Haley's gaze lift. Search for mine in the darkness. I met her eyes, saw the flames of the fire dancing in them. Gone was the dark haze of the fae spells. Gone was her fear and grief. Gone was the sense of defeat.

All that remained was my powerful, determined witch.

A witch ready to detonate.

Haley rose to her feet, the gargoyle following suit. Naked and forced into his human form, ink painting the entirety of his body, he looked as wild and unkempt as our captors. Feral. Beneath the tangle of long hair, those dark brown eyes held the promise of violence.

I was grateful he was on our side. On *her* side.

The three witches turned to face them and said, in a single voice that felt older than the mountains themselves, "The stones whispered to us of your arrival. A powerful dark witch and her consorts. But your intentions... they remain unclear."

"Our intentions are to rid the realm of the poison leaking through our borders," I said firmly, crossing the space to stand at Haley's side. The demon joined me as well, and I continued, "Darkwinter fae invade from the north. The Dark Goddess Melantha is already moving across our southern territories, drawing closer by the hour. We have not come here as enemies with veiled intentions, but as soldiers who seek an alliance."

The general sneered. "And why should the fae who dwell beneath the mountain fight alongside a warlord who's allowed war to rot this realm for millennia? Alongside a witch who is not even of our world?"

I stepped forward, my hands itching to close around his throat, but Haley was already speaking.

"Why should you fight with us?" she asked, her voice controlled despite the fire in her eyes. "Well, let's see. While you've been hiding out under the mountain pulling feathers off birds and drawing on cave walls for the past several hundred years, the entire realm has turned into a fucking powder keg that's about to go full-on nuclear thanks to the Darkwinter fae and a demented Goddess who—along with her legions of undead soldiers—have Midnight in their crosshairs. So unless they've been teaching you undead mortal combat along with those cave art lessons you're getting, you *might* want to shut your smug little fae-holes, stop with the hocus-pocus intimidation tactics, and give us a chance to strategize like grownups."

Her spark was a bright light in the dim hopelessness of the cave, and despite our circumstances, I couldn't help but grin.

If death was coming for us on this night, what better end than watching my witch burn us all to the fucking ground?

The witches remained silent. Unmoving. The other fae in the cave had gone equally still, all of them awaiting some final declaration. The determination of our fate.

The general narrowed his gaze, glaring at Haley with

shrewd eyes. In a low whisper, he said, "Who are you, witch?"

The gargoyle let out a warning growl, but the general didn't flinch.

Meeting his gaze, refusing to be cowed by it, Haley said, "I am the Daughter of Darkwinter. A blood witch of the Silversbane prophecy. I was sent to Midnight under false pretenses by the Goddess Melantha in a bid to break her banishment, syphon the realm's magick, and enslave its people. Now that I'm aware of her true desires, I'm working to stop her and her army, along with my companions."

"And the Darkwinter enemy?" he asked. "Surely you don't mean to take up arms against your own kin."

"The Darkwinter invading these lands, brutalizing its people... They are *no* kin of mine."

The general held her gaze for another beat, then looked to the three witches.

At his nod, they moved to encircle us, assessing each of us in turn.

"We need to see your blood," they said. "The blood will reveal the truth."

Truth-seers, then. Witches who could scry with blood and detect lies... as well as a person's most closely guarded secrets.

Seeing no way around it, I nodded, pushing up my sleeve.

One of the witches produced an obsidian dagger. Another held a silver bowl.

"Do it," I said.

A quick slice across my palm, and I made a fist, dripping the blood into the bowl. They went down the line, taking some from Haley next, then the demon. The gargoyle went last, glaring at them the entire time, as if he might eat them.

When all of our blood had been spilled, the three witches added their own, then swirled the blood together, gazing into the dark pool.

"The Darkwinter witch speaks from a pure heart," the witches finally declared in that singular, eerie voice.

"And her companions?" the general asked.

"The warlord," they said, gazing up from the blood to meet my eyes, "wears many masks. His desire for an alliance is genuine, though his methods of persuasion are less than noble."

Before they could press me for details, they tore their unnerving gazes from mine and moved on to the demon. I tried not to sigh in relief.

"The demon is loyal and strong. He feeds on fear, yet has shackled his own fears deep within his heart, where they fester and weaken his resolve. Guilt will be his undoing."

The demon flinched as if the words themselves were

daggers prying open his chest, but before he could respond, they shifted their attention to the gargoyle.

"A guardian tormented by his past," they said of him. "Haunted by the fae who screamed and bled and fell at his feet while he watched over them and did nothing." Their innate glow dimmed, the bowl suddenly trembling in their hands. Tiny waves rippled across the blood. "It is *he* who failed the Eternal Ones. He who spilled the blood of our noble ancestors."

12

EVANDER

I didn't think it possible for the general and his associates to turn any more pale, yet at the declaration of their witches, they did just that.

Every fae in that cave turned to look at the gargoyle then, a mix of sadness and rage filling their eyes. Creasing their faces. Rippling through the cave with a palpable tension.

My eyes widened as the realization hit me.

The Eternal Ones... the fae children who'd been slaughtered centuries ago. The ones they'd allegedly kept alive by magick, somewhere beneath these mountains.

It was him. Haley's gargoyle. Her mate. He'd been there the night they died at the hands of a gargoyle.

Was it possible he'd been the one to—

"Justice for the Eternal Ones," a fae male shouted from the back of the crowd.

"Justice and vengeance!" another echoed.

The anguish in the gargoyle's dark eyes just then...

Whatever doubts I'd had about him vanished as quickly as they'd appeared. Whatever his crimes, he did *not* kill those children. That family. I would stake my eternal life on it.

"Hey!" Haley shouted, breaking up the chants for justice that were now spreading like a sickness, the fae moving closer, their eyes locked on the gargoyle. "Hudson did *not* hurt those fae. He was attacked by ruthless cowards that night—gargoyles and witches. He would've *died* defending your ancestors, but he didn't get that opportunity, because those vile assholes stole it from him."

"*Haley*," the gargoyle warned, risking a rare moment of speech. But even I knew she wouldn't back down. Not when someone she loved was being threatened.

Ignoring his warning, she went on. "They trapped him in stone with a sunlight spell while they slaughtered his charges. His own kind—along with yours—betrayed him. By all accounts, he should've died that night too, or soon after. But he didn't. He fought to rebuild his life. To protect his friends. And he's here now, willing to fight all over again—fight to the death for a realm that has done *nothing* but brutalize him. Meanwhile, where the hell have you all been?" She turned on her heel, glowering at the fae, at their rage, her own vibrating in her every word. "*You*, who claim you want justice and vengeance for your dead. *You*, ready to attack a man who would sooner let you take his life than spill another drop of innocent fae blood. *You*, the great noble dark fae of old, hiding under the Razorbacks with your heads up your asses while the ones who slaughtered your people go free and the realm shatters to pieces around you."

The fae had fallen silent. All of us had. Only the fire dared break the silence, hissing and popping, flames dancing across the reflection in the blood. *Our* blood.

I chanced another look at the gargoyle, his face impassive now, the pain buried down deep. Most of the information about that ancient attack had been lost to time, lost to the very fae standing before us after they'd retreated beneath the Razorbacks. I'd heard the stories, but I'd never known which gargoyle had been in charge that night.

Which gargoyle had failed.

That he hadn't actually failed at all, but had been betrayed.

Something inside me twisted. Ached for him.

"Wait," said the witches, their attention once again reclaimed by the blood. "The stones spoke to us of five. Only four remain. Where is the fifth?"

"He... died," Haley said, her voice breaking. "The Fog of a Thousand Knives took him during an unprovoked attack by Darkwinter's weather witches."

A fresh slice across my heart, though whether it was for Haley or my brother, I no longer knew for certain.

"He died saving my life," the demon spoke up, reaching out to clasp Haley's hand. "Died in the most gruesome way... And it's just a taste of what awaits us if we don't strike back and strike hard."

The general remained motionless, but something in his eyes had softened.

With a deep sigh, he turned to Haley and said, "I am sorry for your loss. But pure as your heart may be, Daughter of Darkwinter, my people have lived far too long to be so easily swayed by whispers of a fading relic of a goddess and an invasion of dark fae soldiers."

"Seems that fading relic didn't get the memo," Haley replied, "because she's *not* fading. She's making her way across the Boiling Glass Sands as we speak. She'll be here in a few days—maybe sooner. And she'll make the Darkwinter witches look like a few stray cats batting at mice."

"Have you any proof of this?" he asked.

Haley said nothing.

"Even if she *did* break her banishment," he said, "we can't know her true intentions yet. Midnight was her home for a time. Perhaps she's merely—"

"Oh, for fuck's sake," Haley snapped. Then, pointing at the witches, "Give me that bowl. I'll take that shiny dagger too, thanks."

They obeyed at once, stricken by her sharp tone or the determination in her eyes.

I had no idea what game she was playing.

Until she knelt on the ground before the fire, set down the bowl, and slid the dagger across her other palm, spilling more of her own blood.

"*Haley.*" *That* warning was mine, low and menacing, but it was too late.

The witch had already made up her mind—I could see it in those beautiful green eyes. Feel it in the surge of her magick, a soft caress against my own.

She was going to give them that elusive proof—a last-ditch effort to sway our hosts.

She was going to call the Dark Goddess here.

Even the fire seemed to be holding its breath as I bent my head and gazed into the bowl of blood.

Nervousness made my stomach roll, but I forced those jitters down deep, refusing to show a single crack in my facade. It felt as if all my studies and practice sessions on the castle balcony had led to this—not to calling on my ancestors and binding them to fight for us, as Evander had first demanded. But to this bullshit task of proving myself to a bunch of crusty fae fucks who didn't think I had any real juice. Fae fucks who would die just like the rest of us if we didn't find a way to defeat Melantha and Darkwinter.

We needed them. Needed this alliance... Or we were already doomed.

"*Haley.*" Across the fire-lit space, Evander met my gaze, his violet eyes bright with a desperate warning. I held it, waiting until I saw the warning give way to acceptance.

Then, finally—unexpectedly—encouragement. A soft smile. Warmth he'd never dare show anyone else.

The scent of his cold roses filled my nose, and I knew he sensed it too—the connection between us. The deepening of it, made all the more special by our shared loss.

Elian...

Grief slipped into my heart, but I kept it at bay. I *knew* Elian heard me. I felt him. I would try to reach out again as soon as I could. As soon as I got this over with.

Now, holding Evander's gaze, I returned his smile, feeling his magick curl around my heart. Keep it safe.

Hudson had mentioned the mate bond earlier—said I had a similar bond with all the guys, though each one manifested in different ways. With Evander, it was the magick. *Our* magick. I didn't pretend to know how it worked any more than I knew how the gargoyle mate bond worked, but I knew it was real. Knew it gave me strength. Hope.

You can do this, little thief, he seemed to be saying now. *I know you can.*

I shifted my gaze back to the fae—the general. The survival of the realm may very well rest with my ability to convince him we were worthy of their audience. That I hadn't been lying about the goddess and the threat she posed to Midnight.

It was all I could do not to snarl at him. His home was

under direct attack, yet this fae required *proof* before he'd even deign to *consider* offering his aid.

And who was to say he'd accept my version of proof, anyway?

Fucking fae-splaining asshole...

Rage incinerated the last of my unsteadiness.

I clung to it, that fire. That heat. It fused with the love and support I felt from my men—all of them—and strengthened my purpose.

Without further delay, I dipped both hands into the bowl before me, sliding my fingers through the warm, viscous liquid until my bloodstone ring was submerged. My magick responded immediately, warming the blood and giving it a faint glow.

All around me, the assembled fae gasped and tittered.

Oh, how I love when they underestimate me...

I wanted to smirk at them. To roll my eyes. But the resting witch face was in full effect as I concentrated all my efforts on channeling this power.

On finding *her*.

I removed my bloodied hands and lifted the bowl before the fire, then spilled some of the blood across the ancient stone floor, painting a tight circle around me. Over me. Letting it infuse me with the power and magick of my men and the fae witches who'd spilled their ancient blood inside it, too.

With a dark pool of blood still gleaming inside it, I set

the bowl back on the ground and placed my palms flat on the stone. Then, with a deep, clarifying breath, I closed my eyes and gave life to the spell that would decide our fate.

> *Goddess of darkness, goddess of death*
> *I offer this blood, I offer this breath*
> *Across the Sands, I summon thee*
> *Bound by the circle, so mote it be...*

Barely more than a whisper at first, then a soft chant that grew louder and louder with each repetition. The words wound through me and back out, tendrils of power that snaked along the walls of the cave and out into the cool night, up into the sky and past the moons and the stars, past the very darkness itself, and still I kept chanting. Again and again and again until my voice echoed cold and clear off the ancient stone, the fae awe-stricken, and the magick of Midnight finally heard my plea.

> *Goddess of darkness, goddess of death*
> *I offer this blood, I offer this breath*
> *Across the Sands, I summon thee*
> *Bound by the circle, so mote it be...*

Even with my eyes closed tight, I could see the glow of my magick, feel it rising up from the circle of spilled blood like a shield even as it drew the darkness near. Warmth washed over me in subtle waves, magick tingling across my skin, and then... a pause.

The glow held steady. The warmth undimmed. But for an all-too-uncomfortable beat, nothing else happened.

A sigh fell on the air, likely from the general. But before he could follow it with a dismissal, the fire extinguished, throwing the chamber into darkness, lit only by the red glow of my magick.

And then, as if I'd been grabbed and yanked out of the cave and straight up into the sky, I watched the mountains shrink beneath me. I watched as the whole of the realm whipped past in a blur—the Hanging Lake, the leafless black forests. Rivers of blood. Towering cliffs made of ice. Fields of jagged, gleaming obsidian.

And then, at long last—the Boiling Glass Sands, and the terrible sight laid bare across it.

Melantha's army, just as I'd seen it in my previous nightmare vision.

As one, they marched. Thousands. Tens of thousands, a sea of bone that undulated in an single, unrelenting wave that covered the desert as far as the eye could see, moonlight illuminating bare skulls, flames burning in the wake of their gruesome march.

There were more now—the force had nearly doubled in size since I'd seen it last.

A gasp born of both awe and terror escaped my lungs.

The skeletons halted. Looked up toward the moons. Toward me, their mouths open in a unified, silent threat.

Bile burned my throat, but I closed my eyes. Thought of Jax, my fearless demon. Everything he'd ever taught me about the nature of fear. About facing it, even when it damn near paralyzed us.

All fear was rooted in love, he'd said.

So it was love I clung to now—love for him. For Hudson. For Elian. For Evander, too—as new and surprising as it was.

Love for my sisters in Blackmoon Bay. My coven. The friends that had fought by my side back then—another lifetime, it seemed.

Love for the parents who'd adopted me. The grandmother who'd raised me after they died.

Love for myself.

All of it beat inside me like the familiar drumbeat of a favorite song, steadying me. Wrapping me in warmth and gratitude. Reminding me that it was only because I'd been blessed with so much of that love that I was even *capable* of feeling so much fear.

The thought calmed me. Gave me courage.

And when I finally found enough of it to open my eyes again and face what lay before me, she was there, hovering in the dark sky atop her gruesome winged beast.

ELIAN

The red river surged, unleashing the cloying scent of Dream-drenched blood once more, churning up that same mix of hunger and revulsion inside me. Blood filled my mouth again, warm and coppery, the drugs whispering promises so enticing, I nearly dove head-first into that river just to finally claim them.

To succumb to my demons and the eternity of torture they offered, once and for all.

An eternity of torture at the behest of bloodthirsty fiends who would make my nightmares look like old pals.

It was no less than I deserved.

Again, Death extended that pale hand. "You must choose, Elian of Autumnshire."

"Oh, it's *my* choice, is it?" A dark laugh hissed from my lips. "You think I've earned eternal peace?"

"It isn't my job to think or judge—that is for you to

decide. I am merely here to acknowledge your final decision, then escort you on your path, one way or the other."

I glared at that hand, wondering if I could truly accept it. If I could truly rest in peace.

How could it possibly be so easy? For all the terrible, brutal things I'd done—all the pain I'd caused—how could *anyone* believe I'd earned that choice?

It hit me then. The fucking *tsunami* of it—all my worst, most despicable acts.

Murdering those royal fae to earn my first ticket to Midnight. All the monsters I'd killed across the realm on my first tour as I convinced myself again and again I *had* to do it—had to survive, had to find my brother, had to find a way back to Haley no matter what the cost. All the monsters I'd killed this time just to cross that moat into Amaranth City, to ensure safe passage for the ones I cared about—never mind the victims I left in my wake.

So much blood and death...

The lies I'd told. The secrets I'd kept. The hearts and bonds and oaths I'd broken.

Every little black pill I'd popped—little black pills of death that *I* invented. That *I* pushed, far and wide. That *I'd* consumed until they'd begun to consume *me*. Until my need for them obliterated my humanity. Drove me to slaughter a warehouse full of addicts just because I thought their blood would give me one more hit, one more hour of mind-numbing bliss.

All those people, dead. Fae and demons. Vampires. Humans. Mutilated. And the look in Haley's eyes when she'd realized what I'd done... what a monster I'd become...

Yet she knelt beside me anyway, offering up the vein to save my life. Singing me back from the darkness.

Oh, little sparrow...

My god, the things I'd put her through.

Never before had guilt felt so sharp and unwieldy, like a newly forged sword I just kept tripping over and falling on. Everything inside me ached with it. Bled for it.

By the time I opened my eyes, I was shaking so violently my teeth chattered, fangs slicing my lips. It wasn't the fear of death that held me in its grip—even as a so-called immortal vampire-fae, I knew my death had been a long time coming.

This was shame. Regret. Sorrow. All the hurt and pain I'd unleashed, finally boomeranging back to me, carving a wound so deep I was sure it would never heal.

Hell. Hell was where I belonged.

I took a deep breath. Glanced up into the shadows beneath that hood.

But the moment I opened my mouth to hand down my own sentence, something inside me shifted.

I pressed a hand to my chest. And there, fluttering beneath the razor-tipped barbs of my own guilt, beneath the desperate cravings the blood river ignited, beneath the rot of a wasted life, something good and beautiful and whole blossomed in the dirt.

As if in response to my touch, my heart slammed against my ribs, wild and untamed, lighter and stronger than it'd been in years. It was as if it'd been bound with chains and encased in cement, and now—for some inexplicable reason—they'd been obliterated. My heart could finally fucking beat again. And with every one of those wild beats, I heard the name of the woman I loved.

Haley. Haley. Haley...

"It's... gone," I whispered, almost afraid to believe it. "I can feel it. I can fucking *feel* it."

The curse. Melantha's curse. The dark spell that had kept me from truly loving Haley. From truly accepting her love in return.

"You died," Death said plainly. "The curse was placed for your immortal eternity, which has come to its end. The curse holds no more power over you."

And just as quickly as that good, beautiful thing inside me had bloomed, it withered and died.

Never mind Melantha's spell—the price I'd paid to escape Midnight. *This* was the true curse. To be free to love her again... only to have my life ripped from me.

I stumbled backward and crashed to the ground, my chest feeling like it was going to fucking cave in on me. All at once, Haley's words rushed back, echoes that felt as ancient as the stars.

No. You're not that man. You're this man. The one who brought me back from the dead. The one who followed me to Midnight—to the worst hell he's ever experienced—just because I asked for his help. The one who made mistakes but never turned his back on me—not really. And for all those past fuck-ups, for all your present faults, for all the future things you don't even know you should be sorry for yet, you're still mine. Do you hear me? I'm claiming you as mine, even if I can't be yours because of some dark goddess bullshit price. You're my heart, Elian. You've always been my heart. I love you. You. This man, right here. I never stopped, and I never will, and no mistakes or dark goddesses or death sentences in a terrible realm will ever change it. Not for me. So I don't know what that means to you —if it means anything at all—but I'm saying it anyway because I need you to know it...

A rage like nothing I'd ever felt boiled up inside me, erupting in a savage roar. *"No! No fucking way!"*

I'd left her too many times before. Disappointed her. Fucking *failed* her.

I would *not* let my demise be another one of those times.

Fury propelled me to my feet, and I crashed into Death and snatched the scythe from her pale hand, splintering it with a crack that echoed across the black wasteland.

A blinding white light exploded between us, knocking me back onto my ass.

When I finally looked up at her again, the cloak fell away, revealing…

Not a monster. Not a corpse or a skeleton or any of the images I'd always imagined when I thought of Death.

She was a girl. A teenager. Dressed in black leather pants and a bright pink crop top, with dark curly hair and freckles and big blue eyes that held the wisdom of the ages.

Now, fully revealed, she rolled those eyes and sighed.

"You're… Death?" I whispered.

"Um… yeah? Sorry to rain on your whole…" She bared her teeth and formed her hands into claws. "*Grrrrr, I'm a big bad vampire* routine, but the scythe and cloak are just props. I find most people are more likely to take me seriously if I look the part." She lowered her hands and shrugged. "But apparently you're not most people. *Apparently*," she huffed, "you're a *huge* pain in the ass."

I scrambled to my feet, not sure what to make of the turn of events.

The girl stared me down. Narrowed her eyes, sizing me up as if we were about to brawl.

Hell, maybe we were. When it came to dying, clearly I had some knowledge gaps. Or maybe…

"Am I stoned right now?" I asked. "I tried not to swallow it, but maybe… Or did I hit my head?"

"Did I say pain in the ass? I forgot to add *idiot* to the

mix." She rolled her eyes again. "Haley's certainly got her hands full with you, doesn't she?"

I gasped. "You know *Haley*?"

"Oh, your girl and I go way back."

"But you're only... How long have you been here, exactly?"

"An eternity. But by your timeline, it's only been a few months." Then, seeing my obvious confusion, she sighed and said, "TL;DR version? As a human, I was part of Bay Coven. I fought with Haley and everyone in the Battle for Blackmoon Bay. Didn't exactly make it out unscathed, but... the last Death had just become mortal, so there was an opening for a Shadowborn witch, and *voila*! Here I am. But technically, I've only been on the job for a hot minute, so I'd appreciate it if you could cooperate and not make me look bad? I'm still trying to get the lay of the land, so to speak."

I blinked at her. A lot. "Um. TL;DR?"

"Too long, didn't read? Damn. Maybe you *did* hit your head. Anyway..." She held out her hand again. "Despite your theatrics, you still need to make that choice. You—"

Something rippled between us then. Some kind of rift, or...

"Haley," I whispered, her strawberries-and-cream scent wrapping around me, her voice whispering through my mind once more. Only now, she wasn't calling out to me, wasn't claiming she needed me.

It was a spell.

> *Goddess of darkness, goddess of death*
> *I offer this blood, I offer this breath*
> *Across the Sands, I summon thee*
> *Bound by the circle, so mote it be...*

Death's eyes widened, and I knew she could hear it too. Three times. Six. More.

"It's Haley," I said, and she nodded. "How come I can hear her?"

"She doesn't want to let you go. She called to you earlier."

"She said she needed me."

Death nodded. "She was trying to forge a connection. A bridge so you could find your way back."

"Find my way back?" Hope bloomed in my heart. "There's another choice, then?"

"It's... not that simple. You—oh, *fuck*," the girl whispered, her face going pale, those blue eyes dimming. She gripped my arm, and all at once, a great power swept across the land, dark and heavy. Ancient.

And so fucking evil it had me bending over and retching in the black dirt.

"Melantha," Death whispered, confirming my fears. "She's answering Haley's call. She's... connecting with her. Invading her."

"What? What do you mean, *invading* her?"

"For whatever reason, Haley's trying to communicate with her, but the goddess doesn't like to be summoned. She's... she's taking over Haley's mind, rent free."

"As in... possession?"

Silence.

Alarm shot through me like fucking hawthorn poisoning. "Send me back to her. Now."

"Elian, I—"

"I don't care what you have to do to make it happen. What *I* have to do. *That's* my choice. Not eternal peace, not eternal torment. I'll take door number three."

She released me and crossed her arms over her chest. "You do realize I can't just snap my fingers and abracadabra you back to your old existence. Your body's basically gone."

"Surely there must be *something* left of it. I was an immortal vampire-fae, for fuck's sake. I can't just—"

"Dude. That fog turned you into an immortal vampire-fae *smoothie*. An extra-smooth smoothie." She shook her head and blew out a breath, cheeks puffing with the force of it. "Brutal."

Rage boiled up once more. It was an effort to keep the tremble from my voice. "I. Don't. *Care*."

"You. Don't. *Understand*." Despite the bite in her tone, her eyes shone with sympathy, all traces of humor and snark gone from her face. "The pain you'll have to endure just to take another *breath* as a living being, let alone speak or walk or even hold her again... I know you want to be there for her, but... Elian, listen to me. *Trust* me. Going back to a body that's nothing but mush? Zero stars, do not recommend."

"Let me give *you* the TL;DR version, Curly Sue." I stepped close and glared down at her, towering over her by a foot. "I *love* that woman. Love. And I have fucked up so many times, made so many bullshit choices and wrong turns... You wanna talk about smoothies? I put Haley's fucking heart through the *blender*, and she *still* loves me. Still fights for me even now, even after I fucking died. And you're telling me Melantha's curse—the one thing that kept me from loving Haley the way she deserved—the way she was ready to accept again, even after everything I'd put her through—no longer applies?"

"Yes, but that's not the issue. You're—"

"So all that stands in the way of me finding my way back to Haley is the fact that I'm dead and boneless, and that dark goddess bitch is trying to possess her." I laughed at the insanity of it all. "Look, I'm not trying to make your job harder, but if you think I'm going to take your hand and frolic off into the Shadowlands or dive into that river and fuck off to hell just because those options are easier... Sorry, not happening. So whatever pain you say I'm in for, whatever unknown horrors await me in Midnight, you bet your freckles I'm willing to endure it. Whatever it takes to get back to her and my brothers, I'm fucking in, because no, I will *not* leave my woman to face Melantha and the Darkwinter fae without me. I won't leave her to face so much as a damn paper cut ever again if there's anything—even a *single fucking thing* I can do to protect her from that pain. To take it for her. Understand?"

She glared up at me, nostrils flaring, defiance in her gaze.

Then, a sigh. Another roll of the eyes. "Seriously? I'm not sure you really get what TL;DR means, but... ugh. Fine. Compelling points."

"Send me back," I demanded again. "Now."

"You've got quite a fight ahead of you, vampire-fae. And I'm not talking about the war."

"I've been fighting my whole life." I spit out the last of the blood from my mouth and clenched my fists, ready for whatever awaited. "Dying didn't change that, and neither will going back."

Whatever the girl saw in my eyes, she believed me. I saw the change wash over her—from defiance to acceptance. Maybe even a little spark of something else.

Relief? Happiness?

"Just... do me a favor and try not to vamp out on me this time, okay?" she said. "The props aren't exactly unlimited around here."

The robes appeared and shrouded her once more, the

hood casting her face back in shadow. In her hand, a new scythe materialized.

With a wave of of that gleaming weapon, the river of blood vanished. I watched in awe as a wooden footbridge appeared in its place, lined on either side with flowering dogwood trees and pink azaleas.

I recognized it at once. The bridge across my pond in New Orleans, the house and gardens Haley and I had dreamed up together over many sleepless nights in Blackmoon Bay, holding each other as we whispered and laughed and made plans for the future. I'd long since left her by the time I found that house, but I bought it anyway; it was the only way I could keep her close to me.

Now, that bridge called me home to her. I could already feel her pull, a tug on my very soul as all the old memories rushed through me, starting with the very first. The night she'd pushed me into the bay, then dove in after me.

"Why does it look like that?" I asked.

"Haley created it," she said. "From something that binds you."

Our dream, I realized. Our future. She still held that dream in her heart, just as I had.

"Why... why are you just revealing this to me now?" I asked.

"You weren't able to see it before. You weren't ready."

"I'm ready now," I said firmly.

"Follow it," Death said, her voice serene and otherworldly once more. "Follow it back to her. Just know that the moment you set foot on that bridge, you'll be beyond my aid."

"I understand. I... Thank you. Thank you for giving me a chance to..." I trailed off, the words lost to the wave of emotion that followed.

"Elian?" she said softly.

I turned to look at her once more, her robes already shifting back to feathers as her raven form began to take shape.

Hurry, she said, no more than a whispered warning in my mind.

I bowed my head in goodbye, sad that I didn't get the chance to say it properly. To wish her well, though I figured I'd see her again—hopefully not soon, but eventually. The thought gave me a small measure of peace.

When I glanced up again, she was gone, a white feather floating down in her wake.

I caught it mid-air. Held it tight.

Then, I turned back toward that bridge. Took that first step onto it. And fucking *blurred*.

The raven gryphon was massive, its feathers and flesh rotting even as it continued to hover in the night sky, bones protruding from its body. Melantha sat atop it, her own wings tucked behind her. Her sleek ebony skin flickered, revealing the blackened bones beneath—a sign that she still hadn't full manifested.

Despite her lack of substance, untold power emanated from her and the raven gryphon both, wrapping around me like a fist made of invisible iron. Just as it had during my last vision, an icy dread filled my chest, so cold I could hardly breathe.

Melantha glared at me with smoldering-coal eyes— bright red embers in that flickering dark face. A white serpent coiled around her throat, two more around her upper arms, all of them poised and ready to strike.

How dare *you summon me, Daughter of Darkwinter,* she

hissed in my mind, her voice like a sharp talon dragging through the softest parts of me.

I heard myself say the words out loud—her voice on my lips, echoing through that cave—just as I heard the fae in that cave gasp. I was in both places at once—a liminal space that allowed me to communicate with Melantha while my body remained firmly inside the mountain, tethered by the blood of my men and the ancient witches.

Witches as old, perhaps, as the goddess herself.

"Tell us why you're here," I hissed right back, keeping my voice steady despite the suffocating force of her magick. "You were banished from this realm for a reason."

Midnight is mine, foolish girl. Mine.

A shiver rattled my spine at her words, at the unwavering conviction behind them. At the vile sight of her hideous form. Even tucked behind her, those wings promised a painful death, every razor-sharp feather glistening with blood, as though she'd already cut down an entire army. Mutilated them.

Shit. All I wanted to do was flee. Sever the magickal connection and return to my body. But I knew I had to keep her talking—long enough to scare some sense into those fae pricks. Long enough to make them understand that joining us was the only way they'd survive.

That *any* of us would survive.

"You think you can take the realm so easily?" I scoffed.

"Like the people of Midnight will simply hand over their home like you tried to hand me over to Keradoc?"

Keradoc? She seethed, a surge of pure hatred rippling through her at the mention of the warlord's name. *I've no need for such traitors. I will destroy him. I will destroy you. I will destroy anyone who stands in my way as surely as I will destroy the lands you now claim as your home. The men you now claim as your family. All of you will writhe and bow before me.*

Again, I spoke her words aloud in the cave. Felt the answering fear rising among the fae—a fear that mirrored my own. As before, it wasn't the words themselves that sent terror pulsing through my veins—hell, her little speech was straight out of the evil villain mastermind play-book. But that rage inside her—dark and ancient, endless... I had no doubt she held the power to destroy worlds.

"We will fight you, Dark One," I said, aware that the undead army had started up its death march again. Aware that my hold on the spell was beginning to slip, my magick fading. But I needed her to say more. Something, anything... The fae remained unconvinced. As terrified as they were, I still felt their hesitation. Their desperate desire to retreat from a battle they didn't believe belonged to them.

"We will fight until the very last soldier bleeds out on the field," I said. "We will fight until... We... The..." I choked on the words, unable to form another thought. Unable to even draw breath as she tightened that fist of power around my chest and flooded my mind with images so horrifying, I was certain they'd melt my brain.

Black fire consuming thousands of fae soldiers on the stretch of obsidian sand between Vanderham's Wall and the White Cliffs of Oshen, so hot it boiled their blood. The Fog of a Thousand Knives enveloping block after block in the Hollow, turning its people into red mist. That unholy skeletal army flooding over the wall, tearing the flesh from anyone in their path, only to see their victims rise up in death and join them. Wounded guards on the wall and servants in the castle, limbs mangled, eyes burning, all of them begging for someone to kill them, *please* kill them. The screams of fae and vampires and demons and humans alike, a symphony of pain that echoed down every blood-soaked alley, off every obsidian wall.

"No!" I shouted, frantic to find that thread that would lead me back to my body, to follow the blood, to shatter the deadly spell that bound her to me. But all I saw—all I felt—was fire and torture and death. Melantha had fully invaded my mind, her dark talons tearing me apart from the inside...

"Haley!" someone in the cave shouted. Authoritative. Demanding. Fucking terrified...

Evander.

I opened my mouth to call out to him, but no sound came. No words of my own. Only hers.

The Daughter of Darkwinter belongs to me. I have claimed her mind just as I will claim her power.

"End the spell, Haley!" This, from Jax. His voice tight with a fear he'd never before shown. "Damn it! Do it *now!*"

I wanted to tell him I was trying. *Help me...* I tried to reach for him, to follow the sound of his voice, but it was no use.

When I am finished sucking her dry of magick, the goddess whispered through me, *I shall allow my serpents to dine on her blood. My ravens will feast on her brittle bones.*

"Fight her, babygirl. You fucking fight her!" Hudson. His strong hands on my shoulders.

There will be nothing left of your precious witch but the memories I allow you to keep and the knowledge that none of you could save her...

"Release her, you *bitch*," came another command. Sharp and unwavering, filled with a dark terror that rivaled Melantha's.

I couldn't place the voice, couldn't focus long enough to... Everything was spinning, my body wracked with tremors, bile rising in my throat as I gasped for air and—

"Release her or I will drag you to hell myself. *Now.*"

That deep, unbreakable voice again. God... I *knew* that voice...

My heart thudded against my chest as if it'd just gotten

a jump-start, and the invisible fist around my body loosened. A cold wind howled inside me, and Melantha's grip on my mind finally slipped.

I sucked in a deep breath and called to my magick, warmth tingling across my palms. But before I could close out the spell and free myself, the goddess returned, sharp talons scraping through my mind once more, digging in hard.

"I said *release her!*" His voice boomed across the Boiling Glass Sands, rattling the skeletons, rattling the very stars in the sky.

Her grip loosened once more, and in the dark, shuddering space she left behind, another presence flickered to life.

I felt him—his soul, his very essence. Scented him in the air—bergamot and rain. Felt his arms around me and tasted his kiss as memory after memory flashed through my mind...

Then he was inside me, filling me, our hearts and souls merging. The darkness faded from my vision, and...

"Elian," I breathed. And there, standing before my eyes on the bridge in his backyard in NOLA, was my silver-eyed vampire-fae. Live oaks and dogwood trees surrounded him, Spanish moss dripping from the boughs, mist rising from the pond.

"Elian," I whispered again, tears hot on my cheeks. My heart nearly burst with the force of missing him, of longing for him. Of needing him to come back to us more than I needed to breathe.

But just as soon as that unbearable pain carved my heart, it vanished, filling me instead with warmth.

With love.

"I see you, sparrow," he said softly, his silver gaze meeting mine across the mist, that sensual mouth curving into the cocky grin I knew so well. "I won't let her hurt you."

At his words, a shield of silver-white light rose between us, enveloping me. Protecting me.

All too quickly, Elian vanished, and again the vile goddess appeared, her coal-eyes blazing bright. The second Elian's shield touched her, she recoiled, yanking her talons free from my mind as if he'd burned her—as if *we'd* burned her. The fusion of our souls, our love. A bond not even death could splinter.

She glowered at me with such hatred, such determination...

Another image flashed in my mind—Melantha's parting gift.

A woman, bent and broken on a polished obsidian floor. A pool of blood spreading beneath her. Snakes slithering through the dark ruby spill, drinking... drinking... And that high, hollow laughter ringing out from atop the dais as black wings spread across a throne made of rock and bone...

Black roses bloomed around the woman, and I knew at once I'd witnessed my death.

And with that same bleak certainty, I realized it didn't matter whether the feral fae agreed to help us. Didn't matter whether we could pull a miracle out of our collective asses and defeat Darkwinter's forces and all the rebel factions fighting against us.

Because despite this temporary setback, Melantha would not retreat. Not until she'd gotten what she'd come for.

Me.

I will see you soon, Daughter of Darkwinter, the cruel voice echoed as she vanished into the night, the cave finally coming back into view. *Sooner than you think.*

16

EVANDER

he transformation came over her without warning.

Pain twisted Haley's face into something sharp and wicked, her eyes rolling back into her head as the Dark Goddess slithered through her mind. We tried to reach her —to call out to her, to bring her back, to break the spell— but we were powerless to help.

The fae didn't move. Didn't speak. Simply watched her suffering, glazed eyes caught between confused horror and abject wonder.

In that moment, the raging helplessness inside me twined with my magick, no longer leashed by the fae spells and iron chains, and in its wake rose a thirst for violence so complete, so destructive, I knew only one desire.

Blood.

Leaving Haley with her gargoyle and her demon, I took

a step toward the fae general. Reached for him, that smug, emotionless face, the pale skin suddenly so fragile and thin, my hands trembling with the need to rip out his throat and drain him as my half-vampire brother surely would...

A soft sigh in the darkness. A name whispered into the night. And I turned once more to my witch, the bloodlust relenting the moment I saw her face.

"Elian," she gasped. And as quickly as it had overtaken her, the pain vanished.

In its place, the face of my twin shone bright, his silver eyes flickering over her green ones. I heard his voice in my mind, clear as if he were standing beside me.

I see you, sparrow. I won't let her hurt you...

"Elian." I echoed Haley's gasp, reaching out through the darkness for him. For the face that looked so much like my own. Leaving the fae behind me, I knelt down beside Haley and touched her face. My brother's face.

But Elian vanished in a flash, and with him, the very last vestiges of the Dark Goddess.

"Haley?" I asked softly, unable to hide the relief in my voice. In my heart. "Are you—"

"Who was that fae male?" The general's shadow fell upon us, skepticism weighting his every word.

"Elian of Autumnshire," the three witches whispered. I'd nearly forgotten they were still among us. "The missing companion."

Haley flinched at the words, but her eyes were clear, her jaw set. I was still kneeling beside her, and now she reached for my hand. Held it tight.

I'm okay, she mouthed.

It took everything in me not to gather her into my arms.

"Our companion isn't *missing*," the demon said, his blue eye narrowed on the general. "He died fighting the Darkwinter weather witches, as we've already explained."

His tone was murderous, but the general appeared unmoved.

Glancing down at Haley, those ancient black eyes shimmering like polished obsidian, he said only, "The witch can conjure the dead?"

A murmur of unease rippled through the fae, and I sighed.

In calling upon the Goddess, Haley had inadvertently revealed her other gifts. Gifts she wasn't even fully comfortable with— conjuring the dead. Or at the very least, communicating with them. And now it hung between us—the question in her eyes when I met her gaze.

Would we still attempt our original plan? To offer the trade? Their help in the war in exchange for our promise to revive their dead children?

Haley nodded once. Resolute.

Whatever you think is best, she seemed to be saying. *I'll stand with you.*

The murmuring around us turned to bickering as the fae began to question our motives. To question what it meant for a witch to reach across the veil.

"*Deathbringer,*" someone grunted out, the disgust in their voice clear even through the din.

My mind was set.

I squeezed Haley's hand again. Shook my head. No, we would not be offering a trade after all.

We got to our feet, the demon and gargoyle close at our sides. We all exchanged a glance—all seemed to be thinking the same thoughts.

These fae were dangerous. Seeking their aid had been a mistake. If what they'd seen through Haley's spell wasn't enough to convince them of the urgency, I wasn't about to put her through further scrutiny by floating the idea of necromancy.

Their arguing escalated, tension thick in the claustrophobic space. Cursing beneath my breath, I looked around the cave, quickly assessing our options. There was only the one exit. Dozens of angry fae stood between us and our escape.

We could mount an attack, but... no. I dismissed the idea before the thought even finished forming. We had no way of knowing the extent of their power or the size of their forces. Others could be hiding in the shadows, awaiting an opportunity to pounce.

I was still weighing the options when a gruff male voice

barked across the crowd. "Fools! You're all fools! Can't you see? This was nothing but a performance! A trick masterminded by the conjurer of Midnight and the empty-headed *whore* who warms his bed."

I didn't recall leaving her side. Didn't recall charging through the crowd like a wolf on the hunt, sniffing out the bastard who'd uttered those words. Yet suddenly there I was, standing before another cowardly fae, his hair hanging in limp locks to his waist, his eyes black and beady.

My hand was so tightly wrapped around his throat, his parchment-pale skin had turned a shade of lavender I'd never before seen on living flesh.

In a dark, deadly-calm whisper, I said, "I'm certain I misunderstood you, so I'm going to do you the courtesy of asking you to repeat yourself. Think *very* carefully about your response."

Those black eyes filled with contempt. "You and your *whore* have tainted the very air we—"

I didn't grant him the courtesy of finishing before I jerked the obsidian dagger from the sheath on his hip and sliced off the lower half of his face. His jaw and tongue hit the floor, blood pouring from the wound.

"*Choke* on it," I taunted, then took a half-step back as his body dropped.

It took a moment for the rest of the fae to realize what'd happened. I had just enough time to turn and look at the gargoyle, his head towering above all the others, and give him a silent warning before the room exploded in utter mayhem.

He grabbed Haley and the demon both, shifting out of his human form in a blur I barely caught, his wings wrapping around them and turning to stone as the fae mounted their attack—magick and weapons, claws and teeth.

I still held the fae blade, and with it I made quick work of a fae male who lunged for me with his sword held too high, clearly untested in battle. One clean slice, and I opened him up from his throat to his balls. His guts spilled out onto the stone floor, and I braced myself for the onslaught, knowing the fae would converge on me. Knowing I didn't stand a chance against so many foes.

But the attack never came.

17

EVANDER

"*H*alt!"

The single command doused the uprising like a bucket of water poured over a candle.

The general stood among his people, all of them suddenly motionless but for their feral eyes, the three witches standing mute behind him.

"Rennick insulted the witch," the general said. "Gravely. By our own laws, the warlord was within his right to remove his tongue." Then, turning to his witches, "Heal him before he bleeds out, but don't re-attach the..." He made a vague gesture over his face. "Rennick will live with the consequences of his foul words for the rest of his immortal existence."

"And what of Jessian?" someone asked. "He didn't utter a word against the witch, yet the warlord—"

"Jessian's attack was unprovoked and unwise," the

general said. "He knew as well as Rennick that the warlord, however violent, hadn't acted improperly. Jessian is beyond our aid."

Both fae—Rennick, Jessian—lay bleeding at my feet. I stepped aside to let the witches deal with them, adrenaline still surging through my limbs. The blade still clutched in my hand, obsidian gleaming with blood.

Across the crowded room, Hudson shifted from stone to his warrior form, releasing Haley and the demon but keeping them close, his wings out just in case he needed to shield them again.

The general approached me, one silent step at a time.

I made no move to relinquish my weapon.

Stepping over the bodies, his gaze locked on mine, the general arched a pale brow and said quietly, "So *this* is how you treat potential allies?"

"*She* is my ally," I spat, pointing across the room at Haley, unable to keep my simmering rage from boiling over. "Her companions are my allies. *You* are an unknown quantity, having taken us against our will by swords and dark magick both, refusing to even *consider* a partnership despite all that we shared with you about the coming threat. Haley risked her life—her fucking *life*—to secure your so-called proof, yet still, you remain unmoved. So pardon me, *general*, but if the best your people can offer is a childish insult toward the woman and witch who possesses the power to not only contact the Dark Goddess, but to reach across the veil and commune with the dead, perhaps I misjudged your desire to defend yourselves and the legacy of the children your ancestors so brutally lost."

Anger flared in those obsidian eyes, but the fae didn't move to strike. Didn't move to reclaim the weapon I'd stolen from his fallen companion.

With a deep sigh, he said, "You claim the witch has made contact with the realm beyond the veil. And I won't deny what our very eyes have shown us—a dark goddess making terrifying threats and a dead fae."

"Then what else could you *possibly* need?"

"Proof. Proof that this wasn't all some elaborate spell to—"

"Nope." Haley crossed the room to stand by my side, the others close on her heels. "Sorry, but I'm capital-D Done with this shit."

The general blinked, taking in the sight before him. Blood stained her hands, streaked her face. Clung to her hair from where she must've dragged her fingers through it. But that fire in her eyes refused to so much as flicker.

Behind her, the demon glared, unflinching. The gargoyle's shadow nearly eclipsed us all.

"The talent portion of tonight's competition is officially *over*," Haley said. "We didn't leave the safety of the wall and hike through these inhospitable bullshit mountains just so I could do a little song-and-dance routine. You saw what you saw, heard what you heard. After all that, if you honestly believe we're trying to trick you, fine. Cut our throats where we stand and be done with it. But I'm telling you, *sir*, that's the fastest way to ensure you'll *never* reconnect with those you've lost—in this life or the next. Because if you refuse to help us, if you refuse to fight, Midnight *will* fall. The Goddess Melantha and her army will consume this land from the Boiling Glass Sands to the Sea of Tranquility, from the Razorbacks to Dead Claw. Any scraps she leaves behind, Darkwinter will surely claim for their own. And you'd better pray to whatever old gods you still believe in that the two camps don't decide to join forces, or I can pretty much guarantee the caves you call home will be reduced to rubble, and the bones of your precious dead will linger in torment for the rest of their miserable eternity while the rest of you spend *your* eternities kissing the feet of your new dark rulers. Oh, and did I mention Melantha has a fondness for snakes? Poisonous ones who thirst for the blood of their master's enemies? Real cute, those guys. You'll see."

The general scowled at her, but Haley scowled right back.

My heart thundered with awe, with pride.

My little thief had fought for Midnight. For me. Not just in giving the general a piece of her mind, but in agreeing to this doomed trip in the first place. In everything she'd done from the moment I'd taken her captive.

And the moment I'd set her free.

She fought for me. Bravely. Recklessly. But through that fight, she'd... *Fuck.* She'd hollowed me out inside. I hadn't been exaggerating when I'd argued with the general; Haley *had* risked her life to channel Melantha, just to show these fae that she could. Just to give them a glimpse of the enemy's plans.

Her fucking life, just to put on a show. As if it was worth it. As if my powerful, beautiful witch had *anything* to prove to these fucking scum.

That rage bubbled to the surface once more. I stepped between Haley and the general, my eyes narrowing on his.

"We seek an alliance," I said plainly. "As Haley said, we're done belaboring the point. What is your answer?"

There was no conference. No weighing of the pros and cons among his people. The general didn't so much as glance at them as he said, "You needn't have made the journey. My people and I left the politics of this realm behind centuries ago. We've no need to entangle ourselves in yet another territorial skirmish."

"*That's* your response?" Haley stepped out from behind me. "We told you—we *showed* you—that your entire realm is about to be obliterated by a psychotic dark goddess who's convinced Midnight's magick belongs to her. We told you about Darkwinter fae who can wield weather like the deadliest of weapons. We laid all this out for you as plain as can be, and you're just... you're just gonna fuck off under the mountain and bury your heads again?"

"We will allow you and your companions to leave our lands unimpeded, Daughter of Darkwinter," the general said. "Be grateful for—"

"Don't you get it? *No one* will leave these lands unimpeded if we don't win this war," she said, seething. "All of you will *burn*."

"My decision is made."

I felt the shift in her energy, the rise of ire inside her, crackling through the magick that bound us. Her eyes blazed, and before I could draw my next breath, she lifted a hand—to strike him? To clutch his shoulder and beg for the alliance? I knew not. She hadn't even touched him, yet the general recoiled as quickly as an oft-stricken child.

The look on his face wasn't fear, though. It was revulsion.

"You are touched by Death, *witch*," he snarled, all the feigned propriety gone from his tone. "We would no more lift our swords to defend you than we would choose to fall upon them."

Haley got right in his face again. "Death will touch you *all*."

He reached for the dagger at his side, but before he could even draw it, the gargoyle had his arms pinned behind him, and the tip of my stolen blade pressed against his throat. A trickle of blood leaked from a nick above his Adam's apple.

"Be gone," I warned softly, "or I assure you, you won't

need ancient witches and bowls of blood to know just how impure our hearts can *truly* become."

He held my gaze, the promise of death simmering in his. But whether he decided we weren't worth the expense of their magick or their blades, or he simply calculated the odds and decided he'd be happy to let us fight the war for him, he nodded.

"Fight your battles, warlord," he said, and the gargoyle released his arms. "Leave us to our lives beneath the mountain."

"Deal accepted," I ground out, still not lowering the blade.

"Return to these mountains again," he said, "and you will *not* find such a hospitable welcome." A final warning glare. A wave of his hand. And magick flooded the cave once more, that same starlight-flecked dark smoke that had brought them to us initially.

When the smoke receded, the fae and their witches were gone.

Little remained in the cave. The fire, blazing once more. The bowl of half-spilled blood before it. A few scattered supplies, the altar and the dead bird, the fae runes carved into the stone, the stains left behind by the two fae I'd carved.

And the frantic heartbeat thrumming in my chest, the full weight of everything that had happened bearing down on me in earnest.

He could have killed her with that dagger. With his magick. He very nearly had.

As the demon and gargoyle checked her over for injuries, my gaze found hers in the darkness, magick sizzling between us. I had no idea if the others could see or sense it, but in that moment, I didn't care.

Eyes locked on hers, I said to the others in a tone that left no room for interpretation, "*Leave.*"

Silence. Nothing but heartbeats and breaths. The quiet violence of a gathering storm as my gaze burned through her, daring her to defy me. To push back.

Haley said nothing.

"An hour," I said to the men, taking a step closer to her, not once tearing my gaze away from those twin emeralds blazing right back at me. "Do a perimeter check—make sure the fae are truly gone. Haley and I have things to... *discuss.*"

18

lone with my witch, I stared into those fathomless eyes, my heartbeat so deafening I was certain she could hear it.

Thump-thump.

"What?" Haley crossed her arms over her chest, suddenly defensive. She knew she was in trouble. Knew I was damn near *beside* myself with rage. "Why are you looking at me like that?"

I crossed the short distance between us and beheld her up close, firelight casting her blood-smeared face in harsh, terrifying shadows.

Thump-thump.

I couldn't find words. Couldn't form thoughts. Couldn't remember how to do anything but *touch* her. My skin burned with the need to slide against hers, to feel the

137

warm solidity of her body, to know without question she'd survived this fucking encounter.

Thump-thump.

Gripping her arms, I slowly backed her up to the cave wall. Her shoulders hit the rock, and she gasped.

One hand slid into the back of her hair, the other snaking around her delicate throat. My thigh pushed hard between her legs, spreading her. Stealing the heat that radiated from her core. Fucking *delighting* in it.

Thump-thump.

"Evander," she breathed. "What... what are you—"

"*You*," I finally ground out, my voice trembling with fury, "are the wildest, most reckless, most inconsiderate, most... *incredible* fucking witch I've ever known."

Her eyes widened, then narrowed, as if she were trying to decide whether to take my words as praise or scorn.

Behind us, the fire surged. Snapped.

Thump-thump.

After a torturously long pause, a mischievous smile graced her lips. In a soothing, seductive tone clearly meant to distract me from the fact that I was *blindingly* angry with her, the witch said, "And *you're* a schemer, a murderer, and a spy. The devil dressed in high-fae finery who grins as he cuts out the tongues of his adversaries and delivers death with a single thrust."

"Delivering death," I said, "is not all my *thrusts* are good for. Perhaps you need a reminder."

I ground my thigh against her center, giving her just that.

Her eyes shone bright, flashing with some new challenge. "Are you threatening me, warlord?"

A dark pleasure roiled inside me. Oh, how the little thief liked to taunt me. To play such dangerous games. Even before we'd finally given in to our desires last night, she'd always enjoyed walking along the knife's edge with me.

Enemies, lovers. Villains, monsters. A *very* fine edge indeed.

I tightened my grip on her throat, ever so slightly.

And ever so slightly in return, her eyes darkened with a need that stirred my cock to full attention. She felt it immediately, the way it pressed against her lithe body. Knew damn well how deeply she affected me.

How reckless the wild little witch made *me* feel.

A different sort of smile flickered across her lips now—knowing, mischievous—and I wondered if she, too, was recalling that first night in the throne room. Our passionate, all-consuming kiss on the dais.

Or perhaps she was recalling all the things I'd done to her last night. The way my tongue had painted her body with pleasure and unleashed her beautiful, terrible songs...

Before her men had returned with the bitter wind and the news that—

Fuck.

If I were a kind man, a compassionate man, perhaps I would've given her space. Time to grieve the death of my brother. To process the loss and prepare for the danger still lurking on our near horizon.

But the capacity for kindness had been ripped from me long ago, and I had *zero* interest in resurrecting it now.

All I wanted was Haley. To feel the hot press of her mouth against mine, to breathe in the raw scent of her sweat and desire as I fucked her into an oblivion so black it would chase away the pain that haunted us both.

She palmed my rock-hard cock, stroking me through my pants, and a growl unfurled inside me—her only warning before I pinned her against that wall, gripped her jaw, and fucking *claimed* that fiery little mouth with a kiss so rough it drew blood.

Unlike my twin, I wasn't Haley's vampire. But the taste of her blood in my mouth, warm and salty and bursting with life, tinged with the magick we shared...

"*Haley.*" I drew back, barely able to breathe. Barely able to speak the witch's name as my heart thundered into a fierce gallop.

I felt like I was dying. Like this feral heart of mine might very well burst from my chest, shattering the bones around it, leaving me to bleed out as I'd left that fae.

But I couldn't stop. Wanting her this way might end my life, but there was *no* putting this wildness back in its cage

—a wildness that sparked and burned between us like the fire, eager to consume anything in its path.

Another feral growl, and I tore the shirt from her body, ripping it off her arms as I dropped to my knees before her. The pants were next, falling away in tatters as I shredded them in my haste to find that sweet, seductive heat.

"Evander..." She whispered my name like a spell, her fingers knotting in my hair, and I pressed my mouth to the apex of her bare thighs and breathed her in...

And then I licked her. A slow, torturous drag of my tongue across that hot flesh, unleashing a shudder that rolled through her body from her dark head to her toes.

"Please," she rasped. "More. Don't... don't stop."

Unable to refuse her for a single moment longer, I dipped two fingers inside, thrusting slow and deep, then drawing back, again and again, her hips undulating with the motion as her fists tightened in my hair. I licked her again, then slid my tongue inside, alternating with those deep thrusts of my fingers, not wanting to deny any part of me the sweet pleasure of fucking her.

She was so wet for me, so eager, my every touch echoed by her soft moans, by the tiny ripples of ecstasy I felt coursing through her magick. Whatever spell she'd cast tonight, it'd changed something between us, our magickal bond strengthening, intensifying. Driving me to that knife's edge she so loved to dance upon, leaving me aching and desperate to give her this pleasure and make her understand that *no*, we would not be risking her precious life again. Not for this war. Not for anything.

Raw, undiluted fury flooded my veins once more, and I slid my fingers out and gripped her thighs, spreading her wide for me, shoving my tongue deep inside her, fucking her with my lips, my teeth, the hot swirl of my breath, my very fucking soul as I feasted upon her and finally, when I could bear it no longer, growled her name against that hot, silky flesh and made her come, all for me.

Her captor. Her warlord. A dark fae with a withered heart who'd somehow fallen in love with her despite it.

I'd known it the moment I'd seen that fae general's hand twitch toward his blade and I saw her life flash before my eyes, and everything in me turned to ice with the thought of what I'd do to him if he so much as spilled a single drop of her blood.

I fucking loved her. And I would die before I let some fae beneath the mountain cause her pain.

Haley was still panting when I rose to my feet and met her half-lidded gaze.

I was covered in her scent, drugged by her very presence. She was trembling before me as the aftershocks rocked her body. Both of us were exhausted from the trek, from the night we'd endured... But we were nowhere *near* finished.

Shoving both hands into her hair, I claimed another kiss, just as fierce as the last one. She reached for my buttons and buckles, slow and fumbling, and I cursed the fucking gods who'd invented this clothing with all its many deterrents.

I tore away from the kiss only long enough to disrobe, and then I was on her again, hands tangled in that wild hair, mouth kissing and biting and teasing, stealing her very breath as she stole mine. Thoroughly entwined, we stumbled backward from the wall and crashed onto the hard stone ground beside the fire, my body breaking her fall, but I barely felt the crack of rock against my shoulders. Every thought, every breath, every feeling inside me was wholly attuned to her.

The need to dominate her, to protect her, to fucking *own* her was overpowering.

With a possessive growl, I rolled us, knocking over the witches' abandoned silver bowl as I pinned her beneath me. The remaining blood spilled—my blood, hers, the demon's, the gargoyle's, the blood of the truth witches who'd spied upon our dark hearts. It coated our skin and bound us to the ancient rock of the Razorbacks, mingling with the darkness and magick between us, the magick of Midnight, the magick of life and death and every fucking star in the sky, and as I thrust between her thighs and buried myself deep inside her, I felt it rise around us—a great, terrible power. A promise.

Haley arched her back and drew me in deeper, nails raking across my skin, the fire roaring, that dark magick so palpable it felt as if another lover had joined us. And for those long, hot, stolen moments in the cave, we shared no words, no tender touches, no sighs of languid pleasure.

No—my witch and I turned utterly *savage*, bound only by blood and magick, by its dark and ancient promise as I drove into her again and again, our skin slick with blood and sweat, breath mingling, mouths granting frenzied, feverish kisses until she finally cried out to the moons above and I shuddered inside her and came with a thunderous roar, clinging to her, crushing her against me as if I could somehow keep her alive and unbroken if only I held her tight enough.

19

The magick slowly ebbed, leaving a sweet-and-smoky tang on the air. And when that wild, emerald-eyed witch finally opened her eyes and looked at me again, her hair tangled, lips swollen from my kiss, my heart surrendered itself fully. Irrevocably.

As if I'd ever stood a chance at all.

With a soft sigh, Haley rose to her knees, blood streaking her bare skin, the last vestiges of the primal delirium that'd so swiftly taken us both. I turned onto my hip and leaned on my elbow, head propped in my hand as I watched her intently. Waited.

"You're still upset with me," she said, reaching out to trace the crease between my eyebrows. "For speaking out against those fae."

"Not for speaking out, no." I closed my eyes and let out a long, slow breath, gathering my thoughts. "What you did was... I could never fault you for speaking your mind. For standing up for something you believe in." I opened my eyes, met her gaze in the firelight. Finally managed a smile, though it did nothing to ease the pain in my heart. The fear. "I'm sorry I was so... abrupt before. I was more angry with myself for dragging you into this. Putting you at risk was a mistake I—"

"You gave me a choice, Evander. I wanted to be here tonight. No, things didn't go as we'd planned, but still. I'd do it again, even knowing that asshole fae could've actually hurt me and—"

"Don't." I pressed my fingertips to her lips. "I can't think about what might've happened if your gargoyle hadn't been there. If I hadn't seen the fae go for his dagger..." A chill slithered down my spine, and I had to hold my breath to still my nerves, to finally chase it away. "You... you were brave, Haley. Reckless, but brave. You showed more courage tonight than I've seen from all Keradoc's generals combined."

A smile touched her lips, but it quickly dimmed. Lowering her eyes, she said, "None of it mattered, though. In the end, they still turned their backs on us. On Midnight."

"Haley." I sat up beside her, hooking a finger under her chin and tilting her face up toward mine. "It mattered more than I can even... More than I can put into words. You fought for us tonight. You fought for—"

"I don't know *what* I fought for." She turned away from my touch, then got to her feet. Pacing before the fire, she said, "I thought... I thought I could make a home here. I saw it—a future in Midnight. As crazy as it sounds, *that's* what I wanted. What I was fighting for. But now..." A heavy sigh. "I don't see how it's even possible."

I stood up beside her, drew her into my arms. "That path is not closed to you yet. We don't know what awaits us after this war."

"I'll tell you what awaits us." She pressed her forehead to my chest, her whole body trembling in my embrace as some new fear took root. "You are going to *die*, Evander. Either because Keradoc wastes away in his cell or because someone else finds him and does the job. Hudson and Jax are barely holding on after what happened with the weather witches, and Elian... God. I *felt* him tonight. I literally felt his soul, and I know he felt mine, too. He saved me from turning into Melantha's puppet, but... But it wasn't enough. *I* wasn't enough." Her voice finally shattered, and she tipped her head back to look at me, the tears I suspected she'd been holding in all night finally breaking free. "I couldn't bring him back. So yes, we *do* know what awaits us—death. Always. And no, I don't know what I'm fighting for. Not anymore."

"You—*we*—are fighting for a chance," I whispered, tucking a lock of hair behind her ear. "Just a chance."

"It's not *enough*," she repeated, pulling out of my

embrace. She turned away from me, heading off to hunt for her ruined clothes, as if they'd be of any use now.

But I wouldn't let her walk away. Not like that.

"A chance," I said, grabbing her wrist and drawing her in close once more, "is more than most people *ever* get in this life—even as immortals. So yes, little thief. It *is* enough." I cupped her face, brushed a soft kiss to the corner of her mouth. "We will make it so."

Her tears continued to spill, soft and warm on my fingertips, but my witch finally nodded, the tiniest smile curving her lips as she whispered, "We will make it so."

Rummaging through the supplies the fae left behind, I found a few jugs of clean water and a large soup pot. After setting it to boil on a grate over the fire, I headed outside to check on the others, leaving Haley to search through an abandoned trunk of clothing, hoping she might find something that fit and hadn't been torn to shreds by an overeager lover.

True to their word, the demon and gargoyle had granted us our privacy. After confirming they'd spotted no signs of the feral fae or any other trouble, I sent them back to our original cave—I'd been right in thinking it wasn't too far off—to collect our packs. Haley and I needed to be left alone for the remainder of the night, I insisted.

It took some convincing, but ultimately, they agreed. By the time I returned to the cave, Haley was kneeling on a blanket beside the fire, two large mounds of clothing stacked beside her.

"Keeper pile, discard pile," she said, pointing to each stack. "We can divide it up later. I'm too tired to do it now."

I nodded, joining her on the blanket. Steam was just beginning to curl from the pot.

"Your men have... enquired after you," I said, tearing a scrap of fabric from an item in the discard pile and dunking it into the water. "And by enquired, I mean the demon has nearly worn a groove in the mountainside with his incessant pacing and the gargoyle practically tore my arms off when I asked them to grant us a bit more privacy."

"They're... protective." She smiled again, but it was all too brief, not nearly bright enough to chase the lingering sadness from her eyes. "Especially now that—"

"Close your eyes, little thief," I said gently, unable to bear the weight of the words I knew she'd meant to say.

Especially now that Elian is dead...

I still couldn't quite accept those words. Still didn't know how I felt about what'd happened. But even as I thought about it now, I wasn't sure if those words were even true anymore. Elian was *physically* gone, yes. But Haley had made contact with him tonight. He'd saved her from Melantha. Protected her. So how could he be truly lost to us?

I wrung out the makeshift cloth and brought it to her face, gently clearing away the blood. Her blood. My blood. The same blood that ran through the veins of my brother.

Especially now that Elian is dead...

Elian. I took another breath, delved once more into the tangle of my emotions in search of... I wasn't even sure. Regret? Anguish? A deep sense of loss?

Haley and the others wore their pain so plainly, like a second skin they'd never be able to shed. My own pain came in flashes and flickers, if at all. Elian was my brother. My twin. Whether I remembered him or not... If he were truly gone, truly beyond our reach, shouldn't I be able to *feel* it?

I see you, sparrow. I won't let her hurt you...

My brother's words echoed, but a soft sigh brought me back to the moment, to Haley. Blinking away my confusion, I dipped the cloth back into the water, watching the blood leach away before smoothing it over her skin once more.

Upon every inch of clean, bare skin I revealed, I pressed another kiss—softer now. A promise rather than a warning.

I see you, too, little thief. I won't let her hurt you, either.

"Will you stay with me tonight?" she asked, when I'd finally finished bathing her and moved on to take care of my own blood-caked skin. "I... I really don't want to be alone, and I don't know when the guys are coming back. Unless... unless *you* want to be alone?"

Alone. Her voice was low and sweet before the crackling fire, and the word slipped into my heart, poking at old wounds.

"Alone," I whispered, shaking my head as I dropped the cloth into the pot, the liquid inside more blood than water now. "For so long, Haley, all I ever wanted was a night alone. An *hour* alone. One simple hour of peace, sealed away from the blood-curdling screams of the others and all the things I... But then I took on Keradoc's life, slipped into it like it'd always been mine to claim. And from that moment forth, I was surrounded by people. Guards. Generals. Sycophants. Day and night, surrounded." I laughed, dark and bitter. "Yet I never felt so lonely in all my life."

Haley smoothed her hand down my face, her thumb brushing across my lips.

"It doesn't have to be that way anymore. Stay with me," she whispered. Then, lowering her hand, "I... I know you're planning to leave. Things didn't work out with the fae, and now you're cooking up a plan B, and I can feel it, Evander. I can feel you pulling away from us. I don't want you to go."

Something thick and heavy rose up inside me at her words, at the sincerity in her eyes. It made my throat tight, my eyes water, my heart pound as ferociously as it had when I'd watched her deal with the fae. Not with the beat of pride, as it had then. Not with the thrum of fear, as it had soon after.

No. This was the beat of a death march.

For Haley was right. I *was* going to die. Whether on the battlefield, at the hands of the Dark Goddess, or by the very magick that bound me to Keradoc.

I thought I was ready for it. Thought I'd accepted it.

But it was all just another lie I'd been telling myself, night by night, secretly hoping I could somehow outrun it.

"Don't you *dare* leave me, Evander," she said. Demanded. And when I met her gaze again, I watched as a flurry of anger washed away the sadness.

"I'm not leaving *you*, Haley." I cupped her face, her skin so warm and smooth against my palm I wanted to spend the rest of my days caressing it. Kissing it. But I couldn't, because this war was far from over, and every hour I lingered here was another lost to Melantha and Darkwinter's advances. My failure to secure the alliance with the fae only made my mission more urgent.

"I must get word to Oona and the other generals before Melantha completes the desert crossing," I explained. "I want our troops moved from the northern border back to the wall, ready to defend against the Army of the Dead. They are the bigger threat right now. I also need to find Gem and ensure our drug supplies have reached the rebel battlefields. I can move faster on my own, and despite our differences, I trust your men to safely escort you back to Amaranth City before—"

"So that's how it is?" she snapped. "After everything we've been through, everything we've done and witnessed and lost, you're still clinging to those tired old plans? To the hope that your generals—*Keradoc's* generals—can be trusted?"

"There is no one else, Haley. These fae were our last—"

"Keradoc's guards tried to kidnap me, Evander. I only ended up in the moat because I fought back. Trust me—they had something *much* more sinister than death planned for me."

My whole body shuddered at the reminder, rage threatening to turn my vision red.

Through clenched teeth, I said, "Those guards are no longer a threat."

"My point is—we don't know who else was involved, or what they even wanted. So no, your generals can't be trusted. Maybe Oona—*maybe*. But that's it. Meanwhile, you're wasting time and energy trying to take down a bunch of rebel factions with Devil's Dream... This isn't a gang fight, Evander. This is a war."

"Those rebels are my enemies. Which—assuming you mean to survive—makes them *our* enemies."

"Compared to what's coming across the desert, those rebels are nothing more than playground bullies and you know it."

I pinched the bridge of my nose, a headache building behind my eyes. "If you have a point, I'd appreciate it if you'd make it."

"Stop trying to sabotage them with drugs and trickery!" she shouted. "They may be bullies, but they're still fighters. And fighters can be turned into soldiers."

"Soldiers that would just as soon shoot a flaming arrow through my back? Through *yours*?"

"Not if you unite them under a single banner and—"

"Which banner? Mine?" I laughed, rising to my feet and grabbing some clothes from the pile. Yanking a stiff cotton shirt over my head, I said, "Do you honestly think they'd fall in line for the warlord who's been torturing and executing their people for centuries? For the warlord who paraded his own wounded soldiers through the city until they finally succumbed to their injuries, or worse—fell by the swords and arrows of their own men ordered to execute them?"

Haley stood up beside me and took my hands, refusing to release me even as I attempted to pull back.

"No," she said softly, her ire fizzling. "I know they wouldn't fall in line for Keradoc. But for you? For *you*, they might."

I closed my eyes, the realization settling into my gut like lead. "You want me to reveal myself to them. To remove the ring and show them the man behind the mask."

"Not... permanently," she said, touching the ring. The shackle. "I know you can't remove it for very long. Just... just long enough to show them who you are. To explain."

"To what end, Haley?" I opened my eyes to look at her once more, my own ire fading along with hers, leaving nothing but despair in its wake.

"Everyone in the realm will have to choose a side eventually. Even you."

"I choose Midnight. I've *always* chosen Midnight, even when my reasons weren't... weren't noble."

Vengeance. That had been my reason. My *only* reason.

Until I met her.

Haley watched me for a long moment. Then she rested her palm over my heart, a soft gesture in the heat of a brutal conversation.

"You're fighting *for* Midnight, Evander," she said gently. "But who are you fighting *as*? Are you the vicious warlord who executes his own soldiers and brings the people to their knees in fear? Or are you the fae who was stolen from his own life, forced to make a new one in a dark realm, fighting for that chance you whispered about earlier?"

Again, something thick and heavy gripped my heart. Knotted in my throat.

"*You* see the stolen fae," I said softly, not trusting my voice to remain steady. "Evander, the long-lost twin of Autumnshire. But I have no memory of that life, Haley. If there was ever anything good or noble inside me, I've long ago lost it. No, perhaps I'm not the *true* warlord of Midnight, but I'm no savior, either. I'm just one man, one fae trying to... to..." I trailed off, lost to the bleak emptiness that now hung over me like a Darkwinter storm cloud.

"Trying to what, Evander?" Haley's eyes softened, and I felt the touch of her magick curling around my heart. Strengthening me. Bringing me back.

In that moment, I felt more connected to her than I'd ever felt to another person, to a cause, even to the vengeance that had given me reason to keep existing for so many long, brutal years.

"When I look into your eyes," I whispered, "it enrages me to know that darkness and despair are even allowed to *exist* in the same universe as you."

She stretched up on her toes and kissed me, soft and sweet and deep. Another promise. Another tether, bringing me back.

I lifted her up, her legs wrapping around my hips, the weight and warmth of her stirring me to life all over again.

"Reveal yourself to the rebels of Midnight," she whispered against my lips. "The *people* of Midnight. Show them who you really are. Rally them to fight for you. For us."

I ran my hand up her bare back, beneath the dark curtain of hair that had always fascinated me. It reminded me of that first night she'd wandered into the library, fresh from a shower, damp hair curling at the ends. She'd caught me reading Keradoc's diaries over a glass of bourbon. Called me pathetic for it. And through all her taunts and teasing, all I could think about was touching that long, gorgeous hair, grazing my fingers along the back of her neck. I'd wondered if her skin would be warm or cool. If I'd feel the heat of her magick.

Now, her naked body wrapped around me, I had the answers to all of those questions and so many more.

I couldn't keep the tenderness from my voice when I said, "What do you see when you utter such things to me, little thief? A lover? A leader? Or perhaps a monster, no better than the ones hunting us?"

Haley smiled, equal parts sweet and wicked. Tempting and terrifying.

Magick crackled between us once more, her eyes bright with it.

"I see all of them," she whispered. "All of them."

20

ELIAN

e're losing him. Damn it, Saint. Come on, breathe. *Breathe!*"

The harsh commands came to me in bursts, each one punctuated by the unmistakable blow of a fist to the chest.

"Fucking *breathe*, you asshole!"

Another shot to the sternum, and a cough spasmed through my body. Wet, rattling, fucking awful. But when the spasms receded, I finally—*finally*—took that breath. A real fucking breath, cool and deep.

Because I was... alive. Somehow, I'd made it across that bridge. Made it back to some kind of cave, a fire crackling behind me—

As soon as I had the thought, the pain rushed in. Fucking ambush waiting to strike.

Blinding. Soul-shredding. Fucking *devastating*.

I had no idea where I was, who'd been trying to get me

to breathe, but in that moment, I couldn't even open my eyes. I wasn't even sure I *had* eyes—wasn't sure I had anything more than a collection of exposed nerves, every last one of them on fire.

A fierce roar exploded into the night, shaking the very ground I lay on.

It took me a beat to realize that sound had come out of *me*—a sound that tore through my chest and throat, ripping me apart on the way out.

Another cough. The coppery taste of blood in my mouth. Sharp claws and fangs slicing me to ribbons, over and over again as I fought to remain conscious.

"He's not going to make it," the voice said. "He's in too much pain."

"Give him something!" a second voice. Female. Both female.

"We can't risk—"

"Just a little bit. Something to ease his suffering. We can't leave him like this or—"

"We don't have a choice. That shit will *destroy* him. It's too—"

The roar—louder than the first, full of fury and anguish—drowned out their debate. But through the haze of pain, one line rang out loud and clear as a bell that clanged through the searing ache in my skull.

Give him something... Give him something...

Something. The Black. They had the Black. It was the

only thing strong enough to take the edge off this wicked pain, but...

Just ask them for it, the devil on my shoulder said. *You know they'll hook you up. Come on—you need it. It's not even recreational this time. You fucking need it...*

Another ripple of pain rolled through me like a tsunami, taking down everything in its path, no fucking survivors...

"Fuck," I ground out. "*Fuck!*"

The devil was right. I *did* need it—another dance to get me through the night. Another hit to numb the pain.

I. Fucking. *Needed* it.

And that realization woke me up even faster than that fist to the chest.

Because if I couldn't survive this without the fucking Black, I didn't deserve to be here at all.

Death had warned me it would be like this.

The pain you'll have to endure just to take another breath *as a living being, let alone speak or walk or even hold her again...*

I'd sworn I could handle it. That I could face whatever awaited me if only I could go back to my life. Back to Haley.

Now, I was here. Suffering in ways so excruciating, I wouldn't inflict them on my worst enemies—but I was alive. And I had absolutely no doubts that if I gave in now —if I took even one more pill—I'd waste away and end up in that red river bound for hell. *Hell*, where the torment of losing Haley all over again—eternally—would be worse than *anything* my mutilated body could serve up now.

Gritting my teeth, I sucked in another breath and slowly opened my eyes. Glanced down at the naked wreckage of myself stretched out on the stone ground, blood pooling beneath me, the whole sight so fucking gruesome it made my stomach churn. A stomach I could fucking *see* through the mutilated skin. Bare torso full of holes, most of them leaking blood. Bones protruding. The stump of an arm on one side, nothing past the shoulder on the other.

Both legs ended just below the knees.

It was a miracle I still had my dick, but given the state of things, I was pretty damn sure I wouldn't be using it again anytime soon.

I squeezed my eyes shut again as another red-hot fist of pain gripped my chest, so fierce I could've sworn my bones melted. Bile churned through my gut...

I turned my head to the side just in time to puke.

"Easy," came the soft voice. Soothing. Hands in my hair, gently scraping it back from my face as I continued to retch. Someone *else's* hands... because I no longer had my own.

Tears leaked from my eyes at the realization of what I'd become. At the unending fire tearing through me.

Ask her for the pills, you stupid fuck. You're so fucked up right now, Haley won't be able to stand the sight of you anyway, so you might as well just swallow a handful of those little beauties and sail off into sweet oblivion...

"No!" I shouted. "Fuck... *off!*"

"Saint, you need to breathe," the woman whispered, pressing a cool hand to my forehead. "You're body is trying to knit itself back together. You need to relax and let it do its job."

I opened my eyes again and slid my gaze up, following the sound of that voice. A voice I recognized...

A woman knelt beside me. Stoked my forehead, my hair. Her touch settled me—the touch of a friend.

Slowly, her face came into view. Sky-blue hair pulled back into a bun. Violet eyes so much like the ones my brother had borrowed...

Keradoc's eyes.

"Oona?" I whispered.

Tears filled those violet eyes, and she offered a warm smile. "You remember. That's a good sign."

"Where am I? What—"

"Welcome back, Saint." This, from the second female. Sharper. Clipped. "You fucking prick. Thought you were a goner for sure."

She came to kneel beside Oona, her purple hair shining in the firelight.

"Gem?" I blinked rapidly, not trusting my vision, but sure enough, it was her—another old friend.

The old friend who'd betrayed us.

"What the *fuck* is she doing here?" I asked Oona, my heart slamming against broken ribs, the effort of getting angry sending me into another coughing fit.

Gem only laughed. "I believe the phrase you're looking for is, 'thanks for saving my half-wasted ass, Gem. You're a real pal.' But if it's too painful for you to speak right now, you can just thank me later with... oh, I don't know. A fruit-and-cheese basket? Maybe a gift card for a massage?"

I glared at her. "Did you save me just so you could—" *Fuck.* More coughing. Another wave of nausea.

"Kill you?" The flash of her teeth, followed by the flash of a dagger. Gem pushed up her sleeve and drew the blade across her skin, drawing blood. Then, pressing her wrist to my mouth, she sighed and said, "Drink up, Saint. It's story time."

21

ELIAN

I may have needed the Black, but I fucking *needed* the blood. I didn't resist as it slid into my mouth, clear and untainted, an inexplicable richness only a pure dark fae Midnighter could offer.

I lapped it up like a greedy bastard, literally starving for it. And as her decadent blood worked its way through what was left of my body and sped up my lagging vampire healing, Oona kept watch from the entrance of whatever cave they'd dragged me into, and Gem... Damn. That woman wove quite a tale.

She told me about how she'd begun to suspect something was up with Keradoc soon after the boys and I left Midnight the first time around. How the warlord was constantly on edge, but no longer demeaning his people. No longer executing them just for speaking out of turn or failing to deliver victories on Midnight's many battlefields.

Oona, she'd observed, hadn't had so much as a black eye or split lip in months, despite the fact that she was constantly at his side.

"So one night," Gem said, "I was in the castle on business from the Hollow and caught the bastard sneaking away from his war council alone. So, being the intrepid little spy that I am, I followed him—straight down to the dungeons. I knew he'd been keeping a prisoner in seclusion—some fucker known only as prisoner 6712. I figured maybe Keradoc had grown tired of the nice-guy act and needed to spill a little blood. Hear the screams of some nameless victim to help take the edge off."

She shifted her position to give me better access to her blood—every precious drop easing a bit of the pain—then continued.

"But when he got there, he didn't torture the guy. Didn't even open the cell door. Just stood before it and said, 'I want you to remember who put you here.' Then he took off his ring, and he just..." She blinked and shook her head like she still couldn't believe whatever she'd seen. "He transformed. Keradoc literally transformed before my eyes into... Well, I thought it was *you*, Saint. I almost called out to you. But I knew it was impossible. I knew you'd left Midnight—I was still getting your reports from the operations in New Orleans. So I stood there, hidden in the shadows, watching this guy just... just gaze into that cell wearing your face. My mind went over every angle. Maybe he'd seen you in a crowd somewhere in the city, and he'd chosen your face—some random glamor he could slip into. Maybe you'd crossed paths in the castle on some shady deal or another with the guards or the staff. Maybe Melantha had fed him the image."

Sated and exhausted, I pulled away from her outstretched hand and shook my head.

By the time she tugged her sleeve down again, the wound had already healed, and I could finally draw a deep breath without feeling like someone had dipped me in a vat of acid.

Still fucking hurt, but not enough to have me wishing for the Black.

"I kept running through all the possibilities," she continued, "but then the guy wearing your face said to the prisoner, 'I will take *everything* from you, Keradoc, just as you took everything from me. And when it is done, when I've wiped the foul stain of your existence from history, not even your daughter will remember you.' I'm paraphrasing, but you get the idea. He slipped the ring back on, and once again, he became—for all intents and purposes—Keradoc. An ally, I realized. Whoever the guy was, whoever's face he was wearing, he'd found a way to imprison Keradoc, steal his identity, and destroy him. Happy dance, right? Still... I wasn't about to out myself by jumping out of the shadows and suggesting we get matching T-shirts. I had no idea what the fuck was going on—just knew I had to play it cool."

"I found out soon after," Oona said, coming to join us by the fire. "My father had summoned me to his chambers for some briefing or another, but I'd shown up earlier than expected. He didn't hear me approach. I saw him standing before a mirror, the ring held in his palm, the look on his face just... determined. That's the only way I can describe it. Like Gem, I thought it was *you* standing there, Saint— that maybe you'd returned to Midnight to assassinate him. But before I could say a word, he put the ring on and became my father once more. We had our meeting, and I never asked him about what I'd seen. I was too damn terrified."

"Oona was completely freaked," Gem said. "We met up that night for drinks in the Hollow, and I knew something was wrong. Several drinks later, I sort of... let it fly. 'Keradoc isn't Keradoc,' I said. And her eyes got huge, and then we just... It all spilled out. We started comparing notes. Going over all the little things that no longer added up. Things we should've noticed a lot sooner than we did."

"From that night on," Oona said, glancing at Gem, "we decided we'd do whatever it took to help this mystery man bring my father down, even if we couldn't reveal ourselves to him. Even if we couldn't admit we knew his secret. It was all too fragile—too risky. So we just kept playing our parts, gathering intel, trying to suss out his angle."

"Ultimately," Gem said, "we realized he'd spoken the truth that night in the dungeon. He'd told Keradoc he wanted to wipe out his existence—and that was it. Revenge, pure and simple. Which, yeah. Lots of people want to kill Keradoc, but this guy... It always seemed so personal." She shrugged. "I mean, why is he going to such great lengths instead of just shoving a sword through Keradoc's heart and ending it?"

"And why does he look like you?" Oona sighed and trailed a hand through my hair, her face unreadable. "It's... uncanny, Saint. Truly."

I nodded and closed my eyes, trying to process everything they'd told me. The pain had dimmed a bit, but it still hurt to breathe. To think. I tried to shift positions, see if I could lift my head and check whether my wounds had closed, but even the slightest movement sent another wave of agony crashing through me.

"Your body is trying to repair itself," Oona said softly. "Making decent progress, too—the blood will help. When we first found you, you were barely more than a head and a partial torso."

Fuck. How long had I been lying there before they'd found me? I didn't remember anything after I'd connected with Haley and chased off Melantha—whole thing had been over in a blink. But somehow I'd gotten back to my... my former self. Whatever was left of me, anyway.

How long had it taken that vampire-fae smoothie to start knitting itself into a solid form again?

"Where?" I managed, still not opening my eyes.

"We're in the Razorbacks," Gem said. "About a day's march from the city. Darkwinter... they've taken the northern outpost, Saint. Our troops have fallen back to the city center to mount a defense, but it's... not going well. Then we heard rumors about an attack by the weather witches—an attack that supposedly killed a vampire-fae traveling with Keradoc. An attack that Melantha ordered."

My eyes flew open at that. "Melantha? So she *is* working with Darkwinter."

Fuck. We'd known it was a strong possibility. Just didn't think the Dark Goddess had made contact yet.

Gem nodded. "We came as soon as we could. We couldn't risk being tracked."

"We found you on the eastern passage alone," Oona said. "You were exposed on the trail, bleeding out, moaning... At first we thought it was a wild animal left to die by some cruel hunting party, but when we got closer..."

"Darkwinter will come for you again, Saint," Gem said. "They can't risk leaving you alive—not when Melantha is so desperate to take you off the map."

Great. Must've really chapped the bitch's ass when I'd shown up to help Haley.

"Why does she give a fuck about a washed-up fugitive?" I asked. I tried to sit up, but the pain was too much, chewing through every nerve until I was breathless and trembling again.

Oona winced, gently pushing my shoulders back down. "Be still. You need to rest and heal."

Gem said, "You're not a washed-up fugitive, Saint. There's more to this story—so much more."

I glared at her, the old resentments rising. Yeah, she'd probably saved my life with that little blood offering. Seemed to be playing for Team Good Guy again—Oona obviously trusted her. But that didn't explain why she'd fucked us over in the first place instead of just telling us about what she'd discovered in that dungeon. Could've saved us all a lot of blood and tears.

"Is this the part where you tell me why you sold us out to the not-Keradoc guy wearing my face?" I asked, not ready to reveal his true identity. "Why you ordered your men to shoot us full of hawthorn and bolts? Why you—"

"I know what I did, Saint. Every last sin." Gem had the decency to look contrite. "I can't even *begin* to tell you how much I regret hurting you guys. Not just the night of the feast, but... after. With the... Devil's Dream."

She was talking about the warehouse. How she'd threatened us, berated us. How she'd pushed and pushed and *pushed*, then stood by while I lost my shit and massacred all those people...

Guilt burned through me again, a pain almost as vicious as the rest.

"But even knowing how much I hurt you," she continued, "even knowing there was a good chance I'd never get to tell you this story and you'd just go on hating me for the rest of your immortal life... I'd do it again. No question."

"Because you're a fucking sadist?" I asked, not sure whether I should be pissed or disgusted or relieved that maybe I'd been right to think she hadn't actually betrayed us. That I hadn't been such a shitty judge of character when I'd entrusted her with our secrets.

"Because I fucking love you, you stupid asshole," she snapped. "You're... you're my best friend, Saint. You might not want that friendship, but I will *always* cherish it. So yeah, I've made mistakes. I've made bad calls. I've hurt people I care about. But you bet your chewed-up vampire ass I'd do it all over again just to keep you guys safe, and if you don't like that answer, you can fuck off over the side of this mountain."

"*Fine,*" I snapped right back. Then, with a deep sigh of resignation, "But you'll have to throw me over the mountain, Gem. In case you haven't noticed, it's a long walk and I don't have legs."

She stared at me for so long, I worried I'd short-circuited something in her brain.

But then that crazy, purple-haired psycho exploded into a laugh that bounced off the cave walls.

"Sometimes I really hate you," she said, but she was still laughing, tears sliding down her cheeks.

"Then stop checking out my dick and tell me the rest of the story."

One more bout of laughter, then the mood turned serious again.

Oona checked over my wounds, finally deeming them healed enough to earn me a cloak to cover up. She tucked it around my torso and hips, leaving what passed for my arms and legs exposed so she could monitor their progress.

"Haley," Gem finally said, and I could've sworn the fire beside us flickered. "She's the rest of the story, Saint."

"Harder," Jax demanded.

"I... I can't. I can't take another minute of this... this pounding," I panted, sweat burning my eyes. "It's too much. You're... too much."

"Your *excuses* are too much. And frankly, I'm tired of them. You think you can take on the Army of the Dead? Melantha? You can barely throw a punch."

"Jax, I—"

"Hit me," he said. "Fucking *harder*, Haley. Do it."

Frustration surged. My fist rocketed into his face, but he dodged at the last second and my punch glanced off his rock-hard jaw.

"Close, but not close enough, angel," Jax taunted. "You need to give me *more*."

Watching from the sidelines beneath a gnarled, leafless tree, Hudson growled in warning. But my gargoyle had learned his lesson about interfering an hour ago, when he'd swept into the clearing and stolen me away from my ruthless trainer and the two of them nearly came to blows over their differing opinions on what constituted training and what constituted torture.

At the moment, wincing over my bleeding knuckles and the arms that now felt like overcooked lasagna noodles, I wasn't sure where I stood on the matter.

It'd been three nights since the fae had refused our alliance. Three nights since Evander left us. Left me.

My thighs still burned from those wild hours we'd spent in the cave, and every time I took a step now, I felt him inside me again, stretching me, claiming me, grinding my body into the stones beneath us, the very act calling up that ancient, primal magick that still simmered in my veins.

At some point, I'd fallen asleep, curled up in his protective embrace before the fire. But by the time I'd awoken a few hours later, he was gone. No goodbyes. No promises about when I'd see him again, if at all.

Evander, our captor-turned-friend. The brother of my first love. A dark fae who'd somehow slipped into my heart deeply enough to kindle the same sort of feelings inside me as the others... And in the end, he'd left, just like he'd told me he would.

I didn't know whether he'd gone to rally Keradoc's old generals, or whether anything I'd said about uniting the rebels had gotten through to him. I just knew that he was gone, and I missed him in a way I hadn't seen coming—a new hollow in my heart, right next to the one that belonged to his twin brother.

The guys and I had hiked our way down the mountain after that, setting up camp in the forested area that bordered the base of the Razorbacks, slowly making our way back toward Amaranth City. Since our descent, I'd spent my nights alternating between sparring with Jax, keeping Hudson company on his perimeter checks, and spilling my blood in a vain attempt to conjure another spell for Elian. With each passing hour, my magick was getting stronger, my spells more responsive... but nothing seemed to work.

I hadn't felt Elian's presence since that night with Melantha. Not even a flicker of those silver eyes or the barest whiff of his bergamot-and-rain scent. Whatever connection I'd forged in the place where the fog had taken him... whatever connection had allowed him to come to my aid when Melantha had taken my mind hostage...

Nothing but dead air now.

Dead...

The word echoed through my mind, making my knees tremble.

"Haley?" Jax's hands were on my shoulders, his eye full of concern, all traces of the brutal sparring coach gone. "What is it?"

"I… I can't do this, Jax. You guys are counting on me and… and I feel like I'm screwing it up at every turn."

"Ain't one damn ounce of truth in that statement, baby-girl," Hudson said, coming to join us. The fact that he'd spoken a full sentence in front of Jax only proved how worried he must've been. I hated making him feel that way, but I just didn't know how to keep up the brave face.

"It *is* true," I said. "Even after conjuring Melantha, I couldn't convince the noble fae to help us. I lost the connection to Elian. I can't throw a decent punch." I glanced up into Hudson's soulful brown eyes. "You said you're stronger because of me, but that doesn't work if you —if *both* of you—are so worried about me it distracts you during a fight." I shook my head, a dark laugh escaping. "You guys are here because of me. *Elian* came here because of me. You three had a life in New Orleans. No, it wasn't perfect, but it was still a *life*. Then I showed up at the club with my whole dark-goddess sob story, and you just packed up and—"

"We *lived* in New Orleans," Hudson said, tucking a finger under my chin and tilting my face up. "Don't mean it was a life."

"Pretty sure none of us knew what the fuck living even felt like until we met you, angel." Jax tried to smile, but he couldn't hold it.

I knew exactly where his thoughts had gone.

Elian wasn't living. Not anymore.

It hit me then, all at once. The hollow inside me expanded until I was sure it'd swallowed my whole fucking heart. My steps faltered, grief rising once more, a dark wave threatening to drag me down, down, down—so deep I knew I'd never see the light again. It crushed me, this weight. Sliced open some vital part of me I'd never get back.

Overhead, the dark sky flashed with an eerie green light—a light the color of poison. The color of war and rot. Melantha was getting closer, the magick of Midnight responding in kind—fighting. Preparing. I felt it, that magick. The same magick that flowed through Evander. Through the land itself.

The same magick Melantha wanted to steal. To twist and pervert to her own deadly ends.

We'd never even had a chance. Even if the fae had agreed to join us... No. We were outnumbered. Melantha's forces and Darkwinter's hatred... it was all too much.

I'd once told Elian I thought hope was a drug more dangerous than his Devil's Dream, and maybe it was. But right now, as I fell to my knees in the leafless forest and felt the last of my own hope drain out of me, I finally understood why he'd taken all those little black pills. Why he'd never quite been able to walk away from his addiction. The Dream might've destroyed nearly every good thing in his life—might very well have killed him if he'd actually lived through that Darkwinter attack. But it'd given him peace—

enough to get him through the night. The hour. It'd blunted the pain of loss and regret and fear and all the terrible things that made a person wish they'd never even taken their first breath, and right now, if someone had offered me a bottle of those pills, I was pretty sure I would've swallowed down every last one without a second thought.

The shadows shifted around me, and Jax knelt in the dirt at my side, taking one of my hands and pressing a kiss to my palm. Hudson was there too, his big hand stroking my back. And together, without words, without hope, the three of us closed our eyes and wept.

***

By the time anyone spoke again, the sickly green light had faded from the sky, a blanket of clouds sweeping in and blotting out the stars.

I hoped it wasn't the weather witches.

Sluggishly, I dragged myself back to my feet. Brushed the dirt from my ass. Twisted my messy hair into a knot on top of my head.

It didn't matter if grief had swallowed up my heart. I still had to learn how to fight. Still had to try, if only for the men who still lived. The men who loved me as much as I loved them.

I looked at Hudson, my fierce gargoyle warrior. At Jax, my unrelenting, unstoppable demon.

And I thought of Evander. My warlord. My dark fae.

For them, I could do this. I could fight.

"Again," I told Jax, shaking off the haze of my grief. "Let's go."

He and Hudson stood up and exchanged a glance— one I couldn't quite translate.

"You sure about this, babygirl?" Hudson asked, his eyes glued to Jax.

I nodded. "I'm good. Definitely. Let's do this."

Uncertainty flickered through the mate bond, a low rumble of concern humming in his chest.

"I've got her," Jax said to Hudson as he made a show of rolling his neck and cracking every one of his knuckles like some kind of prize fighter. "We're gonna try a new tactic. See if the change-up can inspire a comeback for our feisty little witch."

"Go," I told my gargoyle, rolling my eyes at the demon's theatrics. "I'll be fine. I promise."

Hudson finally relented, and after a quick kiss on my forehead, he was gone, off to scout ahead for the location of our next camp.

When I turned my attention back to Jax, he was grinning at me—the old wolf's grin that had tied my stomach in knots from that very first night at Saints and Sinners.

The one that'd sent chills skittering down my spine and set my heart thundering, just like it was right now.

So my heart hasn't *evaporated, then. Good to know...*

After another beat, the smile fell from his face. And in its place came a look so deadly, so primal, adrenaline flooded my limbs and every hair on my arms stood on end.

Jax folded his arms over his chest, narrowed his eye, and issued a single, bone-chilling command. "*Run.*"

ELIAN

"I'm sorry I couldn't tell you sooner," Gem said, her eyes glazing with raw emotion. "I had to be sure it was safe. Keradoc—the real Keradoc—has so many spies, so many people willing to sell out their own family members for a chance to win favor with him. I couldn't risk it. I had to keep playing my role. I'd already heard about Melantha's deal with Keradoc—well, the man posing as Keradoc. How she'd promised him a powerful Darkwinter blood witch in exchange for him breaking her banishment. Soon after, when I heard you were coming back to the Hollow with a blood witch in tow, I knew. I just knew it was all connected. I also knew the only way you guys would survive was if I kept up the ruse. I helped him take you prisoner the night of the feast because if I didn't, someone *worse* would take you. Fake Keradoc? At least he wanted you alive." She glanced at Oona, who nodded.

"Only the two of us knew the truth. We trusted each other —no one else. And we kept up our little act, played the expected roles, at all costs. Even though it meant hurting you. Even though it meant betraying and losing my friends."

I nodded, still trying to make sense of everything they'd shared so far.

"I suppose you *tried* to tell me," I said with a sigh. "In your own shady-ass way. You were calling me *Elian* when you've only ever called me Saint. You kept telling me nothing in Midnight was as it should be. I thought maybe something was up, but at that point it was too much to hope for."

"I hated keeping this from you. There were so many times in that warehouse when I just wanted to drop the whole charade and throw myself at your mercy, but we couldn't risk it."

"What finally changed your mind?"

A shudder rippled through her body, and it took her a few beats to find the words.

"When I heard Melantha had sent Darkwinter weather witches after you, I made a promise. A prayer, if that's what you want to call it. If you survived and I ever saw you again, I'd come clean—that was the deal. Then we found you and..." She shuddered again, and scooted closer to the fire, eager to rub the sudden chill from her arms. "Took two nights for you to regain consciousness, but here we are."

She reached over and pressed a hand to my chest. "And now you know."

The look in her eyes was so remorseful, so sincere, it shattered the last of my resentments.

She'd sacrificed my trust and friendship just to keep me and my friends alive.

I would've done the same damn thing in her place. Hell, I'd *been* doing the same damn thing… for years.

"I'm sorry I doubted you, Gem."

"After what I put you guys through, I would've been disappointed if you hadn't. But Saint? Let's *never* play that game again, shall we? I fucking missed you. I fucking missed my *friend*."

I put my hand over hers and squeezed, and… wait. My hand?

"I have a hand, Gem. I have a fucking hand!"

"Two of them, you dumb shit." Gem grinned like an idiot. "Look."

I checked it out. Sure enough, she was right. I was recuperating. Slowly, painfully, but damn. Hands! Two fucking hands!

"Tell me about Haley," I said, flexing my fingers, feeling like a badass. "You said she's the rest of the story."

Gem looked to Oona, who said, "Haley is a Silversbane Witch of prophecy, but she's also Darkwinter."

"I'm aware," I said.

"Yes, but just like Silversbane," she continued, "Darkwinter's got ancient prophecies, too. Haley's sister Gray was destined to unite the covens in the earthly realm and bring their oppressors to justice. But you know what the lore says about *your* witch?"

I shook my head, my heartbeat kicking up again, those shiny new hands tingling.

"Haley was never meant for the earthly realm," Gem said, getting up to go check the cave entrance while Oona sat with me. "They're calling her the Balance."

Again, the fire beside us flickered, and I wondered if it was a sign from Midnight itself. An acknowledgment of Haley's gifts. This so-called prophecy.

"The Balance?" I asked. "What does that even mean?"

"Exactly as it sounds," Oona said. "According to the translations, the Balance will bring light to the darkest realm, where the opposing magicks of each will come together in a true balance. Not in a blending, where each of them becomes watered down by the other, but in a way that allows for those unique powers to manifest in tandem. Creation *and* destruction, beginnings *and* endings, good *and* evil, order *and* chaos. An all-encompassing magick that sounds so simple, yet is vast and complex beyond our wildest imaginings. It's the very spark of life itself."

"I'm not sure I follow."

"Essentially, the Balance herself is neutral. She *brings* the light, but she does not seek to illuminate the darkness or stamp it out. She knows one cannot exist without the other, and has learned how to wield them both. To allow them to coexist. And through that union of light and dark, the Balance shall usher in a new world for all who understand and appreciate the duality of such magick."

"Beauty in darkness," I whispered.

Oona lifted her brows in question.

"It's something Haley says. Something she got from Hudson. Sometimes she makes these... these black roses. They bloom from her magick, her blood... I'm not exactly sure how it happens. Used to freak her out, but I think she's learned to appreciate them." A smile touched my lips as I thought of her—the fierce determination in her eyes whenever she was concentrating on a spell. The joy when she got it right. Those gorgeous roses...

"But... how?" I asked, still not sure what it all meant. "Even if the prophecy is real, how can you be so sure Haley is this... this Balance?"

A new light danced in Oona's violet eyes. "I believe you've already answered that for yourself, Saint. But..." She let out a breath, her eyes dimming. "There's another part to the prophecy, and it requires a bit of mental gymnastics to put it all together. It's probably best if I recite it for you."

I nodded for her to go on.

Oona touched my forehead once more, and a deep sense of calm washed over me, as if some part of me already knew what this prophecy would reveal. What it would mean—for all of us.

I closed my eyes, and Oona recited the verse.

> *Deep in the realm where the forests burn*
> *As one becomes two, the wheel shall turn*
> *A bond unbroken but by force*
> *United once more to right the course*
> *The Balance shall mend the tattered threads*
> *All that is false must now be shed*
> *With them she joins, through souls and hearts*
> *What is remade stronger shall never part*

As she spoke, the images appeared in my mind. Where the forests burn—the trees of Autumnshire, red and gold as the flames. As one becomes two—twins, like Evander and me, the one that became two inside our mother's womb. The turning of the wheel suggested the prophecy set in motion, perhaps by our very conception. The bond broken by force—Keradoc, stealing my brother from our family. Evander and I finding each other again in Midnight. And the Balance—Haley. She was the one who brought us back together. Not my searching, not my vow to find him, but Haley. And all that is false... Evander's mask. The lies we'd all told. The truths that had to come out in order for us to win this war. To survive.

And the joining...

"The joining," I said, opening my eyes. "It's literally—"

"Yes," Oona said. "The scholars believe that's a joining

in the physical sense, but also through a deep emotional connection. You obviously have that with Haley, and some of the other pieces align as well."

"The burning forests of Autumnshire," I said, and she nodded.

But I wasn't the only one who had a deep connection with Haley. There was Jax and Hudson, obviously. But Evander... I'd seen it in both of their gazes the night she revealed his identity to me in the library. The night I went from trying to murder him to fighting by his side to take down the guards who'd hurt her.

I didn't know how it happened—only that it had.

Somehow, Haley and Evander had fallen in love with each other.

"We don't know what 'them' means in this context," Oona said. "Whether it's a translation error or a neutral pronoun or—"

"We *do* know what it means," I said. "I know." Then, looking up into those eyes that were so much like her father's, yet so different, I said, "He's my brother, Oona. Evander of Autumnshire. That's why he looks like me. We're identical twins."

"As one becomes two," she breathed. "But you... you never mentioned—"

"Keradoc stole Evander from our home when we were children. Enslaved him in Midnight, where he's been ever since."

"What the *fuck*?" This, from Gem, who immediately abandoned her post by the entrance and joined us. Her eyes glazed with sympathy as she knelt beside me. "Saint, I'm... I don't even know what to say."

I told them the very briefest version of events—my time in Blackmoon Bay, the rumors of Evander's presence in Midnight, my first trip here to find him. The things Haley had figured out about him during our captivity. His memory loss, and finally, his admission that he was not, in fact, the warlord of Midnight.

"Outside you two and our group," I said, "there's only one other who knows about Evander." My gut soured at the thought of her. "Melantha helped him with the spell. The ring that allows him to wear Keradoc's face."

"She knows about the prophecy," Oona said, nodding. "It's why she wants Haley so badly. She knows Haley has the power to manifest all the magick of Midnight—magick she wants for herself."

"It's also why she ordered Darkwinter to kill you," Gem added.

"And why she cursed me. *Fuck*." I hissed out a breath as another bolt of pain shot through my gut, but the realization of what Melantha had done turned that pain into pure fire. "In order to get us out of Midnight last time, Melantha made us each give up something important. The *most* important thing we could offer."

"Haley," Gem said, and I nodded.

"I thought it was just part of her... her Dark Goddess bullshit, you know?" I said. "Nothing without a cost. But this... this was personal. She cursed me from ever truly loving Haley. I couldn't kiss her again, couldn't be with her. Couldn't even tell her that I still loved her." My voice broke as I remembered Haley weeping on the floor in the castle bathroom, desperate for an explanation. Desperate for a reason to hate me.

"Saint..." Gem's eyes softened. "Haley *is* the Balance. And you and your brother are part of this prophecy, too. Melantha only helped Evander become Keradoc because she believed it was in her best interest. She already had Haley in her sights—she was playing the long game here. She wants the magick of Midnight—its very lifeblood— and she'll stop at nothing to get it."

"Few can tap into it," Oona said. "But in the entire history of the realm, *no one* has been able to truly unlock it. Unleash it."

"And you're saying Haley... she has this power?" I asked. "To bring this Balance and unlock it?"

"It's why Melantha wants her," Oona said. "She believes that if she can prevent the joining, she can somehow control Haley and channel the Balancing power for herself." Oona blew out a breath. "Saint, Haley is more powerful than you realize. More than she herself realizes. Her coming to Midnight was no accident. Her arrival here was written in the stars before she was even born.

Melantha knew as much, so she hastened things along by sending her to Keradoc."

"Rather, Evander posing as Keradoc," Gem said.

"But why would she do that?" I asked. "If the Dark Goddess wanted to use Haley to unlock Midnight's potential—to steal all that magick for herself—why would she send Haley here, knowing Evander only intended to use her as a weapon against Darkwinter?"

"Melantha was obviously counting on the fact that Evander didn't know about the prophecy," Oona said. "She assumed he would either honor their deal and accept Haley as a trade for breaking the banishment—thereby allowing Melantha to return to Midnight, where she could reconnect with Haley and set her plan in motion—or he'd break the deal and and betray her. That's why she needed a backup plan."

"She was already working on a spell to break her banishment," Gem said. "If Haley had succeeded in retrieving Evander's blood, or if he'd honored the deal, she would've gotten here a lot sooner. But Melantha was coming back either way, Saint."

"But she hasn't manifested in physical form, has she?" I asked.

"She doesn't need to," Gem said. "She just needs enough of a presence to lead her armies to the city. Now, she's got Darkwinter under her thrall... God, it's the perfect storm. She'll take the realm itself by force, then take Haley and all that magick."

"And what happens to Haley then?" I asked. It didn't sound like something she'd survive.

Their silence was all the confirmation I needed.

Fury tore through me all over again. "Yeah, well, there's one thing that bitch wasn't counting on. When she killed me, the curse died right along with me."

Gem and Oona both gasped.

"Haley and I are *finally* free to love each other," I said. "That's assuming she still wants me. And after everything I put her through—after everything I just went through to get my ass back here—I will *not* let some psychotic Dark Goddess with a lady boner for magick get in the way of me finding my woman and proving to her just how the fuck much she means to me, prophecy or not. So if that bitch wants to come at me again? She can fucking *bring* it."

A dark smile slid across my old friend's face, her eyes alighting with new mischief. "And *there's* that crazy, half-cocked, bastard Saint of Midnight we all know and love."

"*Full*-cocked now, thankyouverymuch," I said, gesturing at the situation below the blanket, which now included all four limbs, hands, feet, and a fully functioning... yeah. That.

Gem laughed. "Like I said, Saint. I'll accept your gratitude in the form of a gourmet gift basket or a spa day. Your pick."

I held her gaze. Her smile.

"A prophecy, on top of it all?" I rolled my eyes. It was all so fucking crazy.

Which—in a place as fucked up as Midnight—only made it all the more believable.

The fire hissed and popped, and I blew out a deep breath, steadying myself. Preparing to move.

"Excuse you?" Gem said, pushing me right back down again.

"I need to get to her," I said. "Tell her about all this. Make a plan to kick some dark-goddess ass clear across the realm."

"You can barely lift your head, Saint. You're lucky to be alive."

"Lucky. Sure." I laughed again. Yeah, I'd been lucky in life before. Lucky for the time I'd had with Haley before I fucked everything up. Lucky I didn't die of an overdose. Lucky my brothers hadn't turned their backs on me completely.

But this time? *This* second chance? No. I made a *choice*. Clear-eyed and clear-headed, maybe for the first time in my entire pathetic life.

"Luck has nothing to do with it, Gem. I *fought* for this honor. And I'd die a thousand times over just to do it again for the chance to protect Haley. To hold her in my arms and keep her safe." Pushing through the agonizing burn in every part of me, I finally—fucking *finally* hauled myself up to a sitting position. Then, with what little strength I had left for the moment, I grinned at my old friend, grateful I could even call her that again. "So are you going to sit there pining away after me and my newly minted cock, or are you going to help me?"

JAX

"I can smell your *fear*, woman." I loped through the dark forest, every one of my senses trained on the hunt. "If I catch you, I *will* bite you."

A rustle ahead. A dark shadow skittering out from behind the trees.

Adrenaline surged inside me, and I shot toward that darkness—the black shadow, the fear, the raw scent of desire rippling from her in hot, intense waves that set my cock on fire.

She was scared. Not because she feared me, but because I'd intentionally triggered her primal instincts, hoping like hell it would be enough to jump-start that innate part of her that wanted to survive. The part that would fucking fight to the bitter end for one more breath —even when her heart was in pieces.

Haley darted out from behind a spindly tree—little

more than a flash of dark hair and the gleam of a dagger strapped to her thigh. She ran deeper into the woods, leaping over roots, charging past trees, pushing herself harder and faster...

Not fast enough, angel.

I caught up to her far too easily, so close on her heels I could taste her. The strawberry scent of her. The sharp, unmistakable flood of terror coursing through her bloodstream.

Good girl.

Sensing me right behind her, she let out a groan of frustration and kicked it up a notch, putting a few more feet between us.

I closed the distance in a heartbeat.

"Haley," I taunted, and my witch made the fatal mistake of looking back at me over her shoulder.

She lost her footing. Tripped on a root. And down, down, down she went...

I caught her and twisted, breaking her fall as we crashed to the ground. Before she could even take another breath, I rolled us, trapping her beneath me.

"*Shit,*" she hissed.

"You're mine now, little mouse. *Mine.*" Straddling her body, I pinned her wrists to the damp earth and leaned in close, licking a path from her neck to her ear, savoring the salty taste of sweat as I growled, "I told you what would happen if I caught you."

I bit her neck, making her yelp, then swirled my tongue over the sting.

"Jax," she breathed, arching her hips. Grinding.

"No, little mouse." I sent another pulse of fear through her mind—the barest brush of my demonic power. "You need to fight me, not fuck me. Fight the big, bad wolf before he *devours* you."

Another bite, harder this time, and Haley's fear spiked again, reacting to the power.

"Get. *Off!*" She shoved against my hold, but I had her at a serious disadvantage, her wrists bound in my grip, my knees clamped tight around her outer thighs, my cock... *Fuck*. I was *throbbing* for her.

"You'll have to do better than that, angel. I'm stronger than you. Faster. I can get inside your head and make you—"

"Stop."

"Stop?" I tightened my grip. Nipped her earlobe with my teeth. "You think that's gonna save you from the *real* bad guys?"

"Jax, I... I'm serious." Defeat flooded her voice, her body going limp beneath me. "Like you said—you're stronger and faster. A fucking fear demon. I can't beat you, so... game over."

"That's your exhaustion talking. Your pain. Push through it, Haley."

She shook her head.

Frustration welled inside me. "Whatever you're feeling, I need you to fight it. Fight *me*."

"No. I can't. I'm too—"

"Damn it, Haley. *Fight!*"

Tears glazed her eyes as she continued shaking her head, then finally just turned away from me completely. Closed her eyes. Sighed.

Gave up.

"No," I said. "You can't quit. Not like this."

No response. Nothing but a tear sliding down her cheek and disappearing in the Midnight earth.

Not because I was pushing her, no. That tear was all for Saint.

And seeing her like this—feeling her defeat, her grief...

I thought of Saint, pushing me out of the way on that mountainside. Exploding.

I thought of all the soldiers the old Keradoc had marched through the streets.

I thought of the oath, blood before roses.

I thought of hell and the demons who'd nearly ruined me.

I thought of my sister, dead at fifteen, bleeding in my arms after a brutal attack because *she* couldn't fight, and the look of terror in my parents' eyes when they found us...

Something inside me snapped. Just fucking snapped.

A roar tore through my chest, and I got to my feet and hauled her up. Got right in her face. "I will *not* stand by and let someone else I love be taken from me because they couldn't defend themselves. So you fight when I tell you to fight. You fucking fight! *Fight!*"

Her eyes blazed—fear, frustration, sadness, rage, all of it colliding into a storm that lit her up from the inside, unleashing a primal scream that echoed through the dark woods. In a flash, she unsheathed her dagger, sliced her palm, and—

Magick. A burst of the brightest red light, and my dark little angel finally fucking hit me.

The magick slammed into me hard, sending me skittering backward and crashing into a tree. She charged in right after it, shoving her bloodied hand against my chest, her eyes wild.

She didn't say a word. Didn't make another sound after that scream finally faded, but oh, that red-hot fury, the tempest in her eyes... it was a fucking sight to behold.

She let it all out, my angel of darkness, hitting me with everything in her arsenal until blood poured from my nose and I swayed on my feet, dizzy from the loss of it, her magick sizzling through my veins.

And then, as quickly as it'd exploded out of her, the magick vanished.

The forest was black once more, lit only by the moons, silent but for our ragged breaths.

I turned my head and spit out a mouthful of blood. When I met her gaze again, the world had stopped spinning, and the heart I was so certain had stopped beating kicked me hard in the ribs.

"Feel better?" I asked softly, reaching for her face.

"Do you?" With a bitter laugh, she took a step backward and scrubbed her hand over her mouth, leaving a smear of blood shining on her lips, rubies in the darkness. "Let's not pretend for a *second* you did this for me, Jax."

"Haley, you're holding it all inside. It's killing you. It's making you weak and sloppy and—"

"No. No fucking way. You wanted me to beat the shit of you tonight—to make you fucking *bleed* because you think I blame you for Elian's death. You think I wish your places had been reversed. That you'd sacrificed yourself and sent *him* back to the cave with the bad news. But that's not how it went down, and now you're trying to convince yourself that if I just hit you hard enough, just *hurt* you badly enough, you won't have to feel so fucking guilty anymore."

Every one of her words hit their mark, igniting a fresh blaze inside me. I pushed off the tree and closed the distance between us. "And what about your guilt, angel? You think I don't see it in your eyes? You think I don't hear you crying in your sleep?"

"You don't know what the hell you're talking about."

"No? So you don't blame yourself for his death? All of a sudden you're done telling yourself he only came to Midnight because of you? That every shitty, terrible, fucked-up thing that ever happened to him was somehow your—"

"It is!" she roared. "It is my fucking fault! It's all of our faults! Don't you get it? Every one of his so-called failures, all the things we've been so quick to judge and condemn... They weren't failures at all, Jax. They were consequences. *Brutal* consequences for the choices he made to save everyone else. He died protecting *us*. Again and again. He fucked up, he made mistakes, he gutted us more often than not, but at the end of the day... Elian put us first, we put him last, and *that* is a shame I'll carry with me forever. And I'll never get to tell him that. That I *saw* him, Jax. Saw the man he truly was. Saw what he did for the people he loved." Her voice broke on the last word, and she fell to her knees as a deafening howl erupted from some deep, dark place inside her.

I dropped down in front of her and pulled her close, wrapping myself around her, my own tears falling into her hair as she screamed and shook and fucking wept.

Wept for the man she'd loved and lost, only to love and lose again.

Wept for the sisters she hadn't spoken with, no idea if they were even still alive.

Wept for the birthmother who'd tried to murder her.

Wept for all the terrible, soul-crushing things that'd tried to take her down. It was as if I could feel her entire history wash through her, crushing her, suffocating her, and all I could do was wrap her up tight and try like hell to hold all the pieces together.

Silence. It settled over us like a shroud—sudden, all-encompassing. I had no idea how much time had passed since we'd knelt on the cold earth, but then Haley sucked in a sharp breath, drew back, and met my gaze.

Her eyes fierce.

I opened my mouth to ask what she needed, whether she was okay, to simply breathe her fucking name, but before I could even get a word out, she was on me. Her hands tangled into my hair, mouth smothering mine with a kiss that damn near sucked out my soul.

Maybe it made me selfish. Maybe it made me greedy. But in that moment, I needed her more than I'd ever needed anything—my lost family, my demonic sight, my missing eye, even my own fucking heartbeat.

I fisted her hair and pulled back just long enough to meet her eyes again. "Angel. You sure this is—"

"Yes. Just... I need to feel it, Jax. Make me fucking *feel* it." She crashed into me again, a violent clash of tongues and teeth and breath. I released her and stripped off my shirt, then hers, before shoving my hands back into her hair. I kissed her hard and deep, kissed her mouth, her jaw, her pale throat. She moaned and arched her body against me, and I bit her neck, her shoulder, my teeth scoring her flesh until I tasted the coppery tang of her blood.

"Jax," she cried out, and that sweet, delicious fear inside her spiked hard, but I knew this pain was exactly what she wanted. Needed. The hurt that would remind her what it felt like to be utterly fucking *claimed*. A reminder that she could still feel anything at all—that both of us could—when all we wanted to do was sink to the bottom of that dark well and never come back up.

"More," she begged. "Don't you *dare* fucking stop."

The intensity in her voice had me out of my fucking mind with desire, with the same need I felt shuddering through her.

I stripped out of my pants, then pushed her back onto the ground.

"You *belong* to me, angel," I said, kissing my way from her mouth to her ear. "To all of us. Saint may not be with us, but you're as much his now as you ever were."

"I know," she breathed. "I know."

"Haley." I wrapped my fingers around her jaw and met her eyes again, my grip unrelenting. "I don't want you to forget that. *Ever.* Tell me you understand."

"I... I understand."

I held her gaze for a long beat, memorizing every fleck of gold in the green, the arch of her delicate brows.

Then, when I felt like my heart might actually explode with all the things I felt for her, I ripped her out of her boots and pants, baring the rest of her naked body to me in the silver moonlight.

Even bloodied and covered in dirt and sweat, she was fucking *stunning*.

"*Good*," I said firmly. Then, lips brushing her ear, I whispered, "Because I need you to know that what I'm about to do to you now has nothing to do with punishing myself for his death and everything to do with reminding you *we're* still fucking alive. That all of this is still worth fighting for. And I'm not going to stop, angel. I'm not going to stop until we're both fucking *empty*."

"I told you I don't want you to stop," she whispered. Moaned.

A cool breeze whispered through the woods, and Haley's eyelids fluttered closed, her dark pink nipples rising.

I lowered my mouth to one of those inviting peaks, licking. Teasing. Scraping my teeth across it until I finally sucked it into my mouth. She moaned again at the contact, and I shifted my attention to the other one, flicking it with my tongue, driving her wild.

But it wasn't enough. Not for my dark angel, writhing and panting in the moonlight.

Not for me, aching to sink inside her.

I shifted and knelt between her thighs, my gaze raking over every curve, my cock hard and eager.

"Take it," she whispered, parting her thighs in the dirt

for me like an offering to the old gods. "Fucking *take* it, Jax."

Another growl vibrated through my chest. I gripped her knees, spreading her wider and dipping my head.

She slid her hands into my hair and sighed for me, sweet and tender, but there was *nothing* sweet about what I had in store for her.

I bit the sensitive skin of her inner thigh hard enough to draw more blood, then licked, dragging my tongue up to her hipbone, then back down, kissing her everywhere but that *one* spot—that one soft, beautiful spot that would make her shatter.

"Sinner," she breathed. "I can't... I can't handle the teasing. I need... all of you. Inside me. Please, I just need... oh, *fuck*..." she gasped, suddenly breathless as I shoved my tongue between her thighs, no fucking warning, no more teasing, no more slow torture. Only the pressure of my thumb circling her clit, the sudden arch of her back, the roll of her hips as I licked and sucked and stroked... *Fucking hell,* the sounds she made, the sudden scrape of fingernails dragged across my shoulders, the warm trickle of blood running from the wounds, the fucking *taste* of her as I devoured that hot, needy pussy with every stroke until—

"Oh god. I'm... Fuck... *Jax!*" she cried out into the night, thighs quaking as the orgasm gripped her tight. I didn't stop, though. Just fucked her harder, faster, sucking her clit between my lips as I slid two fingers inside and stroked, sending her body spiraling into another orgasm that had her panting and thrashing beneath me, cursing my name from this realm to the next.

I didn't even wait for her to come down. Didn't wait for her to catch her breath, didn't wait for that wild heartbeat to settle. She was still trembling when I gripped her hips, flipped her over onto her stomach, and fisted my cock.

"Up," I commanded, teasing her backside with the tip. "I want my angel on her hands and knees for me."

She obeyed immediately, rising up on all fours, arching her back to give me another exquisite view.

"Fuck, angel," I whispered. "You're killing me."

"Take it," she said again. "It's yours, Jax. I'm yours."

"*Mine.*" I ran a hand up her back and grabbed her hair, my other hand curling around her hip.

"Yes," she breathed, so fucking wet for me. So hot.

"*Haley...*" A deep, dark sigh, and suddenly my own words echoed on the breeze, drifting though my mind.

We're still fucking alive...

This is still worth fighting for...

Fucking alive...

Worth fighting for...

"Angel," I said again—a whisper, a plea—and then I fucking *buried* myself. So fucking deep. So fucking hard. Again and again, fucking her beneath a canopy of black branches and Midnight stars until she tightened around me and another blinding-hot orgasm rippled through her body and I spoke those words out loud, those promises, over and over and over until I came hot and fierce inside the woman I loved and I finally—fucking *finally*—believed those promises, too.

"Saint died for me, Haley," I said softly, all the earlier anger gone, burned off by the frenzy of our fight and what had come after. "It wasn't an accident. He sacrificed his life to save mine, and I need to say it out loud because I don't want to forget it. Ever."

She offered a sad smile, curling into my embrace. "You won't. I know you won't."

We'd just finished washing up in a freshwater stream—damn near freezing to death in the process—and now we sat before a small fire, eating the meager meat from a few tiny rabbits Hudson had hunted down. He'd joined us for a few bites, but took off again soon after, wanting to do another sweep of the area. We were still trying to make our way back to the wall, and with every hour that passed, the skies grew more ominous.

The magick of Midnight knew what was coming for it. *Who* was coming for it.

We had no idea what horrors awaited us in Amaranth City—no idea whether Evander had even made it that far or whether he was even still alive. But the city was a destination—a mission. A piece of lasagna, as Haley was so fond of saying. And heading there felt like a better option than sitting out in the open, waiting to get picked off by a squadron of Darkwinter witches on raven gryphons or Melantha's ghouls or any of the other fucked-up monsters headed our way.

"I blamed him for trying to separate me from Oona," I continued. "For being jealous. When all he truly wanted was a chance to get me out of this hellhole. To give his brothers a better life. He was honoring our vow, Haley. Blood before roses. *I'm* the one who fucking..." I trailed off, not even sure what I'd meant to say. Only that it hurt inside. It hurt inside to say all these things, to think about them.

"I blamed him for a lot of things, too." She rubbed her thumb over the scar on her wrist, a spike of old fear hitting her bloodstream. "I haven't even... I haven't even fully forgiven him for leaving Blackmoon Bay without telling me about his brother—about his plans. I understand it, but it doesn't make it any easier to accept. He just... he thought it would be easier on me. Elian... he sacrifices for the ones he loves, Jax. That's what he does, no matter what the cost. What the collateral damage. And he's caused a *lot* of damage in his life—made a shit ton of mistakes. But no matter what the consequences, leaving me to try to find his stolen brother wasn't one of those mistakes. And saving you—sacrificing himself for you—wasn't a mistake, either. It was a choice he made. And even though I want him back —God, more than *anything* I want him back—I can't say I'm not glad he made that choice, Jax. Because losing you would *destroy* me. I—"

I cut her off with a kiss, still not ready to hear her say those words to me. I knew she loved me—it was written in her eyes when she looked at me, written in her touch, in her every kiss. But I just... I needed to get her back to New Orleans, just like I'd told her the other night.

Then, I would let her say it. Then, I would fucking *welcome* it.

"I'm sorry I pushed you so hard tonight," I said.

She tilted her face up to me and grinned, a bit of mischief shining in her eyes. "Right. Because the whole 'don't you dare stop, make me feel it, take it' thing gave you the impression that I wanted it soft and gentle tonight?"

I nudged her in the ribs and laughed. "No, smartass. I'm talking about the sparring. I want you to be strong, but... I could've been less of a dick about it."

"Jax. First of all? I don't ever want to hear anything about 'less dick' when it comes to you. But..." She blew out a breath, the mischief dimming from her eyes. "Being with you... I know you want me to be strong. And I *am* strong—you've helped me see that more than anyone."

"You're the strongest person I know, Haley. I just need you to believe it. To trust yourself."

"I get that. It's just..." A sad smile. A soft shake of her head, the fall of her still-damp hair shimmering in the fire-light. When she spoke again, her voice was barely audible over the crackling fire. "Sometimes I wish I didn't have to be strong at all—even just for a little while."

Fuck, my heart broke for her. All I wanted was to take her into my arms and promise her she'd never have to be strong all the time. That she could sit out a few rounds. That Hudson and I would defeat the enemies of Midnight and take care of her forever.

Hell, I'd even make an allowance for Evander, too, if that's what she wanted.

But that wasn't the world we lived in. Wasn't this fucking place. Wasn't our reality.

"When I was a kid," I said, inching a little closer to the fire. "A *human* kid, I mean. I had a family. Parents. A sister."

Her eyes widened, but she didn't say anything.

"Long story short... I wasn't exactly every parent's dream. Fell in with the wrong crowds, made a lot of shitty choices. Cost my family a lot of money bailing me out of one fuckup or another. Eventually, my parents decided it wasn't safe for me to live there—not with my sister in the house. She was only twelve at the time."

"How old were you?" she asked.

"Seventeen, and they booted my ass out. Wasn't all that unusual for someone my age to be on his own—this was a few centuries ago. But I wasn't ready for it. No job, no prospects. I fell in with an even worse crowd. Gambling, drugs, illegal underground fight rings, all the bullshit you'd imagine. But I missed my sister. She missed me, too. We used to pass letters back and forth through a friend of hers at school—the girl was the sister of one of the guys I ran with. She kept begging me to take her to the fights. Wanted to learn how to throw a punch. Keep the boys on their toes, she used to tease."

I laughed as I remembered how she'd beg me to take her, swearing she wouldn't tell our parents.

"Anyway, this shit went on for a few years. I had *zero* contact with my parents—they were so-called decent, God-fearing folk, and I was a fucking degenerate, so it's not like our paths ever crossed. I got worse. Did things... things I'm not proud of. But my sister never stopped writing. Never stopped trying to make arrangements to see me. I always told her no—I didn't want my parents finding out and kicking her out, too. And I *damn* sure didn't want any of the assholes I associated with to know about her. The guy who exchanged our letters was decent enough, kept his mouth shut about her—probably because he had a sister, too. But I couldn't risk it."

"I... sorry. That's... Shit, Jax. A sister." She squeezed

my hand, and I knew she understood. Haley had been separated from her own sisters as a child, only reunited recently in Blackmoon Bay. She hadn't even been able to see them or talk to them again since then—not since she'd come to Midnight on Melantha's orders.

"One night," I said, "my sister decided to come looking for me. I had no idea. Just got back to whatever shithole place I'd been crashing at—drunk, of course, booze being my drug of choice back then. I stumbled in through the front door, beelining for the couch I slept on, but even in my stupor, I knew something was..." I swallowed and shook my head, the old memories flashing through my mind, tying me up in knots. "I smelled the blood before I saw it. Then I heard the... gasping."

"Oh my god." Haley touched her fingers to her lips, her eyes glazing with tears.

"Room was pitch black. I lit a lantern, followed the sounds. The smell. My sister was... She was on the floor in the back room, curled up in a pool of her own blood. Still alive, but barely. She'd been... brutalized, and they..." I couldn't even bring myself to say the words. To describe it with any more than that single word—*brutalized*. "No one else was in the house. I ran to her, gathered her up in my arms, but there was so much blood and I just..."

A tear slid from my eye, my chest splitting open at the memory, at this darkness I hadn't ever brought into the light.

Haley said nothing. Just held me. Just fucking held me while I got it all out.

"I watched the light leave her eyes, Haley. Held my baby sister in my arms and watched the light leave—a fucking fifteen-year-old girl. And suddenly, out of fucking nowhere, I was surrounded by people. I hadn't even heard anyone come in. Didn't even realize the sun had risen on a new day. Didn't think it had a fucking *right* to rise after something like that, you know? But my parents were just... there. Looming. Gasping. My mother fainted. My father just fell to his knees and took my sister's hand and... He kept saying her name, over and over and over. And all I could think to say to him was, 'you're getting her blood on your knees.'"

I closed my eye and shook my head, the old shame burning through my gut. The memory of how my parents had looked at me after—when the shock had worn off and my mother had come back to consciousness.

A thousand years could pass and I'd never forget the hatred in their eyes. The blame.

"A cop was there, too, and a neighbor who'd claimed he'd heard screaming the night before. But then things got... I don't know. Strange. My parents said they didn't want word getting out about it. They wanted my sister buried privately. Didn't want an investigation—wanted it all swept under the rug. And the cop, for whatever reason, was fine to let it go. Sounded like a family matter, he'd said. To this day, I can't wrap my head around it."

"That's... insane," she whispered.

"Yeah. There's a lot about that night that doesn't add up. Never did."

"Did they ever find out who... who did it? Was it someone you knew?"

"No, I... I never found out. Considering the people I associated with, the shit we were into, the assholes who'd lost money betting on or against me in the fights, the fucking dealers and users flowing in and out of that house every night... There were so many possibilities, but in the end..." I shook my head as if I *still*—after all this time— couldn't fucking believe it. "Haley, my parents... They thought it was me. They took one look at the blood and the dead child in my arms and... that was that. Case closed. No, I wasn't an upstanding citizen by any stretch, but my own parents... My fucking *parents* actually believed I murdered my sister. A sister that I... I fucking *adored* that girl, Haley."

I didn't bother trying to keep my voice steady now. It felt like cheating. Like dishonoring her memory to pretend that speaking these words out loud didn't fucking *destroy* me.

"And here's part two of the short version of events... My parents, in all their infinite wisdom, did what any god-fearing humans with an unsolvable human problem would do. They tracked down a crossroads demon and made a fucking deal. Yeah, we knew about the supernatural back then. Wasn't talked about much, but it was around. I'd tangled with a few demons in my day. Vampires, too—the underground fight clubs were always popular among the bloodsuckers. Fucking buffets, far as they were concerned. Anyway, this asshole promised them he could bring my sister back from the dead—a sister they'd already buried, refusing to let me attend the funeral. And in exchange, all they had to do was sacrifice one little soul to hell."

"Jax. Holy shit. I... holy *shit*." Haley's face was as pale as the moon now, her cheeks shining with tears, her hand trembling as she tightened her grip on mine. "That's... that's how you became..."

"Yep. My own parents sold me out. I'm a demon because they sent me to hell in exchange for my sister's life. But you know the real fucked-up part of this story? I would've gone willingly. If there was actually a chance my sister could've come back, I would've done it in a fucking heartbeat. But I knew it was too good to be true."

"The demon was full of shit," she said.

"Yeah, there was no way to bring her back. She was already gone. Already at peace. So they signed me away for *nothing*, and they left me there to rot. And the demons? Fuck, Haley. They kept me human for years, torturing me at every turn. Then they made me immortal and kicked it up a few notches. And do you know the reason my tormentors in hell were able to do what they did to me? To literally *terrify* me for centuries until I was utterly incapable of fear? Because deep down, I actually *believed* all the terrible things I'd seen in my parents' eyes that night. All the things they'd said to me after. I knew I didn't hurt my sister, but I truly believed it was my fault. I couldn't protect her, therefore, I deserved what my parents had done. What the demons had done. I honestly believed I would never feel love again simply because I didn't deserve it, and—"

"Jax, I don't even know what to—"

"No. *No*, angel, I'm not telling you this because I want you to find some comforting words for me here. They don't exist—not for this. I'm telling..." I let out a deep sigh and cupped her face, some of the bitterness ebbing as I gazed into her eyes. Felt the love. Felt her. "I'm telling you all this because... Look, you were right. You shouldn't have to be strong all the time. You should be able to let your guard down, to laugh, to run through the woods without worrying about some psychotic monster slashing you to ribbons or a dark goddess stealing your mojo and feeding you to her snakes. And someday? I fucking swear to you, angel..." New emotion rose in my chest, my voice thick with it. "I *swear* I'll make that happen for you, but only if you—"

"If I make it out of here alive?" She lowered her eyes and let out a shuddering breath.

I tilted her face back up, forcing her to meet my gaze. "I was going to say, if you'll *let* me." A faint smile curved my mouth. "You're not exactly the sit-out-the-fights, let-the-men-protect you kind of woman."

"No, I suppose I'm not."

My smile faded, emotion rising inside once more. "But until that day comes, Haley, I *can't* let you give in—not even when it's just us sparring in the woods. I pushed you because I *didn't* push her. Didn't teach her how to fight, didn't push back when my parents kept me from her, didn't protect her when she needed it most."

"But that wasn't your—"

"I know it wasn't my fault. I *know* that, logically. But that doesn't change the fact that all of those things are true. I *didn't* protect her, *didn't* fight for her, and she died. I went to hell, but I paid a price more dear than losing my humanity. I lost my *sister*. She died in my arms. I was covered in her blood when I literally felt her soul leaving her body, knowing there wasn't a damn thing I could do about it because I was too fucking late. Because I didn't protect her, didn't get to her in time, didn't try harder to see her so she didn't have to come looking for me. And that image, that memory..." I slid my hand into Haley's hair, gripping her tight, needing her to truly hear these words. "It haunts me more than you'll ever know, angel, but never more than it did the night Hudson brought you back from Beggar's Moat. He's the strongest one of all of us, yet even *he* couldn't stop you from getting hurt. When I saw you in that bed, bloodied and broken and... Fuck, Haley. You were barely breathing. Seeing you like that... I can't get that image out of my fucking head. And the thought of you *ever* coming close to death again... It kills me. And don't think for one *minute* I don't know who saved you that night. Saint healed you. He brought you back to us, and now he's fucking gone. Just *gone.* So I need to do everything in my power to give you the best shot I can at defending yourself, with or without backup, with our without magick, with or without a vampire healer. Even if it means you hate me for what I put you through. Even if it means you walk away from everything we have. I'd risk that—*all* of it—just to give you a fighting chance."

Tears gathered in her eyes again, then spilled, each one leaving a glittering trail down her skin. Trembling, barely keeping it together, I drew her close, kissing one cheek, then the other. Kissing away her tears until there wasn't a single one to be found.

"I know there aren't any words to make this right," she whispered, pulling back to take my face between her palms. "But there's one thing I need to say. One thing I need you to trust me on, okay?"

I wrapped my hands around her wrists and nodded.

"You were wrong, Jax. You *did* deserve to be loved. Your parents failed you. They were supposed to love their son, but they utterly failed. And you don't have to carry their failure for them—that's on them. And you know what? You *are* loved. So just in case you need a reminder of what it feels like when someone loves you—truly, without reservation, without conditions? Well…" She smiled up at me in the firelight, and *fuck*, how I melted for that smile. "It feels a little something like this."

Haley leaned forward and brushed her lips across mine, soft and perfect, and even though I kept telling myself I didn't want her to say it until we got back to New Orleans, I let those words—*her* words—fill me up inside. I let them soothe the ache, let them heal the broken pieces inside me, let them put me back together again in a way *no* one—not in all my long centuries of existence—had ever bothered to even try.

You are *loved…*

It whispered through me like a mantra, again and again, until another word finally filtered in, past the echo inside me, past the sounds of Haley's soft sighs as she kissed me breathless, past the hissing fire and the Midnight breeze.

One simple word.

A word with the power to stop our hearts.

"Sparrow?"

ELIAN

*E*very step on solid ground should've been pure agony. Should've sent me crumpling to my knees, begging for death.

I'd only been on my feet for a few moments. Gem was able to create a portal, using the last of her reserves to transport us out of that cave and into the clearing at the base of the mountains. Every second in that portal had been torture, as if some great beast had reached inside me and tried to wring the last drops of blood from my newly formed veins.

But I'd endured it, following the tug of Haley's magick, the steady heartbeat that pulsed through the bond that now connected us. The bridge she'd built to bring me back.

And now, as I finally stepped out of the portal and spotted her there, sitting with Jax beside a low fire, my pain vanished. My weakness vanished. Everything vanished but her beautiful face and the taste of her name on my lips.

"Sparrow?"

Her eyes went wide, and she and Jax rose to their feet.

With a surge of renewed energy—renewed fucking hope—I blurred. Crashed right into both of them, taking them down to the ground in a hug so fierce it stole the air from their lungs.

"Fucking *Saint*?" Jax was the first to get back to his feet, his face splitting into a grin, tears glazing his eye as he hauled me and Haley back up. "You stupid fae fucking asshole!" He grabbed me again, hauling me against his chest. "You fucking shithead. You fucking fae... *fuck*!"

"I missed you, too, brother."

"But... how... how did...?"

I thumbed at the two women behind me, just coming into view as they walked across the clearing. "They'll fill you in."

"But... Oona?" he asked. Suspicion darkened his voice. "*Gem*?"

"She's with us, Jax. And she'll tell you everything. Just... just go."

I turned around to face Haley, who still hadn't spoken a word. Tears streaked her face, her mouth opening and closing, her eyes bright in the moonlight.

My heart melted. Fucking melted.

Everything I felt for her rose inside me, and I took a

deep breath, then a step. One more, and she was there. Close enough for me to look into those eyes and see into her fucking soul.

"Saint," Jax said again, but I didn't spare him another glance.

"Leave," I ordered, not taking my eyes off Haley. Never wanting to take my eyes off her again. *Fuck*, she was beautiful. So fucking beautiful I could hardly breathe.

A soft sigh, a rustle in the grass, and the three of them were gone, finally—fucking finally leaving me alone with her.

"Sparrow," I whispered again, cupping her face.

And in the long, silent, heart-stopping moments that followed, neither of us spoke, and neither of us bothered to hide the tears that spilled.

Haley's eyes searched mine in the moonlight. After an eternity, she said, "You came back to me."

My hands trembled as I held her face, my gaze sweeping down to her mouth, then back up, slowly cataloging every inch. The precise angle of her jaw. The soft shape of each wave in her hair as it curled over her shoulders. The exact shade of pink coloring her cheeks. The dark, feathery lashes I used to kiss while she slept beside me—a memory that had gotten me through some of the darkest nights of my life.

By the time I met her gaze again, I was panting, my

chest thundering with the beat of a heart that'd been bound for far too long, finally set free.

Death had warned me my return wouldn't be easy. That I would suffer and bleed with every step, with every breath. And I felt it churning below the surface—the burn as my skin and muscles worked to fully heal. The deep ache as my bones worked to grow strong again.

But the pain was a distant hum in the background of this moment. This fucking gift.

"I will *always* come back to you, sparrow," I said.

Another tear slipped down her cheek. "But... how? How is this possible?"

"Haley, you saved me in Blackmoon Bay. You saved me in New Orleans. You saved me here in Midnight so many times I've lost count." I swallowed through the tightness in my throat. "And then you built me a bridge and saved me again. I literally stared into the face of Death, but... One look into your eyes had the power to bring me back home. To life. To you."

"Death," she whispered. "You... you saw her face? Her actual face?"

I nodded, though I still couldn't believe it; the longer I'd been away from that place, the hazier the memory became. But I said, "She was a young witch—and a white raven, too. She said she knew you. That she fought with you in Blackmoon Bay."

"Reva," she breathed, wonder glazing her eyes. Sadness, too. Longing. Relief. "Is she... How is she?"

"She's... intense." I laughed, thinking of the girl's feisty spirit—*that* was something I was pretty sure I'd never forget. "But she helped me... figure out a few things. Well, first she called me a fucking *smoothie*, but then we worked it out."

Haley laughed, the sound of it a balm on my heart. "I can't... I can't believe this is happening. Tell me you're here. Tell me you're really here."

"I'm here. I'm right fucking *here*." I grabbed her hand. Pressed it to my chest. "Do you feel it?"

"Your heartbeat?" She laughed again, tears still falling. "It's racing like the wild mares of night."

"Because it's alive, sparrow. *I'm* alive. And I need to say something to you. I need you to hear it and know it and never, ever doubt it." I threaded my fingers into her hair and stared into those emerald eyes. *Fuck*, how I wanted to eat her whole. To taste every inch of her. To claim her so fiercely, not even death would ever dare part us again.

But first, I needed to get out the words. Words that'd been trapped inside my heart, bound by that fucking curse for far too long.

"I was *with* you," I said, my voice quaking with the force of it. Of her. Of *us*. "All those three-thirty-threes, those stone-cold lonely mornings when all you could do was stare out the window and wonder what the fuck went wrong. I was right there with you for every single one—missing you, aching for you, dying inside for how badly I hurt you. I know you felt alone, and I know my telling you this doesn't make up for the pain I caused. But you *weren't* alone. I was with you. Every time. Because I love you, Haley Barnes. With all that I am, I *love* you. I have *always* loved you. You're my heart, my family, my fucking *soul*. Melantha's curse died with me. And I promise you—here and now and forever—I will *never* walk away from you again. From us. You are *mine*, little sparrow. And I'm yours, in any way you'll have me. And anyone—*anyone*—who tries to come between that again will fucking *burn*."

By the time all the words were out, I was panting again. Breathless. My heart thudding so loudly in my ears, I was pretty sure there *was* a wild mare in my chest.

But I waited. I waited and waited. I'd told Haley how I felt, let it all out, and she... she was still here. *We* were still here. Warm and solid and real and unbreakable.

"Tell me what you're thinking," I whispered, afraid that anything louder would pop this dream like a bubble.

Her eyes drifted closed, that heartbreaking smile gracing her face. In a soft whisper, she said, "I'm thinking I'll die if you don't kiss me, Elian of Autumnshire."

"A kiss?" I teased, my lips so close to hers I could already taste them. I bit down gently, my fangs descending, scraping across her lower lip and making her shudder. "Is that all my sweet little sparrow wants?"

"Is it true?" she whispered. "The curse is really gone?"

"Yes."

"Then no, Elian. I don't want a kiss." She opened her eyes, fire blazing inside them. "I want all of it. All of *you*."

I slid a trembling hand into her hair, the other down the front of her pants, her skin hot and smooth. I brushed past her clit and dipped two fingers inside her, and when she gripped my arms and gasped in pleasure, I captured her breath in my mouth and held it, memorizing the taste of it. Of her.

A tremor rolled down my spine, the last of my fear giving way to pure, red-hot desire.

I pressed my lips to hers, savoring the silky touch as she slowly parted for me. My tongue swept into her mouth, tasting every curve as I slid my fingers deeper into that soft, wet heat.

"It's been *far* too long since I've had the taste of you in my mouth, sparrow," I whispered, drawing back and bringing my fingertips to my lips. Still half-kissing her, I licked my fingers, savoring the twin sensations of her sweet mouth and the familiar, sweet-and-salty taste of her desire.

It unleashed something wild inside me, that kiss. That taste. Something that'd been chained up like an animal, finally cut loose.

With a growl, I unzipped my pants and freed my cock, then spun her around and fisted her hair. Lifted it up to reveal her bare neck. Kissed a blazing hot path from one side to the other, teasing and licking, biting, damn near weeping to even be *allowed* to worship her like this again.

"Elian," she breathed, trembling with every kiss. "You feel... you feel amazing. Everything you do to me is..."

"I know. I remember how you like it," I said softly, releasing her hair and wrapping a hand around her throat. With my other hand, I fisted my cock, teasing her from behind as she lowered her pants. "I remember *exactly* how you like it."

Fuck, how many times had I played this movie in my mind, so desperate to hold on to the memory, to find a bit of warmth and comfort during too many dark and endless nights to count. I would always be grateful for those memories, but now that I had her in my arms again, in my mouth... *Fuck*. Those memories felt like cheap imitations, and they would never be good enough. *Nothing* would ever be good enough—only this. Real. Fucking real.

"Tell me you want this," I whispered into her hair. Begged. "Tell me you still want this."

"I want this. I want you, Elian. More than you could even—"

I didn't give her a chance to finish before I slid inside her from behind, claiming her in one hot, slick thrust that had us both crying out into the night.

Buried inside her, my mouth on the back of her neck, hand still wrapped around her throat, I went completely still.

Being with her like this again felt like coming home. Home to all that I'd turned my back on. Home to all the things that'd kept me going, even when I'd wanted to give up. Home to the woman I'd never stopped loving.

And home to myself.

But as much as I'd fantasized about this moment, as much as I wanted to give it to her hard and fast from behind in all the ways I knew she loved... Tonight, I needed to see her face. To see the light glowing in those beautiful green eyes as I made her come, all for me.

I pulled out and slowly turned her to face me again.

She smiled, soft and sweet. And the love I saw there, the intensity...

My chest tightened, my eyes blurring with tears.

"Sparrow," I breathed.

She nodded, understanding without words, without explanation.

We stripped out of our clothes, then laid down on the soft earth, Haley on her back as I kissed her shoulder, her collarbone, her breast, her stomach, slow and decadent, nothing between us but skin and heat and love—so much love it filled me up, smoothing all the jagged edges inside me. The black holes. The rage and the fear, the mistakes, the emptiness. Death.

She tugged on my hair, gently urging me back to her mouth, to another perfect kiss, and she parted her thighs for me and arched her back, and I slid inside her once more, whispering her name with every breath like a prayer of thanks to all the gods of every fucking realm I knew.

There was no awkwardness, no re-learning. Our bodies remembered. *We* remembered. She felt at once familiar and new, the years that'd passed changing her in small ways, the men she now loved changing her even more.

I nearly laughed at the thought. All those years ago, making love to her in Blackmoon Bay, I would've murdered anyone for even *suggesting* I might one day share her with another man. But now she had two other men. Three, if my suspicions about her growing feelings for Evander were true. And though it defied all logic and reason, I wasn't jealous, wasn't spiteful. They made her happy. Fulfilled her in different ways—ways that made her eyes light up. Ways that gave her happiness and hope, and through her, gave me happiness and hope, too.

I loved them for it. All of them.

Now, my sparrow in my arms once more, I took my time, savoring every stroke, every fevered touch, every sweet moan as I moved inside her, our bodies drawing close, our souls knitting back together, the old rifts repaired. Strengthened. In this moment, there was no war, no enemies, no fear. Only love. Only this perfection between us, my every kiss another promise—one I made to her. One I made to myself.

Death had given me a second chance, and I wasn't about to squander it. I had no illusions that it would be easy, but I was ready to fight for it. To fight to stay off the Black—that old demon I no longer feared, though I knew it still had sharp claws. I would fight to stay present, releasing my old resentments, the old wounds. I would fight for my brothers and the woman I loved. I would fight for Midnight.

And every day, I would earn that second chance I'd been given. I would fucking *earn* it.

I shifted and moved deeper inside her, and Haley gasped, her body tightening around me.

I pulled back and gazed into her face.

"Open your eyes, little sparrow," I whispered. "Let me see you shatter for me."

She did as I asked, dark lashes fluttering as she opened her eyes and looked at me again, her lips parted, her heartbeat wild, blood and magick singing through her veins as the pure pleasure swept her up and spun out inside her, making her quiver, making her cry out my name into the darkness, again and again.

Still trembling, she lifted her head and kissed me, and that was it. Everything inside me exploded, fucking supernova, and I came with a shudder and a roar in a blinding rush that made my whole world shatter, then come back together, piece by piece, breath by breath, until we were a single soul once more. A single heartbeat.

When I finally broke our kiss to look into her eyes again, tears streaked her face.

"Elian," she whispered, her palm warm against my cheek, and that was the last of it. No more words but the ones written in her eyes.

"I know, little sparrow." I turned and pressed a kiss to the center of her palm, my chest tight, my heart full. "I know."

I rolled onto my hip and shifted her so her back was against my chest, and I held her close and breathed in the scent of her skin. Her hair.

Moments later, with a deep, satisfied sigh, my little sparrow began to sing. Her chest vibrated with the sound of it, soft at first, then steadily growing until it echoed out across the clearing. Echoed through my heart.

And there, in those sweet, off-key notes, I found my salvation.

live? What the fuck do you mean, he's alive? Move!"

Ignoring the halfhearted protests of Gem, the demon, my lieutenant commander, and the gargoyle—all of whom attempted to keep me away from the clearing where my dead brother had apparently manifested hours earlier—I barreled through the trees and headed straight for him.

Straight for them.

My witch... and my brother.

Elian.

Back from the dead, they said. Alive.

I'd been tracking Haley and the others for half the night, having only just secured the allegiance of a scant few of Midnight's most brutal, bloodthirsty rebels. Most of the others I'd found hadn't even granted me an audience. Many had already fallen prey to the enhanced Devil's

Dream we'd pushed out through the ranks, the addiction spreading like wildfire, decimating entire camps in a matter of nights. Others had tried to kill me on sight, their hatred and bloodlust staunched only by my own cunning and quickness with a blade.

The few rebels who'd finally agreed to fight with us were a motley crew of barbaric demons and imps, dark fae mercenaries, and vampires from the human realm who didn't much care *where* their next meal came from so long as it screamed while they ate it. Their fealty had come at a cost—not just the revelation of some of my longest held secrets, as Haley had implored me to share, but the promise of full pardons for all past crimes, more money than I'd ever be able to produce, and precious real estate in the city... assuming we could save it.

Amaranth was already under Darkwinter attack, their forces moving in from the north, their weather witches controlling not just the Fog of a Thousand Knives but other phenomena as well—earthquakes. Floods. Just as Haley had predicted, most of Keradoc's generals had turned traitor the moment the enemies closed in, joining forces with the Darkwinter troops who promised to spare their lives.

Fools. Fucking fools.

Now, just about five miles south of the wall, I'd finally found her again. Them.

And learned that my brother was alive.

I stalked across that clearing, stopping only when I saw them lying in the grass, naked and entwined beside the fire.

My witch. My brother. Their bodies gleaming.

Whole. Alive.

Inside the darkest depths of my heart, twin flames burned bright.

One—relief and awe at the presence of my once-dead twin.

Two—a raging, unfathomable jealousy that he and Haley had already... reunited.

Liar. I closed my eyes, the word sliding through my mind. *Fucking liar.*

For when I searched my heart, I knew it wasn't their reunion that had set me ablaze. Haley was happy—I wanted that for her. Truly. I wasn't jealous of her love for Elian.

I was jealous, I finally realized, of her relationship with him. That she'd known him for so many years. That she had actual memories of him, a shared history that'd bound them, that'd allowed him to turn his back on death and follow her love home.

And I had... nothing. No memory of my twin brother, no matter how badly I wished for it now. No shared history, no matter how desperately I despised the yawning ache of that blank space in my mind. My old life.

"But... how?" I blurted out suddenly, startling them both.

They turned and gazed up at me in the moonlight. Haley smiled. And Elian... he smiled too.

Together, they rose, neither covering their naked bodies.

It was Haley, not my brother, who responded first.

"He heard me that night, Evander," she said softly, her smile as bright as the first moon. "He *felt* me. And when he sensed Melantha's hold on my mind, he..." She glanced over her shoulder, where my brother was standing at her side. "He broke it. And then, somehow, he fought his way through hell to come back to us."

"Not hell, exactly," Elian finally said, reaching for her hand. "I managed to avoid that particular destiny for now. But..." His silver eyes clouded, the usual smirk settling into a grim line. "It wasn't an easy journey. I'm still not entirely... healed."

I couldn't help my scoff, that irrational jealous ire flaring to life inside, looking for some target to hit—*any* target.

"Apparently you're healed enough," I said, raking my gaze down his naked form. Then, with no trace of emotion, "Get dressed and find some weapons. We march for the wall at—"

"He's still in pain, Evander," Haley said, her touch on my chest making my breath catch.

Glaring at his nude form once more, I said coolly, "If he's well enough to *fuck*, he's well enough to fight."

A growl. A shimmer in the air. A blur in my peripheral vision.

I was flat on my back and blinking up at the stars before I could even draw my next breath.

The vampire-fae had knocked me on my ass, and now he loomed over me, knee pressed to my chest.

"You're right, brother," he sneered. "I *am* well enough to fight. Are you?"

I shoved him off and tried to get to my feet, but another blur slammed me flat on my back once more—*this* blur accompanied by the bright red light and the smokey taste of magick I recognized as Haley's.

My only comfort was the fact that my brother had suffered the same fate.

"Really?" Haley stood over us, hands on her naked hips, green eyes rolling to the sky. "Look, I know you two are still coming to terms with this whole twin-brothers-reunited-after-one-was-kidnapped-and-the-other-one-*died* thing, but... guys. Seriously? You need to work it out."

"Because we're brothers?" I grumbled, getting to my feet and dusting the dirt from my backside. My brother did the same, finally locating his pants.

"Because you're family," she said. "*My* family. Look, I'm not forcing you into this just because you're blood relatives. I'm doing it because you're brothers in an even deeper sense. You care for each other—it's obvious. And we're all in this war together now. Fighting amongst ourselves is only going to make us easier targets for the real enemies."

"I *will* fight by his side for you, Haley," I said. "For this realm. That's not even a question."

"You know I'm with you on that, too, sparrow." Elian handed her some clothes.

With another roll of her eyes, she quickly dressed, then said, "What about fighting for each other? For our family?"

Neither of us responded to that.

Silence, for now, was better than coming to blows.

After a long, tense beat, Haley blew out a breath and said to me, "Tell me about the rebels. Were you able to scrounge up any additional fighters?"

I gave her the update—the rebels I'd secured, the ones I'd fought off. The ones the Devil's Dream had ruined beyond help.

At the mention of the drugs, Elian shook his head, his silver eyes bright with new anger.

I drew in a sharp breath at the sight. It was as if a veil had fallen away, and now I was seeing him for the very first time.

Guilt bubbled up inside.

My brother—my twin brother—was addicted to the very drug I'd forced him to work on, night after night. Forced him to deliver.

I couldn't hold his gaze. When I spoke again, my voice was tight. "Elian, I... I'm sorry."

"For what, exactly?" he snapped. "Shooting me full of hawthorn the night of the feast? Taking me prisoner and throwing me in the dungeon? Lying about your identity so the rest of us would continue to fear you and do your bidding?" He stepped closer, his eyes glowing even brighter, his entire body vibrating with rage.

I could nearly taste it.

Clearing my throat, I said, "I was... speaking of the Devil's Dream."

Elian scoffed. "Oh, don't give me that pitying tone, *brother*. I *invented* Dream. I earned every bit of torture those little pills put me through."

"No, I... I should've been more... understanding. About your situation. Haley tried to tell me and I..." I trailed off. This wasn't something I could fix with words, no matter how earnest.

"Did it work?" he asked. "Did you weaken any *actual* enemy forces, or just the ones who might've joined us?"

"Dream is a poison, like any other," I said. "Once it starts to spread, it's very difficult to contain."

"Quite an astute observation, Evander. Keradoc teach you that skill?"

Disgust rolled through my gut at the mention of the warlord's name, igniting a new fury inside me... But it faded quickly.

For all that I didn't remember him, Elian was still my brother. Not just by blood, but by the simple fact that Haley loved him. That he'd come back for her. That he was still willing to fight.

"I don't wish to battle with you, Elian," I said. "Haley's right. Our fight lies elsewhere."

"I suppose when you view the world through the eyes of a warlord," he said, "everything's a battle, isn't it?"

"Elian," Haley warned, her gaze darting between us. Then, with a sad sigh, "Guys, I don't... Look. I know you've got some things to... unpack. No one is saying you have to do that right now. I'm just asking you to drop the defensiveness and try to... I don't know. See each other the way I see you."

"And how do you see us, sparrow?" Elian asked.

She looked to me, her eyes brightening, her smile warm. It disarmed me, that smile. Always.

"Evander," she said, the sound of my name like the sweetest music, "is so much more than a warlord, Elian. He's decent and kind, he fights for what he believes in, and... and he's someone worth knowing as a man, despite the fact that you lost the chance to know him growing up."

I returned her smile, dim compared to the light gracing her face, but genuine nevertheless.

"And Evander, you need to know... Your brother *never* stopped looking for you. He walked away from our life in Blackmoon Bay—from love—just for a *chance* to find you.

A chance—that thing you told me most people never get in this life. That thing we're supposedly fighting for."

I looked at my brother, waiting for him to deny it. To set the record straight. But his gaze was fierce. Unwavering.

"And as for the rest of this... situation," Haley continued, and I knew at once she was talking about our relationships. Our feelings for her. The tangled, thorny things I now found myself wanting. "Elian, I never stopped loving you. Not for a second. And I know you never stopped loving me, either. Now that I've finally got you back, I'm not letting you go again. And Evander?" She turned to me once more, lighting me up inside, obliterating the last of my earlier jealousy. "You... I'm not even sure what to say. You snuck up on me. My feelings for you are... complicated and surprising, but real. I can't deny them. I *won't* deny them. All I can do is give you the same choice I gave Jax and Hudson when I told them I wanted us all to be together. But that choice is about us—our relationship. It's not about the two of you working it out. That is *not* a choice."

Once again, I felt myself smiling at her. Completely undone by her. "That your heart has such a boundless capacity to love is a wonder and a gift, Haley Barnes. I would no more seek to dampen it than I would seek to dampen your magick."

"Well, other than the time you put an *actual* dampener cuff on her," Elian quipped, but there was no real anger there. The ghost of a grin twitched his lips, and Haley glared at him with the blazing heat of a thousand starshowers.

"What part of *working it out* don't you understand?" she asked him.

I tried but failed not to smirk.

Then, whirling on me, "And *you*? Wipe that look off your face before I blast your ass into the dirt again."

I raised my hands in surrender.

Elian sighed. "So you two," he said. "You're a thing, then."

"We've... gotten closer," I admitted.

He narrowed his silver eyes. "Define closer."

"Oh, for fuck's sake." Haley laughed. "Let's save the dick-measuring for *after* the war. We can make a game out of it. Family date night!"

Elian's eyes blazed, then dimmed, acceptance settling over him. "You know there's nothing I wouldn't do for you, sparrow. That *has* not and *will* not change. So if you have..." He swallowed hard and sighed again. "If you have romantic feelings for my brother, then I accept that."

"Accept, but not embrace?" she asked.

To his credit, he didn't scoff. Just met my gaze, assessing.

"We just... need time," he finally said. "To get used to your... feelings for us."

I nodded, grateful he was willing to leave it at that.

"And what about your feelings for each other?" she asked.

"Time," I echoed, and Elian—for once—agreed with me.

———

While the gargoyle and demon did another perimeter check, the rest of us sat around the fire, and I finished updating the group about the intel I'd gathered, the fighters I'd arranged to rendezvous with at the wall later. Oona and Gem shared what they'd learned, and we began to cobble together some sort of plan.

Get to the wall. Find the other fighters. Defend our city.

It was bare-bones at best. Hopeless at worst, but...

A chance, I reminded myself. *Just a chance. That's all we need.*

Haley smiled at me across the dark space, her eyes golden in the firelight, filling me with a sliver of hope.

A hope that my brother shattered with a single word.

"*Fuck.*"

We shot to our feet just as the demon came into view, running toward us across the clearing. By the time he reached us, he was panting and covered in filth. The gargoyle landed beside him, his face grim.

"A rift," the demon managed. "Melantha made some kind of rift. The Army... they're here."

He'd barely gotten the words out when I felt the telltale rumble in the ground. I met Haley's eyes again, the ripple of dark magick hitting us both.

I had just enough time to reach for her.

"*Fight*," I commanded, gripping her jaw. "You fucking fight with every bit of magick you possess, every bit you can take from this realm, and don't you go down for *anything*."

I kissed her. And then I was off, sword drawn, charging straight into the mayhem with the others.

Straight into our end.

HALEY

A wave of nightmares broke upon the hill, the skeleton army I'd seen so many times in my visions finally here. Black blood oozed from their mouths, clung to the white bone, glistened in the moonlight.

And the sounds—the endless droning of their empty moans, the clattering of bone against rock as they moved across the land...

Nausea churned in my gut. I wondered how many fae they'd already consumed. How many had risen again.

Overhead, a dark shadow blotted out the moons, and I glanced up to see it—that giant, rotting raven gryphon. And though I couldn't see its rider—still formless, still unable to physically manifest in the realm she so desperately wanted to claim—I felt her.

Her voice echoed through my skull.

Here is where your friends perish, Daughter of Darkwinter. Here is where you bow to me.

"Attack!" Evander roared. "Attack!"

And my men—along with Oona and Gem—followed the order. Swords flashed, striking bone. Shattering it. Some of the ghouls dropped. Others... others kept right on coming for us, seemingly unaware of their missing limbs, missing teeth, bashed-in skulls...

A bright flash of pale blue magick, and I turned to see Gem hitting the front lines with a blast that took out a few dozen at once. She couldn't hold on to her magick, though—it was as if it had grown unstable, just like the magick of Midnight. I could practically feel it—feel it thrashing around beneath the ground, upended by the chaos that had broken upon the realm.

Gem's magick finally fizzled out, and she followed up with her crossbow, shooting bolt after bolt through their skulls.

I lost sight of Elian. Of Evander. Of Jax. I had no idea if Jax's powers would even work in a fight like this—if the undead had fears he could manipulate.

Nearly impossible to kill in his warrior form, Hudson sailed out across that sea of death, grabbing skeletal soldiers and smashing them to bits. Dropping them, only to do it all over again. Again and again.

Chaos. There was only chaos. Chaos on the battlefield.

Chaos in the magick as it shuddered beneath this dark invasion, this unnatural blight.

Chaos in my heart.

I dropped to my knees. Sliced my palm, letting the blood trickle over my ring. Magick whispered across my skin, tingled down my spine. Time slowed to a crawl, and I closed my eyes, trying to breathe. To focus.

My first love had just returned to me. Defied death, fought his way back to a body that hadn't even existed, fought through insurmountable pain... all for a chance—just one chance to tell me he loved me. To tell me our curse had been obliterated.

To stand by our side as we faced our enemies.

He'd also told me about the Darkwinter prophecy. The Balance. The seeds that'd taken root in my heart from my very first steps in Midnight and had since bloomed into something so vast, so all-encompassing it didn't even occur to me to question his story. The lore. The legacy. As soon as the words were out, I just knew. Knew they were true.

This was my destiny.

And the guys—Elian, Hudson, Jax, Evander—they were a part of that destiny, too. Part of my magick. My courage. My capacity for love and forgiveness.

We were a family in the truest sense of the word, and my heart had never been more full. More content.

Something else tingled down my spine then. Not magick. But fury. Cold, hard fury.

How *dare* the Dark Goddess try to take this from us. Try to shatter this bond. How *dare* her minions try to hurt the people I loved.

"Come see what happens when you piss off a Scorpio blood witch, you *assholes*." I slammed my bleeding palm into the dirt. A flash of red exploded around me as the magick of Midnight—the magick of my home—surged up my arm, straight into my heart. It filled me. Fortified me. Set me on fire with a single purpose:

Take back what the goddess had so wrongly claimed as hers.

The ground trembled around me, and all at once, hundreds—thousands of black roses burst from the mud, blooming to brilliant life in the moonlight. The magick surged again, righting itself as if it was finally shaking free of the chaos, finally finding its purpose as I had found mine.

I closed my eyes, and images flashed unbidden through my mind—the vision Evander had shown me on the balcony during my first weeks here. Before I'd known he wasn't really Keradoc. Before I'd come to care for him— to love him.

Flame and shadow bending at my command, breaking the laws of physics and magick both.

Power surging through my veins, crackling at my fingertips.

Death rising, a thousand raw-boned corpses clawing out of the black earth and bowing at my feet...

As the vision played out in my mind, his words from that night echoed as well.

It's not diamonds or oil we're fighting for. It's magick. A magick that runs through every rock, every tree, every lake of blood in this realm. The magick of Midnight is a precious thing, Miss Barnes. Far more valuable than our cities and walls...

I'd admitted to him that I'd felt it, that magick. Like a hum in the air. A vibration in the ground. A subtle glow upon everything I looked at.

He'd insisted it was because that very magick was part of me—my Darkwinter legacy. The longer I remained in Midnight, he'd said, the more connected to it I would become. And even though I'd insisted—*insisted* I wasn't dark, he didn't back down.

What do you find when you search deep in your soul, past all the things you believe make someone a good person, past the things you believe keep you safe from the dark? When you sleep, little thief, where do the nightmares take you?

He'd said those words, soft and seductive, and then he'd touched me—traced a soft line across my forehead— and unleashed that vision. And rather than being terrified, I was excited. Filled with sheer wonder at the possibility. Hoping that one day, all of those things he'd shown me would indeed come to fruition.

I felt it then. The blood and magick of Midnight, of my ancestors—Darkwinter and Silversbane both. The blood and magick of the prophecy.

My blood and magick.

Now, when I opened my eyes and raised my arms, power crackling between my hands as if I'd reached into the skies and plucked the lightning from a storm, that same sense of wonder filled my heart.

And all of those things, those visions, came to life before my eyes.

"Fall back!" I shouted into the night. "Fall back!"

Hudson was the first to hear me—to sense the urgency through our bond. He swept down and grabbed Elian and Evander from the melee. A flash of blue hair, then purple, and Oona and Gem were clear as well. Jax came last, a final swing of his sword taking down another skeleton before he bolted out.

Power surged again, heat and starlight, building and building inside me until I could no longer contain it, and then—

A wall of blood-red fire exploded across the front line, rising into the dark night, consuming the bones as the bones had once consumed the living. The dead howled, an unholy wailing that made the very trees quake, but I didn't relent. Not for a fucking second. I lifted my hands higher, and the flames followed my command, surging ahead and chewing through Melantha's forces, destroying, devouring, turning everything in their path to ash.

Overhead, the raven gryphon shrieked, and an explosion of the darkest light burst through the sky, like a star going supernova, a black hole that swallowed the beast and the goddess both.

I lowered my arms. The flames vanished.

The men returned to my side, speechless, breathless. Awed.

For across that field of black, barren death, the Army of the Dead rose from the ashes, the bones reforming.

My friends gripped their swords and crossbows, ready to charge in once more.

But I merely stepped forward. Raised a single hand.

And tens of thousands of skeletons bowed before me.

"Are they... surrendering?" Jax whispered.

"Not surrendering," came the reply. Not mine. Not any of ours.

We turned toward the sound of that ancient voice, watching as hundreds of pale faces emerged from the trees behind us.

"The Army of the Dead is swearing fealty to its new commander," the fae general who dwelled beneath the Razorbacks said. "As are *we*, Daughter of Darkwinter. Deathbringer. She For Whom the Bones Bow."

Evander leaned in close, lips brushing my ear with a whisper meant only for me. "It appears I was right all along, little thief. You really *are* the secret weapon to turn our fortunes in this war."

Despite the insanity of the night, I laughed. "And to think you had me wasting all that time on ancestor spells."

"I should've known you'd only disregard my orders and do things your own way."

I brought my mouth to his ear, making him shiver. "*Always.*"

Turning back to the general, Evander cleared his throat and said, "Does this mean you'll fight with us?"

"We will fight the Darkwinter enemies for the death-bringer," he said. "It is written."

"*Written?*" Evander tensed beside me, clearly gearing up for a fight, but I put a hand on his arm and nodded. I didn't care what reason the old fae had for joining us. I only cared that they were here. That with them and the Army of the Dead, we actually had a fighting chance.

"Thank you," I said.

The general turned to his people. Raised his obsidian sword, the blade catching the moonlight.

"She For Whom the Bones Bow!" he shouted again, and the gathering fae echoed the call, a dark chant on the breeze as they all dropped to one knee. Then, as one, they raised their obsidian swords and let loose a fierce cry into the night. "To war!"

HUDSON

The sky over Amaranth City was as black as death, every last star blotted out by smoke and ash and the dozens of raven gryphons the Darkwinter witches now controlled.

Every few seconds, another flash of color exploded—magick, lightning—illuminating the burning city below.

Standing beside me at the top of the White Cliffs of Oshen, Haley said, "You'll need to bring me in close, Gargs. *Very* close."

"How close we talkin'?"

"I need to be *in* that moat."

"No."

She laughed. "Hudson. When I told you I'd have to spill my blood in the moat, I meant that literally. In the moat. There's no way around it."

I blew out a breath and tucked her in close, doing a

partial shift from my human form so I could fold a wing around her body. "How the fuck did I already know you were gonna say that?"

"Because deep inside that strong, overprotective heart of yours, you know I'm always right, and you know I always get my way."

"Yeah." A low chuckle rumbled outta me, despite the fucked-up shit we were jumping into. "Pretty sure I heard that about you, babygirl."

She nuzzled in close, and together we continued to watch the wall, waiting for the signal.

Waiting for Evander to lead the others across the drawbridge and into Amaranth City.

My insides were all tied up like a damn pretzel. I hated that we'd split up, but they needed to get inside and start beating back the Darkwinter forces, and I needed to get Haley into that moat.

To round up the very last fighters Midnight could offer us.

The fucking ghouls.

After the feral fae had sworn their tenuous allegiance to our girl, Haley had ordered them to follow Evander's command. Saint, Jax, Oona, and Gem were under his command now, too.

And the Army of the Dead?

I shook my head, still not believing the damn sight.

They were already crossing the bridge over the moat.

Tens of thousands of 'em, all marching on Haley's orders. Bound to her magick. Obeying her command through whatever dark Midnight mojo she'd harnessed.

Couldn't help but smile at that, my heart nearly bursting with pride.

Spooky little monster girl.

Now, we watched as the last of her skeletons finally cleared the wall. Watched as the city itself seem to ripple in the wake of their dark, all-encompassing wave.

Then came the screams.

They echoed out from the city, floating across the black sands between the wall and the cliffs, rising up to surround us both. If I closed my eyes, I could almost pretend it was an outdoor concert—cheering and whistling. Music. Life.

But this was no concert. No life. This was war. And those screams? They were merely the final, desperate, bloodcurdling cries of the enemy that had invaded our home.

So? Fuck 'em. Every last one.

"There," Haley said, pointing. "They're going in."

I peered out across the darkness, watching as Evander and his charges began crossing the drawbridge, following the Army of the Dead's path straight into the city. The feral fae went first, led by Oona and Jax. Gem was somewhere in the middle. Then came Evander's rebels.

Evander and Elian brought up the rear.

"Come on," Haley muttered, bouncing on her toes as she watched them disappear behind the wall, a few at a time. "Come on, come on, come on."

I tore my gaze away from our fighters and peered down at my girl, drinking in the sight of her. The dark hair, pulled back into a tight braid. The fighting leathers she'd pilfered from whatever the feral fae had left behind. The weapons—daggers and stakes, mostly. Her weapons of choice.

She was fierce, my little monster girl.

And she'd have to be. Tonight, more than ever.

My gut rolled again, and I bit back a dark curse.

We'd all seen Melantha vanish after her Army basically told her to get fucked. But according to Haley, Melantha wasn't actually gone. The Dark Goddess, she'd told us, would be waiting for her in Amaranth City. Waiting to exact her revenge and claim Haley's magick... and her life.

I had no idea how my girl knew all that, but I trusted her.

Just didn't like it. Not one fuckin' bit. And if she thought I'd let her march into that bitch's trap alone like some kind of sheep led to the slaughter—

"Now, Hudson," she said, scattering my dark thoughts. "They're in. We need to move."

I scanned the black obsidian sands once more. Sure enough, the bridge was empty. "You ready?"

She nodded, and I gathered her up in my arms. Then, just before I shifted into my full warrior form, I kissed her. Fucking breathless.

"For luck?" she asked, beaming up at me in a daze.

"Nah, babygirl. We don't need luck." I ran my nose down the length of hers, then kissed the tip. "We got *you*."

With that, I took off, leaping over the cliff and shifting into my warrior form, sailing us right down to that moat.

If I thought the sounds of Darkwinter's screams were loud before, this was... this was fucking deafening.

"Let's be quick," I said, then dropped us both down to the bottom, keeping a close watch as she knelt in the dirt.

She unsheathed a dagger and sliced her palm, the spell already on her lips as the blood welled, then spilled.

> *Blood of hell, blood of night*
> *I call on the darkness to show us the light*
> *May evil and malice and violence intended*
> *Return to its hosts uprooted, upended*
> *Magick of Midnight, hear now my plea*
> *Grant me this power, and so mote it be*

The ground trembled beneath us, and Haley got to her feet. "Up," she said. "Now."

I grabbed her and flew us back up to the ground level, landing on the south side of the moat just as those fucking ghouls exploded out of the ground like a goddamn oil strike.

Haley lifted her arms, magick red flames glowing in each hand, and I watched with my damn jaw on the ground as the ghouls—for the first time in their miserable eternal existence—climbed the north side of the moat.

They looked like them Army of the Dead skeletons at first, but then they started solidifying, rotten skin clinging to their bones, the stench of them making my eyes water as they kept coming and coming and coming, flowing out of the ground like cockroaches, like water, obeying the silent command of her magick.

She lifted her palms higher, and once more, the ghouls began to climb.

Not the moat.

Fucking Vanderham's Wall.

I took a breath to say something—anything—but before I could even get a word out, shadows eclipsed us and I felt the ground quake behind me and I knew... I fucking *knew* it wasn't from the ghouls.

I turned and shoved Haley behind me. Blinked as the full bullshit spectrum came into view.

My old fucking pal, Garrison. Two dozen Stone City meatheads I didn't know. And there, stepping out from behind the line of gargoyles who didn't deserve to call themselves warriors, Mad fuckin' Marco.

So the whore is *still alive,* he said through the gargoyle connection, that gap-toothed grin glinting in the moonlight. *Excellent. Now I'll get a chance to hear beg before I kill her.*

A fierce growl ripped through my chest, but before I'd even settled on whose wings I'd be tearing off first, a blast of red exploded into the night, illuminating every one of their stone-gray faces and sending them stumbling backward.

Haley stepped out from behind me and sighed. "I warned you, Gargs. Told you if I ever saw him again, I'd kill him."

I cocked my head smiled. Fucking woman would never stop surprising me.

"With a dagger, magick, or your bare hands," I said. "Ain't that right?"

"Aw, you remembered!"

"Sure as hell did. Thing is, babygirl, they ain't dead. Just stunned."

She shrugged. "Details."

Haley snapped her fingers, calling another red flame to life in each palm. Behind us, another wave of ghouls scurried out—this time, on our side of the moat.

Flowing around us like a river over rocks, they headed right for the shell-shocked gargoyles still bumbling around like dickless shitheads after Haley's blast.

I laughed. Couldn't be helped. This was gonna be fuckin' awesome.

One more smile for my woman. My mate. And then, together, we charged.

She headed for one of the nameless assholes in the middle. Me? I went right for Marco.

I grabbed him, slammed him into the ground. The impact must've jarred something loose in his head, because the bastard finally blinked up at me, awareness rushing back into his dead eyes.

He growled at me, then shoved me off, rolling on top of me in the black dirt. All around me, red magick surged and sizzled, Haley ordering her ghouls to feed. To feast.

And oh, how I welcomed *those* screams. A beautiful fucking symphony—the perfect accompaniment to the taste of their blood on the air as the ghouls devoured them. Wings, arms, torsos, heads.

But I wouldn't let them anywhere near Marco. He was mine.

"This ends *tonight*," I ground out, slamming a fist into his face, rolling us once more and pinning him beneath me.

He hit me with a jab to the throat, momentarily stealing my breath, but I managed to hold on. Got in another punch to the face, blood gushing from his nose. One more, and I finally knocked out those fucking teeth.

"Better," I said. "But you're still an ugly motherfucker."

He let out a roar, and before I could get in another hit,

one of his asshole wingmen leaped on my back, an arm locking around my neck.

Fucking Garrison.

He wrestled me off Marco, forcing me onto my feet. Marco shot up in front of me, smashing my ribs with a battery of jabs to the chest, each blow more punishing than the last.

I twisted out of Garrison's death grip long enough to smash the back of my head into his mouth. He stumbled back a step, and I whirled on him, grabbed his head, and slammed my knee into his face.

T. K. motherfucking O.

He fell to the ground in a bloody heap, and Marco was on me once more, kicking out my legs and dropping me to my knees. He pounced on me, knocking me face-down, a knee jammed into my back, right between my wings. I thrashed, trying to throw him off, but before I could get any fucking leverage, another one of the bastards grabbed my legs, pinning them down.

I heard the sing of a sword drawn from a scabbard.

Saw the flash of that blade as Marco yanked my head back, exposing my throat.

Knew what he was planning.

But then—

"Oh, I don't fucking *think* so, asshole," Haley snapped.

Marco turned toward her. Toward the pulse of magick

flickering around her. Toward the ghouls gathered at her sides, bloodied from their feast. Still hungry.

And with that single moment of distraction, she'd given me my opening.

I pushed up hard, finally throwing the fuckers off, then jumped to my feet and spun to face them head-on. Haley sent a blast of magick barreling straight into the nameless asshole. He wheeled back and fell into the moat.

The ghouls down there converged. Consumed.

And once again, my enemy was in my sights.

I didn't fucking hesitate. Just lunged for him. Tackled him to the ground. Pinned him on his belly like he'd pinned me, my knee digging into his back, his wrists locked in my grip, my other hand smashing down on the back of his head, grinding his face into the dirt.

I felt the rumble of that roar in his chest. Felt him squirming beneath me.

And suddenly, I thought of those kids. Those innocent fae kids he and his friends slaughtered, all because of some slight against his family. Some petty jealous bullshit.

The old rage rose up inside. Centuries upon centuries of it.

But then it faded away, and a sense of deep calm settled over me.

And without ire, without bloodlust, I released his head. Grabbed a wing.

And fucking ripped it out of his back.

He howled in pain, writhing, begging, but I was just getting started.

All around me, the remaining gargoyles went down, felled by my girl and her gang of ghouls.

And with that sense of calm still intact, I ripped off his other wing. Tossed them both into the moat for the lingering ghouls. I heard the crunch of muscle and bone as they bit and tore, fighting over the scraps of him.

After she'd finished decimating the other gargoyles, Haley came to join me. To bear witness. Her magick surged through the mate bond, lending me strength. Power. Without a second thought, I punched a hole in Marco's lower back. Gripped his spine.

Tore it halfway out before the fucker finally—thanks to some latent, ancient survival instinct—turned to stone.

But that wouldn't help him now.

That only made my mission easier.

I got to my feet. Pulled the half-mutilated statue upright and turned him around so I could see his face.

Twisted in agony. In terror. Frozen. His final act.

For so many centuries, I'd wanted him dead. Wondered if I'd been saving up all my words just for this moment, when I could finally let him have it—all the rage and disgust that'd been festering inside me all those years. The betrayal, the hurt, the fucking shame. I felt the words gather, churning inside me like a Louisiana hurricane.

But then, just like my fury, they fell away.

Marco didn't deserve my words. Not the ones in my mind, and sure as hell not the spoken ones. Haley was the one who'd helped me find my way back to those, and I had no interest in cheapening what we shared by wasting so much as another *breath* on this asshole.

So instead, I released the statue and took my woman's hand. Felt the strength of her magick once more. Her loyalty. Her love.

And with nothing more than a boot to the chest, I kicked that motherfucker into the moat.

He exploded into pieces so minuscule, not even the wind bothered to blow him away.

Haley leaned over that great gash in the earth and spat.

Me? I couldn't even work up the gumption for that.

A low, strangled moan drifted across the darkness, and together we turned to see Garrison—the only fucker still alive after the massacre—just getting to his feet.

"I got this one, babygirl."

"You sure?"

I ran a bloody hand over her head, ruffling her hair. "Yeah."

I didn't give Garrison the chance to fully regain his footing. Just slammed him to the ground and tore that fucking bastard apart, wing by wing. Bone by bone. He didn't bother turning into stone, and I didn't bother caring.

Just shredded him. Watched his blood spill into the

earth. Then got to my feet and booted his carcass into the moat.

By the time I wiped the blood from my face and turned to take in the scene once more, the gargoyles who'd betrayed me were finally gone, nothing but dark wet stains on the earth to prove they'd even been here at all.

But Haley's ghouls were gone, too.

And so was my woman.

"*Fuck.*"

I could still feel her, though. Her courage. Her determination. Her magick, more powerful now than ever before. Every part of her, every feeling came to me through the mate bond, giving me more strength. Giving me hope.

I looked up at the wall. Behind it, the battles raged, every army in the realm converging in a clash of steel and obsidian and magick.

I took another deep breath. Sighed. And then, I ran. Leaped over the moat. Flew up into the darkness and sailed right the fuck over that wall, straight into the jaws of death.

Fear. I tasted it with every breath I drew, let it linger in my mouth like a fine wine. Marveled at the subtle differences in flavor.

Maybe I should've felt guilty about this simple pleasure, but I didn't.

I absolutely *relished* in it, because I knew that every single one of these Darkwinter motherfuckers meant my woman harm. And *that* was a sin even a demon called sinner couldn't forgive.

So I made my way through the city, block by battle-ravaged block, following the enticing pull of that wild, delicious fear as it led me to our enemies.

Not as efficient as Haley's Army of the Dead or the Beggar's Moat ghouls that had arrived soon after us, sniffing out pockets of Darkwinter troops and consuming them in a frenzied feed. Not as elegant as the dance of a proper sword fight, the clanging of metal on metal that echoed through the night as Evander and the Razorback Mountain fae fought their way through the city. Not as brutal as the breaking of bones, the rending of flesh, and the spilling of blood Saint's vampire attacks offered. Nor was it the stunning visual beauty of black feathers and blood raining down from the sky every time Hudson took out one of those fucking raven gryphons.

But hell... It was a damned good time.

Now, ducking down the alley that ran behind our old pub in the Hollow, I zeroed in on my next target. A Darkwinter grunt. Seemed to have lost his way, the poor fuck.

I cleared my throat. Welcomed the hit of fear that flowed through me as his adrenaline spiked. He drew his dagger, but didn't make a move as I stepped closer, rifling through his mind until I found his oldest, darkest fear.

Fire.

I grinned. A classic, to be sure.

With little more than a thought, I conjured an inferno in his mind. One that chewed through the buildings on either side of us, rising higher and higher, the heat nearly melting his skin.

He barreled past me and charged out onto the street, right into the path of another group of Darkwinter assholes parrying with some of Evander's rebels.

Safely hidden in the shadows of the alley, I watched as

he stopped short behind his own men. Knew the moment he believed they'd all burst into flames.

At first, he tried to save some of them. Pushed them to the ground, one after the other, battering them, desperate to tamp down the flames even as they shouted at him to stop.

Another group merged in, Darkwinter about three dozen strong now, confusion spreading among them as quickly as that imaginary fire as my target continued to shove and batter. To scream. To turn their confusion into sheer fucking panic.

Some were trampled in the commotion. Others left themselves open to the thrust of a rebel dagger. The bolt of a crossbow.

Oona's, this time.

She stepped out from behind me and sighed.

"Let me guess," she said dryly. "Fire?"

"Wow," I said. "You're getting pretty good at this."

With a dark grin, I let the illusion drop away. The solider regained his mental faculties. Took one look at the surrounding carnage. Realized what he'd done. And then... the dumb bastard shoved his own dagger through his chest.

"Brutal," Oona said with a mock shiver.

We moved on to the next alley, locating two more enemies. I slipped into the mind of one—fear of the hybrid mutant shifters his own kind had created. He turned to his companion, his eyes narrowed in sudden suspicion.

Only a single heartbeat passed before he sliced the guy's throat.

Oona lifted her crossbow. Shot the fucker before I even had a chance to reveal the illusion to him.

"You are *no* fun," I said.

"I am *very* fun." She slung the crossbow over her shoulder and unclipped the water bottle hanging from her belt, downing half of it before passing it to me.

I nodded my thanks, then took a few sips. Smiled at her.

Somehow, bound together by this ruthless mission, the two of us had finally made our peace.

It'd begun after Saint's miraculous return, as she and Gem told me the story—his death, how they'd found him, the prophecy about Haley. How the two of them had been working together ever since the rest of us had left Midnight the first time. All the betrayals that weren't actually betrayals after all.

And then later, as Oona and I had peeled off from the group and begun our block-by-block sweep, that conversation continued, edging closer and closer to the real issue that had risen like a wall of ice between us. We worked in tandem, taking down hybrids, taking down dark fae soldiers, until she'd finally said, "I know the past is the past, and our lives have... diverged along very different paths. But for what it's worth... I'm glad you got out of Midnight, even for a little while. And though I regret hurting you, I can't say I wouldn't do it again if it meant giving you that same shot."

I'd stopped her then, right in the middle of crafting a mass hallucination about a cloud of poison gas, and looked into her violet eyes. Probably for the first time since I'd seen her in that fucking dungeon the night Saint and I had been captured. The night they'd admitted to faking her death just so I'd leave Midnight.

And when I saw the earnestness there, I knew. Knew I'd already forgiven her.

There was a saying about hatred. Something about drinking poison and expecting the other person to die. And in that moment, I realized I'd been doing just that.

Besides, deep down, I didn't really hate Oona. And despite Saint's miraculous return, we all knew life was too fucking short to hold petty grudges against people who might just turn out to be damn good friends.

"Admit it," she said now, bringing me back to the moment. "I'm *very* fun. Admit it or I'm not guessing any more of your fear tactics or shooting another Darkwinter."

I returned the water bottle and rolled my eye. "Fine. You're very fun. The funnest. Now, can we please go scare the life out that fucking general over there?"

I pointed at another Darkwinter fae just before he slipped into an abandoned building across the street.

Checking to be sure we were in the clear, we crossed the street and ducked behind the building, knowing he'd be coming out on the other side eventually.

As we waited for him, Oona locked another bolt into place on her crossbow, then said, "You and I had some good times back in the day, Jax." Her voice turned serious, her violet gaze soft. "I cared for you, and I know you felt the same."

I nodded. No point in denying it.

"But," she said, "Haley makes you happy in a way I never did. It's obvious what you all have together is special. Real. I've always wanted that for you, Jax. That kind of family. That kind of love. I... I hope you know that."

I opened my mouth to tell her that I did, but before I could speak another word, a door banged open and our target emerged, two others in tow.

I reached out for him. Slipped into his mind.

The general had a fear of spiders.

I nearly laughed at my good fortune. Arachnophobia —another classic. *Very* easy to work with.

With a gentle pulse of my magick, I crafted the illusion, turning his companions into six-foot-tall spiders with hairy legs and iridescent bodies, crawling toward him, touching him, devouring him...

In his rush to escape, he lost his footing, crashing down flat on his back.

The other two tried to help him up, but our general

saw only those spiders, ready to devour, ready to wrap him in their sticky web and suck him dry.

He stabbed them both through the belly with a sword, their hot guts spilling out all over him. And with another little nudge from me, those guts exploded into a million tiny spiders, all of them scurrying over him, covering every inch of exposed skin, slithering into his open mouth...

A bolt right between the eyes, and the general's misery ended.

Glaring at Oona, I said, "I take it back. You are so *not* the funnest."

She shuddered. "I don't like spiders either, asshole." Then, pressing the crossbow to my chest, "And if you *ever* use that fact against me—"

"I don't turn fear on my friends, Oona. Not like that."

She blinked at the sudden ferocity in my tone. "Is that... what we are? Friends again?"

I didn't hesitate. "Yeah, Oona. We're friends again." I put an arm around her. "Assuming you don't fake your own death to get rid of me again."

Oona laughed. "As if I could pull off a ruse like that more than once. I'll have to think of something *much* more sinister next time."

"Just remember, I know your deepest fear now." I wriggled my fingers in front of her in the approximation of a spider.

Oona shoved me away, but that smile still held. "You are *seriously* disturbed. You know that, yes?"

"*Some* women actually appreciate that quality in a man."

She sighed. "I can't decide whether I should congratulate Haley or warn her."

"Let's see how you feel at the end of the night." I jerked my head toward the street again, and together we crept back out, resuming our mission.

Block by block, enemy by enemy, each sweep bringing us closer to the castle. To the rally point Evander had established.

I wasn't sure how much time passed. Three hours. Eight. But eventually, we made it, ducking into the shadows behind the castle, heading for the servants' entrance off the kitchen.

We stepped inside, checking to make sure we were alone.

No enemies. No one.

Closing the door behind us, I leaned against it and let out a breath. Oona went to refill the water bottle, and I closed my eye, taking a moment to just breathe.

Outside, the battle raged on. Swords clashing. Magick exploding. Blood running red down every street, mingling with ash and fallen bodies and the feathers of dead raven gryphons.

But the fighting was starting to ebb. Battle by battle, we were gaining ground. Taking back our city.

Oona returned a moment later, nudging me with the water bottle.

I opened my eye. Took the offered drink.

Then, passing the bottle back, I said plainly, "Thank you."

She knew I wasn't just talking about the water, or even about having my back out there tonight.

Because of her, I'd gotten out of Midnight before. I'd survived. And that survival, as much as I couldn't see it at the time, was the only reason I was here now.

The only reason I'd found Haley. The woman I loved. The woman I wanted to build a life and family with—a future I never could've imagined when I was just a fucked-up, one-eyed fugitive.

As if she could read my thoughts, Oona smiled, emotion glazing her eyes. "You're welcome, Jax."

I held her gaze for another beat. Then said, "We should head up to the ballroom. See if the others made it yet. And if they haven't, we need to make sure we're not dealing with an ambush."

"Lead the way."

We'd just made our way through the kitchens and out into the main parlor when we spotted them—Saint and Gem, racing down the stairs from above.

Panic bleached the color from their faces.

"Melantha," Gem panted as we approached. "She's barricaded herself in the throne room. Spelled the doors and windows."

"If she wants that throne so badly," a dark voice seethed, "she can claim it."

We all turned to see Evander striding across the room, Hudson just behind him. It was clear they'd only just arrived.

He looked us over quickly, then turned to Gem and Saint. Relief shone in his eyes at the sight of his brother, but when he spoke again, that same dark rage echoed in his voice.

"I will burn this entire castle to the *ground* if it means ridding the realm of her foul presence once and for all."

Saint took a step toward his brother. Put a hand on his shoulder. A single tear glittered on his cheek—silver, like his eyes.

Then, in a voice so soft and broken it sounded like air leaking from a balloon, he whispered, "She's not in there alone, Evander."

And all at once, we knew.

Haley.

"I've been expecting you, Daughter of Darkwinter."

Sneering at me from her perch on the throne of obsidian and bones, the Dark Goddess Melantha lifted a lazy hand, and the doors to the throne room slammed shut behind me. I had no doubt she'd spelled the windows, too.

A death trap, if the visions I'd seen when I'd conjured her were true.

My death trap.

She'd finally manifested in physical form. She was nude, her ebony skin gleaming, her eyes burning red. Long, dark hair fell in waves over her breasts. No wings.

For now, she looked... mostly human.

Didn't make her any less creepy, though.

With a hiss that slithered across the polished floor like the serpents coiled at her bare feet, she said, "So entitled, making me wait for your arrival as if *I* were the commoner and *you* the queen."

A shiver gripped my spine at the raw power in her voice, the promise of death whispering beneath every word, but I refused to shudder in her presence. Refused to show even a shred of fear.

Melantha had laid this trap for me, but I'd walked into it by choice. My own fucking free will.

I'd come too far, fought too hard to fall apart now.

I lowered my head and took a deep, calming breath. Steadying myself. Gathering my strength. My magick.

Beyond these dark obsidian walls, the battle for Amaranth City raged on. Through the thick velvet curtains, I could just make out the flickers and flashes of colored light—magick from the Midnight witches who fought on our side, magick from the Darkwinter weather witches who didn't. The violent tempests of Midnight herself, stirred to life by the utter *wrongness* of what was happening here.

I knew my armies were out there—the ghouls of Midnight, the dead Melantha had once commanded—all of them bound to me now, devouring Darkwinter's ground forces as they broke upon those enemy lines, wave after wave of destruction and ruin. Every grisly attack rippled through my magick like an electrical current.

And my men... my men were out there, too.

I closed my eyes and reached out through our bonds—

magickal, fated, love—and tried to hear each of them. To draw strength and courage from them.

Evander, my dark fae warlord, shouting orders to the troops he'd rallied, to the feral fae who'd finally agreed to follow him in my stead. For all that he'd lived most of his life as Keradoc's prisoner, Evander had learned the role well, his fierce command inspiring courage despite the bleakest odds.

Jax, my demon, fearless in the face of our enemies, baiting the most terrifying Darkwinter soldiers with their own worst fears as he and Oona worked to secure the streets of our city, block by block, home by home.

Elian, my vampire-fae, tearing out the throats of every abominable creature Darkwinter had shoved through its portals and packed onto its ships. Creatures like those I'd fought in the Bay—hybrids, vampires who could turn into wolves, fae who could steal souls like demons. The magick in their blood would infuse him, every kill making him stronger and faster as Gem fought by his side with magick and weapons both.

Hudson, my warrior gargoyle, patrolling the dark skies and fighting off raven gryphons and traitorous gargoyles alike, breaking them, slaughtering them, finally freed from the shackles of his old enemies. His betrayers.

They all fought hard. For Midnight. For each other. For me. I desperately wanted to be with them, to fight with them, but in the battle for Amaranth City, I was hunting a different sort of beast.

I'd sensed the Dark Goddess's foul energy the moment Hudson and I had reached the wall. As soon as I knew for certain Marco and Garrison were dead, I'd followed that wave of Beggar's Moat ghouls straight into the city. Straight into the castle.

Straight into the place where Melantha had shown me a vision of my death.

Not on the battlefield. Not at the hands and teeth of her skeletal army or the poisoned swords of Darkwinter.

But here, from her self-appointed place of honor on the throne, where she planned to spill my blood, steal my power, and claim Midnight once and for all.

The worst part? She hadn't even risen to her feet. As if the task of ending my life would be nothing more than a minor inconvenience—something to pencil in between a manicure and drinks with a friend.

Magick simmered in my veins at the sheer *audacity* of this bitch.

I lifted my chin. Met her glowing red eyes. And said only, "You are *no* queen."

She shook her head, clucking her tongue. The serpents at her feet uncoiled, slithering down the dais, as lazy and unhurried as their master seemed to be.

"You've come alone, then?" she asked.

"The first time I faced you in the Temple of the Dark Moon, I was alone."

"And in all this time, you haven't managed to make any friends?"

"Oh, I've made plenty of friends." I grinned, taking a few steps closer to the dais, ignoring the warning hiss of the serpents now coiling at the base. "But sending you to hell doesn't require an audience."

Those red eyes blazed bright. Her anger rippled outward, thick and palpable. A crack shattered the obsidian floor behind me.

I raised my hands in mock surrender. "You're right, I misspoke. Sorry." Then, with a deeply put-upon sigh, I said, "I'm *not* actually sending you to hell. I'm just... eliminating you. Kind of like when you spill tomato sauce on your favorite white blouse, and you think it's totally ruined, but then you attack it with that stain remover stick and it just... vanishes? Poof! Gone! Where does it go? No one knows." I lowered my hands and bared my teeth, taking a step onto the dais. "It simply stops... *existing*."

"Do *not* disrespect me, child," she whispered. Then, with nothing more than another lazy flick of her wrist, both serpents sprang for me.

My magick shot up around me of its own accord, a shimmering red wall of light. Both snakes crashed into it and vanished.

The magick fell away.

Melantha finally had the decency to show a little surprise.

Still didn't move her ass from that throne, though.

"I swore an *oath* to you," I gritted out, taking another step up. "I vowed to do what you asked of me, and I would've gone to the ends of the earth to see it through, because I truly believed that however dark, however terrifying, *you* were a goddess worthy of my allegiance."

She gripped the arms of the throne, dark fingers morphing into talons that gouged the carved obsidian.

"Yet here you are," she shot back. "Simpering like a coward."

"Simpering. Right. Says the woman who slithered back into Midnight after she'd been banished? The woman who gave up her own army because she was too scared to face me?"

"You have no power over me, Daughter of Darkwinter."

I cocked my head, letting a little zing of magick sizzle up the dais. "You sure about that?"

She flashed a feral grin, teeth as sharp as swords. In a sickly sweet voice, she said, "Perhaps if you'd spent less time spreading your legs and more time practicing your spellwork, devoting yourself to your goddess, you would not find yourself in such—"

"Goddess?" I laughed. "You don't deserve the honor of such a title. You don't deserve the blood and magick of this land. You don't even deserve another breath." I lifted my hands, calling up my reserves, ready to eliminate this stain once and for all. But before I could unleash a single bolt of magick—

A wave of dark power slammed into me, knocking me on my ass as a thunderous crack echoed through the room. The throne and the dais crashed to the ground, and when I glanced up again, the Dark Goddess was standing on the rubble in all her nightmarish glory. Black wings dripping with blood, four more white serpents twining around her gnarled limbs, those deadly talons poised and ready to strike.

Blood spilled from my nose, my ears ringing, the room spinning, my vision turning gray at the edges...

"I warned you this night would come," she hissed. "Warned you that you and your men would writhe and bow before me."

She leaped from the rubble and landed beside me, eclipsing me in her dark shadow, her magick syphoning my power, my strength, my hope, all of it.

"Foolish girl," she sighed. "There was a time when you called upon me for help."

She was right. In my most desperate hour, I *had* called upon her. And she'd answered, granting me the power to fight enemies that were so much stronger than me. Than my sisters.

My sisters...

I thought of them now, my three beautiful sisters—

Gray, Addie, Georgie. Sisters I would gladly die for, wishing I'd gotten just one more chance to hug them.

I thought of the other witches of Bay Coven. Witches who'd fought by our side. My friends. Reva, the shadow-born witch who'd become Death. Who'd help send Elian back to me.

I thought of Gray's men—how they'd protected and loved her through it all, just as my men protected and loved me.

I thought of them, of course. My men. My monsters. Fierce warriors who would fight until the bitter end for us. For Midnight.

I thought of the realm. A land of darkness and death. The place where I'd found light and love. Home. Belonging.

And then, I thought of myself. How far I'd come from that broken woman in the bathtub, desperate for an escape. I'd carried her with me all these years, and now, upon my death, I could finally set her free knowing I'd saved her. Knowing I'd made her proud.

The vision from the night with the feral fae flickered to life behind my eyes. Me, lying in a pool of blood. This blood, this room, this moment.

And I knew, without a doubt, I was going to die.

And that... that was just... fucking *unacceptable*.

Blood leaked into my mouth. Filled it. Filled *me*. Magick simmered in my veins once more, twining with my rage, and despite the pain in my body, I rose to my feet. Shaky but unbending. Determined.

Melantha only laughed. "Who will come to your aid now, little witch? Not the Dark Goddess. Never again will I heed your call. Never again will I help you fight your battles."

The magick inside me surged, chasing away the last of my weakness. The last of my tremors. The last of my fear.

I met her gaze, and I knew my own eyes glowed just as fiercely. And when I finally spoke to her again, my voice held the power of a thousand eternities, a thousand moonless nights, a thousand dark realms.

"I don't need to call upon the Dark Goddess to fight my battles." I lifted my hands, magick exploding from my palms, bathing the entire room in my red light. "I *am* the fucking Dark Goddess."

The floor rumbled and cracked, the polished obsidian splitting. Tendrils of dark mist curled up from the fissures, slowly taking form.

The restless spirits of all who'd died here. All who'd been executed before the throne, right or wrong.

Now, they would fight for me. Deathbringer. The Balance. She for Whom the Bones Bow. The true goddess of Midnight. A goddess that had the power to imprison them for eternity... or set them free.

I lifted my hands higher, and the dead rose to their full height. Their gruesome glory.

And there, in the eyes of the once all-powerful goddess of darkness and death, true fear shone bright.

Ignoring the wings and talons, I grabbed her throat. Smiled. "Time for you to writhe and bow before *me*, bitch."

And with little more than a nod, I unleashed hell.

The dead swarmed her, devouring her as I held her in my grip, watching her glowing red eyes turn black, then burst. Black blood spilled from the sockets, eating through her face like acid. Skin melted from the bone, revealing an ashen skull and rows of those razor-sharp teeth.

And the power... so much power. It leaked out of her and poured into me, weaving with my own magick, filling me, healing me.

Remaking me.

And when it was done, the feathers and bones of Melantha turned to ash, and the dead of Amaranth City vanished, and I fell to my knees and wept.

"Come back to us, sparrow. Come back." A gentle voice, a soft whisper caressing my cheeks.

Warm hands in my hair, on my shoulder, rubbing my back, squeezing my hand.

I sucked in a sharp breath and opened my eyes. I was still on my knees in the broken throne room, but I was alive.

They were alive, I realized. Kneeling in a tight circle around me, covered in blood and filth, but unbroken.

Which meant... it was over. The war was over.

I looked at each of them in turn.

Hudson, my fierce winged warrior with a heart as big as Midnight.

Jax, the fiery, passionate demon who pushed me to my limits and refused to let me give up on myself.

Evander, our captor and warlord. Our commander. Our friend.

And Elian, my first love. The silver-eyed vampire-fae who'd refused his own death and found a way back to us. *For* us.

My monsters. My family.

Mine.

I felt it settle inside me then—all that wild, dark goddess magick. Felt it finding its home inside my heart just as I'd found my home in Midnight.

We'd done it. We'd defeated Darkwinter and Melantha both.

A smile burst across my face, and I rose to my feet, feeling lighter and happier than I had in years.

The guys rose, exchanging nervous glances.

"Does this mean you're well?" Evander asked.

"Take it easy, angel." Jax put a warm hand on the small of my back. "Just tell us what you need."

I laughed. "Totally appreciate the concern, guys, but

seriously? What your girl *needs* is a hot bath, a hot meal, and some filthy, raunchy, *epically* hot sex... not necessarily in that order."

Evander's eyes widened.

Jax shook his head and laughed, his blue eye sparkling beneath a mask of blood and gore. "Good to know you're still *you*."

I shrugged and turned my palms up. Twin red-and-black flames danced to life across them, and my fingers curled into sharp talons.

"Mostly me," I said with a wink. "Just a few modifications."

"A *few*?" Evander said, at the same time Hudson said, "God *damn*, babygirl."

"*Fuck*," Elian said. "I think I just came."

Jax laughed again, giving Elian a playful shove. "Good to know *you* haven't made any modifications, asshole."

"So..." I doused the flames and talons and stretched my arms over my head, my back popping. "About those needs of mine..."

"Soon," Evander said, leaning in to brush a kiss to my forehead. Then, his eyes darkening, he clamped a hand over Elian's shoulder and said, "There's something I... Something I need to take care of first. And I'd appreciate it if my brother were at my side."

32

ELIAN

"Haley was right last night," I said as Evander led us into the cramped dungeon beneath the castle. For its lone prisoner, death was close at hand. The smell of rot nearly overwhelmed me. "When she said I never stopped."

A low chuckle. "No one in their right mind would stop loving that woman. I'm quite certain it's categorically impossible."

"True, but... I was talking about what she said about *you*, Evander. How I never stopped searching for you. Not when we were kids. Not when I turned my back on Haley and the closest I'd ever come to being happy. Not even after, when I was back in New Orleans and struggling to find a reason to get out of bed every day—stoned out of my fucking mind, totally lost, wishing death would finally claim me... Fuck. I still wanted to find you. Still hoped it was possible... Somehow."

He stopped in the center of the room and turned to face me, the torch he carried casting his face in a soft orange glow. "I'd like to think that deep down, maybe there was some part of me that never stopped hoping you'd find me." Genuine warmth glazed those strange violet eyes, but his smile turned sad. "I just don't remember it, Elian. I'm sorry."

Fuck, how my heart broke for him—for the childhood he lost. The innocence that Keradoc had stolen from him. All the good things in his life he'd forgotten, because it'd taken every bit of his focus and will just to survive Midnight. To survive all that Keradoc had done to him.

"No," I said, struggling to keep my voice even. "I'm the one who's sorry. *Truly* sorry for all you've endured. If we could trade places, I—"

"Don't even think it," he said, suddenly harsh. Then, with a sigh and a wry smile, "Besides, if it'd been you, I wouldn't have the pleasure of killing the bastard." He shoved the torch into the sconce on the wall and slid his blade from its scabbard—an obsidian dagger with a handle of carved bone, sharp and deadly. Perfect. "For as much pleasure as this filthy animal found in torturing me, I found *my* pleasure in imagining the night I could look into his eyes, look upon his wasted face, and decide the *exact* moment at which he'd draw his final breath."

In the cell before us, the lone prisoner rattled his chains and let out a watery groan, but he had no real fight left. He'd wasted away in here, his body kept alive—barely —just so my brother could exact his revenge.

"Haley told me your life is bound to his," I said. "That if you remove the ring or kill him—if *anyone* kills him— you'll..."

I trailed off, unable to finish the sentence. I'd only just gotten Evander back. And though I wasn't foolish enough to think we'd pick up where we'd left off as children, I'd started to allow myself the tiniest bit of hope that maybe... maybe we could start over. Not as brothers, but as friends. As men who'd fought for each other. Men who'd fought for the woman they both loved and the home they hoped to make with her.

"It's a distinct possibility, yes," Evander said, no hint of concern in his voice. "But with Melantha gone, I feel..." He pressed a fist to his heart and shrugged. "I can't explain it, Elian. It's almost as if she left a piece of her dark magick inside me—a splinter in the heart, festering. Poisoning. But now it's just... gone."

I nodded. I'd felt similarly when my death had broken Melantha's curse.

"For so long," he went on, "I assumed I'd die with him, and I made my peace with that. All that mattered to me was destroying his legacy, eradicating his name, and ending his life. If mine had to end as well? So be it. Collateral damage, a risk with any war. But now... honestly, brother. I believe with my whole heart I can be free of him. That I can go on living my life as I was truly meant to. I'm not sure I'd risk it otherwise."

"No? Even though you've been jerking off to visions of his dead corpse for centuries?"

Another low chuckle. "Yes, but you see... I have a lot more to live for now than I did when I first made this vow. This grand plan." He turned to me once more, his hand gripping my shoulder as his laughter faded. "I don't actually *want* to—you know. Cease to exist. But there are no guarantees with magick, and if the worst *does* happen, I thought... I would ask that you... I wanted..." He blew out a sigh of frustration and closed his eyes, gathering his thoughts. When he finally met my gaze again, his own was rock steady. "I wanted it to be you, Elian. The one to witness my final breath, as it was you who witnessed my very first."

My chest tightened, tears stinging my eyes. I was terrified—fucking terrified of losing him again. But my voice was resolute when I gripped his shoulder and said, "I'm honored, brother. But it won't be your last. I feel it, too. So let's end it. *End* it so we can return to our friends and our witch."

He held my gaze for another moment, then finally nodded and turned away, closing the short distance that remained between him and his prisoner.

I grabbed the torch from the wall and joined him at the bars, shining the light into the darkness. Keradoc recoiled and hissed, but I didn't draw back. He was a wraith—little more than a collection of bones sheathed in a translucent layer of skin marred with open sores and deep purple bruises. His mouth hung slack, gums bleeding, no teeth to speak of. Most of his hair had fallen out as well. The violet irises that had once been so vivid were little more than a pale wash of lavender.

He tried to rattle his chains again, but couldn't even lift his arms.

My brother unlocked the cell door. We stepped inside, the stench of waste and decay making my eyes water.

I shook my head, shocked at the sight. "Keradoc was truly a fearsome beast—I remember him, Evander. His cruelty. His utter lack of remorse."

I was pretty sure I'd never lose those memories. The blood running through the streets of Amaranth City as he paraded his wounded men before their families, some twisted punishment for their perceived failures. The roses, trampled underfoot by the mares of night and the soldiers who remained standing. The bodies he'd dumped over the wall for the ghouls of Beggar's Moat. The screams that echoed through the city streets whenever he came near.

"How did you manage to turn him into this... this *thing*?" I whispered, as though anything louder might reverse the spell and give the old beast his claws back.

"I didn't turn him into anything. I merely revealed him for the worthless coward he always was." Evander glanced at his sword, the black blade glittering in the torchlight. "That's the thing about power, Elian. He was so seduced by it, so convinced it was his by right, so secure in his belief that he himself *was* that power. He saw me as weak. As one more *thing* to be dominated and controlled, just like he controlled the others. It never once occurred to him that the fae he stole and ruined as a child would one day grow into a man who could ruin *him*."

We stood in silence for a moment, watching the ruined beast trembling on the straw-covered stone floor. He coughed again, and the scent of fresh piss filled the cell, a thin river of it trickling along the stone.

"I have to imagine there's a chance for all of us," my brother said softly. "A chance for a better life, even in a place as harsh as Midnight. And that chance starts right here—with trust. With me trusting the magick of Midnight. Trusting my own magick. My own power."

He wasn't talking about the power of a crooked warlord, the power that corrupted and destroyed. He was talking about the power inherent in all of us, if only we found the courage to claim it.

Haley had made me believe in it.

And now, as I stood beside my brother in the final moments of the darkest chapter of his life, I felt it swell inside me, too. Power. Courage. Love.

"It's strange," Evander said, testing the edge of that blade against his thumb. A bead of blood welled on his skin. "In all my fantasies of killing him, I never imagined he'd be so pathetic. So broken."

"You broke him, Evander. You truly shattered him."

"Do you judge me for it?"

"Wouldn't be here if I felt that way. Besides..." I smirked and thumbed at my face, a bit of levity to chase off the lingering darkness. "You're about to get your old face back. You think I'd pass up an opportunity to see which one of us wears it better?"

He arched an eyebrow. "Seems you've already made up your mind on that."

I laughed, and he returned it. Still restrained—still nowhere near the full and boisterous laughter I remembered from our childhood. But I welcomed the sound of it anyway. Just one of the many things I'd have to learn about my brother—his laugh.

Emotion rose inside me again, churning as swiftly as the river of blood that'd nearly swept me off to hell. I looked down at the vile beast on the floor. The beast who'd stolen my brother and hurt him in ways I couldn't even let myself contemplate for longer than a few seconds. The beast who'd destroyed my family and rerouted our entire lives.

"You mean to give him a painless death?" I asked. That blade was sharp enough to kill a man before the first trickle of blood showed on his skin.

"I have been giving him death for many, many months, brother. And it has been anything but painless. This is merely the end." He bent down and wrapped a hand around Keradoc's throat, hauling him to his feet as if he weighed no more than a child. The chains rattled with the movement, but the man himself remained utterly silent now, tears staining his sunken face.

Evander said, "In all my dreams of this moment—and there were many over the years—I always felt his blood on my hands."

"And now?"

"I won't let so much as a *drop* of it soil my skin," he said. Then, to Keradoc, "Your daughter has known for some time about my ruse. I offered her a chance to say goodbye, but she declined, sending no parting words to the father who brutalized her when he should have loved and cherished her. You were an abomination in life, and the stain of your foul deeds will linger in the scars of all those you've harmed. But eventually, you'll fade from our collective memory. With every home and business we rebuild, with every wounded soldier we heal, with every family we welcome into this realm, your deeds will be undone, your story rewritten. And the night will come when your memory is nothing more than a shadow, and then mist, and then... nothing. You will be nothing."

With a final exhale and a quick thrust, Evander shoved

the obsidian dagger through Keradoc's chest, then dropped him and the dagger both. The Warlord of Midnight landed in the pile of his own waste, skull cracking against the wall, his final strangled breath sputtering out before the blood even rose to the wound.

Evander removed his ring. Dropped it into Keradoc's lap. And turned away.

Meeting my gaze again, he said only, "it's done."

His eyes were still violet, and something dark and sinister flickered behind them, but then it was gone. All at once, the light returned.

"I need to burn it," he said. "The body. The ring. All of it."

"Do you want the dagger?" I asked.

Evander shook his head.

"Then allow me." I was still holding the torch, and now I stepped forward to stand over the body. "I've never been one for big speeches or blathering on with pretty words, so—"

"Blathering on?" Evander said, feigning insult.

Turning to look at him over my shoulder, I said, "You did get a bit long-winded there, brother."

A smile. A little more light in those violet eyes. "I suppose you think you can do better?"

"Watch and learn, brother. Watch and learn." I grinned and turned back to the body. "Fuck yourself off to hell, asshole. I'm sure they've got a nice room waiting for you."

I tossed the torch into his lap, and together, Evander and I backed out of the cell and closed the bars.

The flames caught, the fire crackling to life.

I put a hand on my brother's shoulder. Not an embrace. Not the casual arm of an old friend. Just a touch. Just enough to let him know I was still here. Still with him. Always.

Side by side, we watched in silence as the flames chewed through the straw and cheap rags that clung to his body.

Watched as his skin blistered and split, ignoring the stench of burning flesh.

Watched until it peeled away and all the bones beneath it turned as black as his heart.

Watched as the metal ring glowed bright, then melted.

Watched until the fire retreated and the beast of Midnight was nothing but a pile of ash.

Evander turned to me and drew in a deep breath, then let it out slowly, as if he were blowing away the last of Keradoc's terrible hold.

And there in the darkness, revealed only by my vampire sight, my brother transformed.

His cheekbones sharpened, his mouth and jawline a mirror image of my own. His hair retained some of the black, but most of it had turned silver. Our build was the same, too.

The eyes, however, remained violet.

Still, the sight of him—the sight of my brother, my twin...

"Not bad." I coughed, loosening the knot lodged in my throat. "A little wrinkly around the eyes, and that hairline might be receding a bit, but... I suppose you're passable."

"You suppose I'm *passable*?"

I shrugged. "I've always been the good-looking one. *Everyone* knows that."

Evander laughed. Not the smooth, cultivated laugh of the warlord, or the bitter laugh of a man who'd clawed his way back from a life of torture and pain, but a *true* laugh, rich and warm, the promise of something better alive in every note.

Clapping a hand on my shoulder, he guided us out of that rancid pit and said, "Perhaps, *brother*, we should let the Dark Goddess be the judge."

I leaned back on the cool obsidian ledge, gazing up at the two fae warriors that towered over me. One was carved of moonstone, the other of onyx, their swords held high, clashing in their eternal battle. Spilling eternal blood.

That blood filled the fountain I now sat upon, the dark ruby liquid swirling in a dance as endless as their swordplay.

The first time I'd seen this fountain, Jax and I had been trying to escape the castle. He'd told me the fountain held the blood of the realm—that no one really knew where it came from, only that it never evaporated or froze. And all who attempted to touch or drink it perished, as evidenced by the collection of decaying vampire skulls around its base.

At the time, its sinister presence terrified me, but now I

found it beautiful. Calming. This fountain, these warriors, they represented all of us. Strong, but flawed. Warriors who could just as easily destroy as we could create. Darkness and light. Death and life.

The Balance.

It was magick that'd kept the fountain flowing. Blood and magick. So many, many things in Midnight came down to that. So many things in my own *life* had come down to that.

Now, scrubbed clean of the blood I'd spilled in battle, I sipped from a fresh mug of lavender-mint tea and gazed up at the warriors once more, drawing a sense of safety and certainty from them. A reminder that Midnight would always be worth fighting for.

Blackmoon Bay would always be a part of me. And I couldn't wait to go back and visit my sisters. My friends. But Midnight?

Through all of this—the capture, the fear, the fighting, the blood and the magick...

Midnight had become my home. And I was staying.

While Evander and Elian had gone down to the dungeons to deal with the prisoner whose name I would no longer utter, Hudson and Jax had gone to the city center to check on Oona and Gem. They'd set up a triage at the former Devil's Dream warehouse with some of the realm's healers, all of them working diligently to treat the wounded. From what I'd seen and heard of the battle, I knew they'd have their hands full tonight. Tomorrow night. For many nights to come as we all worked to assess the damage, bury the dead, and slowly—ever so slowly—rebuild the realm.

I wasn't sure how many of Midnight's citizens had died tonight—on *either* side. How many would carry the scars and memories of all we'd done. But we *had* done it. Defeated Darkwinter, defeated those who'd sought to tear the realm apart, to destroy its magick, to claim it or bend it to their own ends. We'd united some of Midnight's warring factions—not all of them, of course. In a place as harsh as Midnight, there would likely always be strife. But every soldier who'd sacrificed his tribal allegiance for a chance to help the realm? He represented another bridge. And bridges could be built. Fortified.

And Melantha? She was gone. Not merely vanquished, not merely dead, but her very essence... well, that essence was mine now. Not to control and manipulate, but to nurture. In destroying her tonight, I'd become her. The Dark Goddess as she always should have been.

The creak of old metal hinges cut through my thoughts, and I glanced toward the gate, smiling at the welcome sight.

Two silver-haired brothers emerged from the darkness, freshly showered, exhaustion heavy in each step, but smiles gracing those mouths. *Twin* smiles, crooked and mischievous. Warm and familiar. Mine.

"Evander," I gasped as he knelt before me and placed his hands on my knees. The face that gazed up at me now was no longer the face of our warlord, but the face of the man I'd first glimpsed in the throne room the night of the feast. The man I'd kissed.

His eyes, though... They'd remained violet.

Sensing my confusion, Evander said softly, "I wore the mask of that man for so long, I suppose he's become part of me. A reminder of what happened here—all the things Midnight doesn't want us to forget, lest they happen again."

"I don't want to forget," I said. "Any of it."

"None of us do," Elian said, sitting on the fountain beside me and wrapping a hand around the back of my neck.

Still kneeling, Evander closed his eyes and let out a deep sigh, and together the three of us sat in the dark, peaceful shadows cast by the moonstone and onyx fae, listening to the gentle trickle of the blood fountain. Out beyond the walls of the courtyard, the sounds of recovery filled the night—shovels and pickaxes slamming against rock as the fae dug for survivors. Shouting—orders, questions, cries for help. The moaning of the injured, the weeping of all who'd lost someone they loved. Smoke and magick filled the air, barely perceptible over the smell of death.

"Thank you," I whispered to my men, tears slipping

down my face. I didn't finish the thought, but the words flowed through my mind anyway. *Thank you for surviving. For finding your way back to each other. Back to me. Thank you for loving me...*

I didn't need to say them out loud. They understood.

When Evander finally met my gaze again, I cradled his face between my palms, still marveling at him.

Every facet in those violet eyes glittered. "Does it... displease you?" he asked.

"Is this your true face now?" I asked. "Your true self, fully embodied, because the warlord is finally gone?"

Evander hooked his hands around my wrists, squeezing gently. "He is *gone*, Haley. Nothing but ash. The man you see kneeling before you is me. Only me." Then, with a soft chuckle and a glance over at Elian, "Well, maybe a *little* of my brother as well."

"It's the hair," Elian said.

"As you can *clearly* see," Evander said, "it looks better on me."

Elian laughed. "We're supposed to let *her* be the judge, dickhead."

Violet eyes caught my gaze once more, his brows lifting in question.

"I'm not displeased, Evander," I said, tracing his cheeks with my thumbs. "You're beautiful. You're you, and you're beautiful."

The relief on his breath was palpable, then quickly

turned into another laugh. "So this means we're in agreement about which of us is the handsome twin, yes?"

The three of us got to our feet, and I narrowed my eyes at Evander, then Elian, assessing. "I don't know, guys. It's not something I can just *declare*. I need more information."

"What sort of information?" Evander asked, brushing a soft kiss along one corner of my mouth, then the other.

Elian shifted to stand behind me, hands on my hips, breath warm on my ear as he said, "You know we're happy to provide some... additional evidence." He nipped my earlobe, and I leaned back into his warmth, that so-called evidence pressing urgently against my backside.

"If it's evidence the goddess demands," Evander whispered, biting my lower lip, then kissing a path from my mouth to my throat, "evidence we shall provide."

With slow, deliberate movements, he worked his way down my body, gingerly unbuttoning my shirt and unfastening my bra, sliding both off my shoulders, tracing swirls across the top of my breasts with light fingertips and teasing, languid strokes of his tongue. Behind me, Elian gathered my hair and lifted it off the back of my neck, replacing its warmth with the heat of his mouth, his breath, his increasingly passionate kisses.

"Beautiful, reckless little thief," Evander teased, then closed his mouth around my nipple, sucking hard as he palmed my other breast, stroking and teasing, all of my awareness zeroing in on the intense pleasure of his tongue, his teeth. I slid my hands into his hair—long and silver, just a hint of black remaining—and arched my back as he continued to lick and suck, flooding my core with hot, molten desire.

Elian's cock twitched against me, and a low moan of pleasure escaped my lips. Evander groaned, his kisses growing more urgent as he made his way down to my stomach, unzipping my pants and sliding them down my hips. I stepped out of them, and the panties quickly followed; eager fingers hooked inside the waistband, then ripped them away like tissue paper.

When I glanced down again at Evander, there was no hiding the bulge in his pants, his cock straining against the fabric as he brought his mouth to my flesh and inhaled.

"So fucking wet," Evander whispered, one finger gliding over my clit, teasing my entrance. "So fucking delicious."

I let out a whimper, everything in me winding tight, my entire body pulsing with an insatiable need for them.

"Do you like making my brother hard for you, sparrow?" Elian asked, a dark whisper against the shell of my ear as he snaked a hand around my throat, squeezing it just... God, just right. "Do you like bringing your captor to his knees?"

His other hand slid up to cup my breast, fingers tugging and teasing where seconds earlier, Evander's mouth had nearly unraveled me. Every part of me ached, throbbing and oversensitive and desperate for more.

"Yes," I breathed. "Fuck, yes."

With another groan of pleasure, Evander slid two fingers deep inside me, then pressed his hot, lush mouth between my thighs, unleashing that wicked tongue once more.

"Evander," I gasped, fisting his hair, tugging him closer.

Behind me, Elian stepped backward, releasing me. I was about to demand his immediate return when I heard it—the clink of a buckle, the whoosh of a zipper, the unmistakable whisper of fabric sliding off skin. Seconds later, he was back, one hand curling around my throat again, the other fisting his cock as he teased me from behind.

"I'm going to fuck you now, little sparrow," he warned. "While my brother sucks on your sweet pussy until you're singing your greatest hits."

"Please," I whispered.

Evander slid his fingers out but didn't tear his mouth away, his tongue drawing slow, deliberate circles over my clit.

And Elian—who knew my body so well, knew just how hard I liked it—tightened his grip on my throat, pushed his cock between my thighs, and fucking buried himself.

"Elian!" I cried out, my voice hoarse beneath the unrelenting hold on my throat as Evander sucked my clit between his lips and moaned, the vibrations humming across my flesh, my body pulsing as Elian dragged himself out slowly, then slammed right back into me. The orgasm was already building inside, glowing embers sparking to life, and then—

The creak of that gate. Shadows shifting across the courtyard.

Hudson and Jax both met my gaze, their own burning bright as they took in the scene.

"A demon and a gargoyle," Elian teased, slowing his thrusts but not stopping. Not releasing me from the choke-hold that was driving me absolutely wild. "And what are you two reprobates doing in a nice place like this?"

Hudson let out a growl, but Jax laughed.

"Trying to decide if we should be offended that you started this party without us," my demon said.

"Less gawking, sinner," I panted. "More stripping. Both of you. I need... I need to feel you. *Taste* you."

Eyes widening, they both looked to Elian, who only laughed.

"You heard the goddess," he said, then slammed inside me once more, making me gasp. Evander licked another hot, delicious path along my clit, then sucked it hard between his lips, thrashing me with his tongue as Elian rocked against my backside, driving in deeper, harder, hitting that perfect spot inside me, his grip tight on my throat, the light dancing behind my eyes and then—

Elian released his hold, and the air rushed back to my

lungs just as the fire inside me roared to life, heat sizzling across my nerves, the intensity of it spinning me out to the stars and moons and back again as wave after wave of pure, white-hot euphoria crashed over me.

A deep growl, a shudder from behind, and then Elian came inside me, thrusting against me as he tumbled head-long into those same euphoric waves.

Evander got to his feet, his mouth glistening, violet eyes dazed as he gathered me into his arms and kissed me. I tasted myself on his tongue, and I sighed into his mouth, reaching down to palm his cock as Elian slumped back-ward against the edge of the fountain.

I pulled back from Evander's kiss just long enough to glare at my demon and my gargoyle, who I just realized had been staring at us in utter silence for the past several minutes, mouths hanging open.

"Apparently, you two have difficulty following orders," I teased, raking my gaze down their fully clothed forms. "Do you really want to piss off the Dark Goddess on her first night?"

A burst of bright-red magick shimmered in the air between us, and I laughed as they gasped and finally obeyed, stripping out of their clothing.

"You, too, Evander," I teased. "This is not a clothing-optional event."

The magick faded as my men approached, naked and strong and beautiful in the moonlight.

Despite the teasing, a heaviness still hung on the air—the weight of all we'd lost, all we'd witnessed, all we'd survived. Maybe it was wrong to want this right now—to want this pleasure so soon after the chaos and destruction.

But the warrior fae towering above us reminded me once more that all things were a balance. Life and death. Order and chaos. War and love.

And tonight, right now, even for just a little while, I wanted love. Only love.

Silently, I beckoned all of them closer. Ran my hands over velvet-smooth skin and the hard muscles coiled beneath. Kissed the freshly healed wounds, the ancient scars, the trails of old hurts that could no longer be seen. Whispered away the pain, the loss, the fear, until all that remained was the bright beacon of love—a love we'd all fought so hard to protect.

Then, it was me falling to my knees, stroking my demon's cock in the moonlight, my tongue darting out to swirl around the tip, making him shudder.

"*Fuck*, angel," he growled, his fingers knotting in my hair. "You... you're..."

I moaned as I opened my mouth and took him in deeper, sucking him, worshipping, making him tremble and gasp. Behind me, Hudson knelt and ran his hands down my sides, my hips, gripping my thighs and urging them apart to make room for that perfect, stone-hard cock already sliding between them. I obeyed at once, and my gargoyle pulled me into his lap, impaling me as Jax slid all the way down my throat, making me choke. Making me gag. Making me so hot and wet, I feared I would literally melt.

Hudson growled in my ear, thrusting in deeper, circling his hips, spreading me, stretching me as Jax fucked my mouth.

Evander knelt beside me, kissing another blazing fiery trail from my jaw to my neck, and I reached for him and fisted his cock, teasing him with a soft, light stroke, my thumb brushing across the tip as I slowly increased the pressure.

Elian was in the dirt on my other side, mirroring his twin's movements, a trail of warm breath and soft lips that soon turned into the delicious graze of fangs. He scraped them across my nipple, then licked, making me moan. Jax hissed at the sound against his sensitive skin, and Hudson drove deeper inside me, my grip on Evander's cock tight as I stroked him harder. Faster.

"Open wider for me, sparrow," Elian whispered, that hot mouth sliding down my chest, my belly. "Now it's *my* turn to make you come on my tongue."

Evander captured my nipple between his lips, nibbling and teasing as Hudson gripped my thighs and spread them even wider, making room for Elian as he lowered his head between them and kissed. And sucked. And feasted until those embers inside me ignited once more.

It was wild. It was filthy. It was love. So much love, I felt it rise up around me like my own magick, radiating warmth and security and possibility and a promise that this was ours. That we *belonged* to each other. That every kiss, every touch, every deep stroke was another sacred vow to honor and cherish this. To fight for it, no matter what. To never give up.

In the long span of our collective lives, all of us had lost so much.

Evander was stolen from his family as a child, leaving Elian to wade through the wreckage, eventually losing the family he'd known and loved too. Jax lost his sister, only to have his parents abandon him to the most barbaric torments imaginable. Hudson was betrayed by his own people, scorned and exiled, never able to truly mourn the fae children whose gruesome murders he'd been forced to witness.

I was torn away from my sisters as a child, all of us hidden to protect us from a mother who'd wanted our magick so badly she'd tried to kill us for it. And though my adoptive family was loving and kind, they died young—to young—and I was left alone.

All of us were orphans. Outcasts. Yet somehow, we'd found each other.

We were part of each other's histories now, each other's hearts. And I was honored and humbled by it, this belonging. This love we all shared. I felt it glow and expand inside me with that fire—the knowledge and comfort that I was theirs. Their little sparrow and their little thief. Their babygirl. Their dark angel. And I was *me,* too. All me—the Dark Goddess, the Silversbane-Darkwinter Scorpio blood witch, wielder of magick and eater of lasagna, a woman who'd finally come to truly appreciate her life.

To appreciate all the beauty in that darkness, however painful, that had brought me here.

A deep throb pulsed through my core, and my body tightened around my gargoyle's cock as the fire inside me ignited again in earnest. I stroked Evander with a fevered touch, his body trembling beside me, Elian's silver head thrashing between my thighs, licking and sucking, Hudson sliding in deep as I moaned around Jax's cock in my mouth and then...

The orgasm detonated, bursting like a Midnight starshower inside me, hot and bright and endless as I shattered for them—all of them, my men, my heart.

Hudson was next, slamming inside me with a shudder and a growl that had me moaning all over again, and then Jax, fisting my hair as he spilled down my throat.

"Haley," Evander ground out, barely breathing, and then he was trembling again, his hot release spilling as he thrust into my hand.

Spent and sated, all five of us fell onto our backs on the dirt, panting. Dreaming. Breathing each other in. I curled my fingers into the dirt, and then, as if in response to some ancient call inside me, the ground rumbled, vines pushing up through the damp earth, reaching for life.

Jax sucked in a sharp breath, no doubt remembering our last encounter in this courtyard. The chokeweed that'd sprouted up in the darkness, nearly killing us both.

But even without looking at them, I *knew* these plants. Knew we had nothing to fear.

The blooms that caressed our bare skin tonight weren't chokeweed.

They were my roses. Black and lush and perfect. A gift from Midnight herself, welcoming us to the realm.

My men gasped as we leaned up on our elbows and took in the sight of this strange, wondrous new garden.

It was, most surprisingly, Hudson who spoke first.

"Beauty in darkness," came his deep, soothing rumble.

"Beauty in darkness," I echoed.

And when I leaned back again and glanced up into the Midnight sky, the triple moons all seemed to be smiling, and I let out a deep sigh and smiled right back at them, knowing in my heart that this view had *always* been meant for us.

Knowing we were finally, truly, irrevocably home.

One month later...

Memory was a strange thing. A curse or a gift, I still knew not, though lately I'd been more inclined to hope for the latter.

I used to tell myself I was better off without my past—that it could only ever be a burden that would weigh me down and distract me from my mission.

I no longer believed that. Our pasts were an integral part of us—part of who we became, who we were *always* becoming as one moment slid into the next. It was only in the present where we made that choice: would we allow our histories to be our burdens, or would we invite them to be our blessings?

Perhaps there was room enough for both. Perhaps, in the fine balancing of the two, we could find our peace.

I still didn't remember my childhood or my brother—not in a way that made sense. But things were coming to me more often now—a scene playing out in a dream. A flash triggered by my brother's laughter. A memory unlocked by the scent of fresh-baked bread cooling on the kitchen's obsidian countertop.

For so long, I couldn't see any of these things—not even the barest glimpse. But in saving our realm, in severing the chains that had once bound me to my vile captor, I'd finally shed the soul-crushing despair that'd hung over me like a death shroud for centuries. And in that place inside me where only darkness and nightmares lived, a light had finally begun to shine.

Not the light of memory, but the light of possibility. Of hope.

Haley had given me that.

"Is she ready, Evander?" one of my household employees asked as I paused before a decorative mirror outside the ballroom to check the fit of my clothing. Again. I'd lost count at how many times I'd changed, but every-thing had to be perfect tonight—my gift to her. Beauty in darkness.

And it was—I noted with no small amount of relief—perfect. The sleek, tailored jacket and pants, black as the Midnight sky but for their faint silver-and-violet whorls. I'd selected the pattern for Haley. The hint of color brought out my eyes—the violet irises I'd finally come to accept. To appreciate, if only for the way she looked at me each and every night.

"The people are eager to see her," he continued.

"As am I." I smiled and peeked inside the packed ballroom. For once, it wasn't just a crowd of sycophantic nobles who'd paid for the privilege of attendance, but the people of Midnight themselves. Those from the Hollow. Those who dwelled in the shadow of Dead Claw. The imps and the demons, vampires and fae, witches. Men and monsters all. Even the feral fae had re-emerged from their caves in the Razorbacks tonight—not to fight, but to celebrate with us. To rebuild. To remember those who'd come before us.

Their people. *Our* people.

Together, we'd buried the Eternal Ones—the children of their ancestors—in a place of honor on a high cliff overlooking the Sea of Tranquility, along with many others who died fighting for their homeland.

Hudson had spoken for them. Before a group of hundreds, he'd remembered them. Their light. Their boundless capacity for love.

In the month since our victory over Melantha and the Darkwinter fae, we'd made other changes as well.

Night by night, the people of Amaranth City were rebuilding. Homes, businesses, open spaces... More than ever, the city glittered like a jewel in the north, a beacon for all who wished to follow it home.

We'd signed treaties and trade agreements with many of the surrounding territories—Stone City, the Razorbacks, Dead Claw, Hanging Lake. Now that we'd gotten a taste of peace, very few wanted to return to the brutalities of the past.

Not everyone was so eager to make amends, however, and none of us were foolish enough to believe there would never be another skirmish, never be a territorial dispute or invasion, never be a battle for resources or weapons or drugs.

But we had to start somewhere. We'd fought and bled and died for the realm. For each other. Now, it was ours to protect.

We'd taken down most of Vanderham's wall so that no one would be denied passage into our city again. Part of it remained intact, however. A memorial to the fallen, as well as a reminder of our dark history—a history that could shape a better future, but only if we remembered it.

Beggar's Moat had been filled in, the magick that'd bound the fallen dead to the city eradicated, their trapped spirits finally set free—along with Haley's Army of the Dead.

From now on, the dead of Midnight would *always* rest in peace, no matter the manner of their deaths. No matter their deeds in life.

In the end, all of us deserved peace.

As for the living, Haley and I had worked with Oona,

Gem, and some of the other purebred Midnight fae to reconfigure the portals so that anyone who wished to travel to and from our realm could do so freely—no spells or dark bargains required. Midnight would no longer be a realm of exiles, but a realm of free people. A realm of possibility.

And tonight, exactly one month after the attack on Amaranth City and the victory snatched from the claws of death, the castle reconstruction was finally complete, and our people were more than ready to celebrate.

Excusing myself, I headed into the throne room to await Haley's arrival. The others would be meeting us shortly, but I'd asked for a few moments alone with her first.

A few moments to just... be.

My back was turned on the dais, but I knew it the moment she stepped into the room. I felt her presence, the magick that connected us. The love.

I hadn't seen her all week—she'd been in Blackmoon Bay visiting her sisters. And now, I held my breath and turned to see her, my heart nearly bursting with antic-ipation.

I'd missed her. More than I could ever express.

Entering through the door behind the dais, she met my gaze and smiled, her green eyes glittering. She wore a deli-cate black-and-silver dress that clung to her curves like water, arms and shoulders bared, tiny blood-red jewels sewn into the hemline. With each step, the dress caught the light and shimmered.

Her hair was woven into a series of intricate braids that fell down her back. Behind her ear, a single black rose bloomed.

Resplendent. That was the word that came to mind.

The very sight of her brought tears to my eyes. I had never seen her so lovely. So fierce.

"Well," she mused, raking her gaze over me as I ascended the dais to join her. "You clean up well, warlord."

I didn't speak. Couldn't. Not until she said, "And how do *I* look? I wasn't totally sold on the dress at first, but Gem talked me into it. She said it would show off my—and I quote—hard-on inspiring shoulders."

"You," I finally whispered, daring to brush a single kiss to one of those shoulders, "look like the Dark Goddess and queen you were born to be. And allow me to be the first to concur with Gem's assessment."

I shifted on my feet, attempting to adjust the sudden bulge in my pants.

Mischief danced in Haley's eyes, the magick bond sizzling between us.

In that moment, I wanted nothing more than to drag her into that secret room behind us, shred her delicate dress, and—

I cleared my throat. Refocused on the matter at hand.

"I have something for you," I said, holding out my arm for her.

Her eyes raked down my body once more. "I bet you do."

"Something *else*, incorrigible little thief."

She finally took my arm, and I led her around to the front of the dais. To the new throne that sat atop it.

The room had been scrubbed clean of the stain of Melantha, the ancient throne of skulls replaced with something much more suitable.

A high-backed throne of polished obsidian, hand-carved with black roses and vines that twined around the arms and up along the top, where the triple moons—forged from the steel of melted swords—met in the center. Tiny flecks of amethyst and diamond sparkled down the back—the stars of the Midnight sky.

"It's... its beautiful," she breathed, running her hand along the rose motif.

"It's yours, Haley."

She stilled, and when she glanced into my eyes once more, I saw the hesitation there.

"Tell me," I whispered. "If you'd prefer a different design, we can—"

"No, it's not that. It's beautiful. It's perfect. But... I didn't get here alone, Evander. I haven't earned this."

I retrieved the wooden box I'd hidden beneath the

throne earlier and held it out to her. "For millennia, Midnight was ruled by self-appointed kings and warlords."

"And now you think we need a war *lady*?"

"No, Haley." I unlatched the box and revealed the crown inside, finely-wrought silver vines blooming with flowers of onyx and moonstone. Delicate and fierce, just like she was. "Now, we need a queen."

Haley gasped, her eyes shining.

"Sit," I said softly. "Grant me the honor of being the first to bend the knee."

Her gaze snapped up to meet mine once more. A mischievous smile curved her lips. "The last time you ordered me to sit on the throne, it didn't end well."

I laughed at the memory. "As if I could forget. You blasted me with a blood spell and destroyed half the room. But I assure you, little thief. My commands can be quite... enjoyable. With the right intentions, of course."

She narrowed her eyes playfully. "Is that what you have? The right intentions?"

"Shall we find out?"

She lifted the crown from the box. "One condition."

"Name it, queen."

"You call me by all the names."

I arched an eyebrow. "*All* of them? But there are so, so many."

With another devious smile that sent a bolt of pleasure straight to my still-hard cock, she placed the crown atop her head, settled herself in the throne, and said, "Then I guess you'd better get started."

Resting my hands on the arms of the throne, I hovered over her, my mouth brushing across hers. In a dark whisper, I said, "Wicked little beast."

Then I dropped to my knees.

I pushed up her dress, revealing her bare thighs and the jewel-encrusted daggers strapped to each one.

I couldn't help but laugh. "I'm beginning to think you love your weapons more than the beautiful dresses that conceal them."

"Weapons are *always* the priority, Evander. Dresses are just the frosting on the cake."

"And oh, what a decadent cake it is." I gripped her thighs, spreading them apart as I brought my mouth to her hot, wet center. She wore a scrap of violet lace over smooth, bare skin, the thin fabric already damp with her desire.

After our victory, it didn't take long for word to spread about Melantha's defeat. About the Silversbane Darkwinter blood witch who'd fulfilled an ancient prophecy and brought peace and balance to the realm. They'd given Haley more names than we could count —names lauded in the taverns over wine and ale, names praised in the chapels, names exalted in every shop and home throughout the city and beyond as Haley had helped her people rebuild, wielding her magick as readily as she'd wielded a hammer and nails.

I'd memorized each and every name. Loved them, as much as I loved her. And now, I would show her just that.

"Haley Barnes, the first of her name," I murmured, then licked a hot path across the lace, making her shiver and writhe.

"She Who Claimed the Darkness," I said, unsheathing one of her daggers and slicing through the lace, baring her to me.

Another lick, this time directly across her hot, naked flesh. "Bane of the Enemies of Midnight."

"Oh, God," she breathed, her eyes fluttering closed, her body melting at my every kiss.

"The Great Balance." I gently bit her clit, flicking her with my tongue as I slid a finger inside her.

"Breaker of Walls, Builder of Bridges." Another finger to join the first, teasing her with long, slow strokes. I kissed the sensitive skin at the top of one thigh, then dragged my mouth across to the other. "Deathbringer. She for Whom the Bones Bow."

I curled my fingers inside her and slid in deeper, *deeper*, once more lowering my mouth to her flesh, tongue swirling over the sensitive apex.

"Dark Queen of the Realm," I whispered, my breath as shallow as hers, heart thundering in time with the red-hot pulse of magick emanating through our bond.

Fuck. I could no longer hold back. No longer tease and taunt.

With a final growl, I said, "*My* dark queen."

And then I was on her, my mouth devouring her as I fucked her with my hand, every part of me conspiring to give her this pleasure, to taste her, to feel her, to make my Midnight queen come for me.

I thrust inside her once more, hitting that perfect spot.

"Evander!" she cried out, and I moaned, licking her madly as she thrashed against my face and took every last bit of pleasure, every hot mist of breath, ever last silken kiss.

"What are you thinking about?" she whispered, fingers drawing lazy circles on the back of my hand.

I was seated on the throne now too, Haley curled into my lap, her lovely dress smoothed back into place.

The crown glimmered in her dark hair.

I could still taste her on my lips.

Pressing a kiss to her temple, I said, "Just recalling the time a devious little thief and her friends crashed my party in a vain attempt to steal my bodily fluids."

Haley laughed. "We've come full circle."

"And yet so much has changed."

"True." She shifted in my lap, her sweet berries-and-cream scent floating to my senses. "Last time, you didn't make me come on the throne."

"If you'd given me the opportunity, I assure you... I *would* have."

"Well, at least now we've got a fun game for later. And by later, I mean every time I'm sitting on this thing in a dress."

"Understood. I shall order you more dresses at once."

"Great." She ran a hand down the carved arm of her throne and grinned. "Now I'll *never* be able to walk into this room again without thinking of your *very* talented tongue."

"Indeed you won't. And don't believe for a second *that* was unintentional."

"My warlord," she teased with a roll of her pretty green eyes. "Ever the strategist."

She shifted again, drawing closer. I wrapped my arms tight around her and pressed my nose to the soft skin beneath her ear, breathing her in.

After several silent heartbeats, I said softly, "Do you remember when I told you my mind had blocked out all of the good things in my life, magnifying only the worst?"

She nodded, her body tensing.

"It's different now," I said.

She glanced up and met my gaze, her eyes sparkling. "You've remembered something?"

"Your dress," I said. "From the Feast of Midnight. You

were a dark flower blooming in an even darker realm, and the sight of you stole the very breath from my lungs."

"You remember my dress?"

"You've beguiled me since our first encounter, Haley. I knew you were a spy—possibly even an assassin. Knew I should have ordered my guards to seize you at once. But one look, and I was just so desperate for a dance. A single dance, I promised myself. But then you were in my arms, and we were talking—all those little threats hidden behind teasing smiles—and somehow I'd fallen into those gorgeous emerald eyes, and I was already half enamored of you before the first waltz had even ended." I smiled, basking in the memory of that night. That dance. "I spent the next several weeks trying to convince myself it wasn't happening. Truly, I didn't believe my heart had the capacity to feel such things."

Her eyes misted. Through a soft grin, she said, "Only half enamored, huh?"

I laughed and closed my eyes, focusing on her warmth. The feel of her soft skin. The sound of her heartbeat. The magick simmering in her veins—the magick we shared.

"Maybe a bit more than half," I admitted.

The rest... it'd come to me slowly after that, sneaking in behind the cracks of my armor night by night, moment by moment. A mug of lavender-peppermint tea offered in my library after a nightmare. A stolen glimpse at a beautiful witch dancing on the balcony after accomplishing a spell.

A gentle touch on scar-ravaged skin. The realization that this was a woman who would fight tooth and nail for the ones she called friends. The ones she loved.

"The truth is, I..." I swallowed hard and opened my eyes, meeting her intense gaze, losing myself in those eyes once again. "You saved me. You... you pushed me when all others cowered in fear. You believed in me when all others had turned their backs. And somewhere over all those nights, all those arguments, all the questioning and shouting and blood and tears and stolen kisses... *Moons and stars*, those kisses... I fell in love with you, Haley Barnes." I cupped her face, brushing away her tears with my thumb. "I *love* you. You have my *entire* heart, and even that doesn't feel like enough. It will never feel like enough because you deserve so much more. But if you'll grant me this chance, I vow to you I'll spend the rest of my immortal life trying to be worthy of all that you've already given me. Of all that you are to me."

"Evander," she whispered, her eyes fluttering closed, the tears falling freely even as she smiled.

When she finally looked up at me again, there was so much light in her eyes it made me gasp.

"Terrible things and terrible people have the power to make us feel unworthy," she said. "But only if we allow them to. Don't give them that power, Evander. You *are* worthy. I love you. And I'll spend the rest of my life taking care of your heart just as you've taken care of mine."

It was more than I could've asked for. Not just the words, but the promise behind them. The truth.

And yes, the hope.

———

The others were waiting for us as they'd promised, standing just outside the grand entrance in their Midnight finery.

As we approached, all three of them stared at her open-mouthed.

"Can we... skip the party, maybe?" Elian said, his gaze roving down her curves, then back up. "And just go back to the bedroom and—"

"No," I said.

"What if we just... show up a little late?" This, from Jax, who leaned in to brush a kiss to her cheek. In a low whisper not quite soft enough for me to miss, he said, "Our closet's still intact, angel. Maybe we should—"

"*Maybe* you should stop drooling before you stain your formalwear," I said. "Honestly, the three of you are so uncouth, it boggles the mind you even learned to walk without dragging your knuckles on the ground."

Hudson glared down at me. "Says the man who clearly enjoyed a little... ahem... *dessert* before the party." He swiped his thumb along my lower lip. "Speaking of staining the formalwear."

Haley laughed, stretching up on her toes to plant a kiss on his cheek. "Plenty more to go around later, Gargs."

"Enough salivating," I said to the men once more. Then, to Haley, "It's time to give the people what they so desperately need."

"Wine and chocolate?" she said, bouncing on her toes. "Oh! And those little pastries with the baked brie inside? I love those."

"I'm aware. And yes, all of those things await you. But I meant..." I took a breath, the mood turning serious once more. "A dark queen worthy of the title. Worthy of our loyalty."

At this, all four of us bowed our heads.

Haley allowed it... but only for a moment. Then she laughed and said, "I'll be *more* than happy to put all four of you on your knees for me later. But right now, your girl is hungry and those pastries are definitely calling my name."

She turned and opened the grand ballroom doors, revealing the vast sea of people behind them—dancing, laughing, some of them meeting and embracing one another for the first time after centuries of bloodshed.

All because a thieving little green-eyed witch crashed upon my castle and turned the whole realm upside down.

I watched as they noticed her entrance. Cheered for her. Offered her drinks and hugs and gratitude, and warmth filled me at every smile, at every teary-eyed kiss on her cheeks.

The magick of Midnight had chosen Haley as its keeper, as our goddess and queen. But unlike those who'd come before her, she wasn't interested in power and domination.

Only in peace and prosperity. In friendship. In family.

And now, as the many peoples of our realm celebrated the start of this new era, it wasn't the grandeur of the reconstructed ballroom I noticed, or the symphony of the realm's very best musicians, or even the crown glittering atop her dark head.

It was Elian. My brother, my twin. The fae Haley had fallen in love with years ago—lost and found again, brought back to me for a second chance just as he'd been brought back to her.

It was Hudson, the fiercely protective gargoyle who was just beginning to find his voice again. His place—the place of honor and friendship he deserved.

It was Jax, a brother to us all, the demon who'd taught Haley about love and fear and courage, more courageous himself than he even realized.

And it was Haley. It was her eyes and her laughter. Her heart. That boundless capacity for love. Her ferocity.

They were my family. Midnight was our home.

And together, we would continue to rebuild. To negotiate. To laugh. To honor. To love.

To fight for each other and for our realm.

And together, come what may, we would cherish the

beauty that bloomed in all the darkest places, tonight and always.

Thank you so much for coming along on this twisty, turny, happily-ever-after journey with Haley and her sexy monsters!

It's always so hard to say goodbye to my characters, and these guys were among my favorites to write! I loved getting to know each of them, smashing all their hearts to bits, and then—of course—putting them all back together again (what kind of romance series would it be without that last step?).

I put them through the ringer in this story, but I know I've left them all in a good place—together, in love, and ready to build their new life in Midnight.

If you haven't read Haley's origin story in the Witch's Rebels series yet and want to jump in, now is the perfect time! Set in Blackmoon Bay, this spicy urban fantasy RH series is where it all began for Haley and her sisters. Start with book 1, Shadow Kissed!

If you're all caught up with the Silversbane witches and

you're ready for what's next... How do you feel about GARGOYLES?

Hudson fans, this one is for you! Claimed by Gargoyles is a sizzling hot reverse harem paranormal mafia romance series... with gargoyles.

That's right, friends. Our lucky witch teams up with not one but four fierce, brooding, *insanely* overprotective gargoyles to break an ancient curse and get revenge on the cruel dark mages bent on destroying her.

If you enjoy dark, supernatural thrills and *crazy hot* spicy romance featuring... *ahem...* special equipment, sensitive wings, and oh-so-dominant dirty-talkers, I've got you covered. **Start with book one, Wicked Conjuring!**

Are you a member of our private Facebook group, <u>Sarah Piper's Sassy Witches?</u> Pop in for sneak peeks, cover reveals, exclusive giveaways, book chats, group therapy to deal with these killer cliffhangers, and plenty of complete randomness from your fellow fans! We'd love to see you there.

XOXO
Sarah

MORE BOOKS FROM SARAH PIPER!

Looking for more Reverse Harem romance?

THE WITCH'S REBELS is a supernatural reverse harem series featuring five smoldering-hot guys and the kickass witch they'd kill to protect. If you're wondering about Haley's sisters and the Battle for Blackmoon Bay, this is the series where it all begins!

TAROT ACADEMY is a paranormal, university-aged reverse harem academy romance starring four seriously hot mages and one badass witch. Dark prophecies, unique mythology, steamy romance, and plenty of supernatural thrills make this series a must-read!

ABOUT SARAH PIPER

Sarah Piper is a witchy, Tarot-card-slinging paranormal romance and urban fantasy author. Through her signature brew of dark magic, heart-pounding suspense, and steamy romance, Sarah promises a sexy, supernatural escape into a world where the magic is real, the monsters are sinfully hot, and the witches always get their magically-ever-afters.

Readers have dubbed her work "super sexy," "imaginative and original," "off-the-walls good," and "delightfully wicked in the best ways," a quote Sarah hopes will appear on her tombstone.

Originally from New York, Sarah now makes her home in northern Colorado with her husband (though that changes frequently) (the location, not the husband), where she spends her days sleeping like a vampire and her nights writing books, casting spells, gazing at the moon, playing with her ever-expanding collection of Tarot cards, binge-watching Supernatural (Team Dean!), and obsessing over the best way to brew a cup of tea.

You can find her online at SarahPiperBooks.com, on TikTok at @sarahpiperbooks, and in her Facebook readers group at Sarah Piper's Sassy Witches! If you're sassy, or if you need a little *more* sass in your life, or if you need more Dean Winchester gifs in your life (who doesn't?), come hang out!